MW00883678

# SHATTERED DAWN

## THE ETERNAL FRONTIER BOOK 3

# ANTHONY MELCHIORRI

Shattered Dawn (The Eternal Frontier, Book 3)
Copyright © 2017 by Anthony J. Melchiorri. All rights reserved.
First Edition: June 2017
http://AnthonyJMelchiorri.com

ISBN-13: 978-1548664145
ISBN-10: 1548664146

Cover Design: Illustration © Tom Edwards, TomEdwardsDesign.com

No part of this book may be reproduced, scanned, or distributed in any printed
or electronic form without permission. Please do not participate in or encourage
piracy of copyrighted materials in violation of the author's rights. Thank you for
respecting the hard work of this author.

This is a work of fiction. Names, characters, places, and incidents either are the
product of the author's imagination or are used fictitiously, and any resemblance
to locales, events, business establishments, or actual persons—living or dead—is
entirely coincidental.
10 9 8 7 6 5 4 3 2 1

# ONE

The faint glimmer of Meck'ara's sun filtered through the ocean above Tag Brewer, a commander in the SRE navy and former chief medical officer, now captain of the SRES *Argo*. Millions upon millions of tons of salt water teemed with all kinds of sea creatures, vague analogues to the denizens of the deep found on Earth. A beast roughly the size of an SRE strike fighter craft passed above him, skirting upward along the massive polyglass bubble protecting Tag from the ocean's crushing pressure. His eyes followed the sea monster as its tail whipped in circles, akin to a propeller, pushing its rotund, cilia-covered body. Its shadow passed over the spiral trees and bunches of bush-like vegetation in the park Tag walked through. Soon the beast followed the curve of the bubble back down, disappearing behind the silhouettes of buildings covered in black sheet-alloy that made up the Mechanic city of Deep Origin.

The polyglass and alloy structures reinforcing the gargantuan bubble creaked under the weight of the ocean, accompanied by the soft sounds of artificial breezes caressing the parks and city beneath it. Mechanics striding along the streets gave Tag the occasional curious glance, and their soft chatter followed in his wake. Most of the Mechanics in the bubble cities had been saved from the scourge of the nanites. Tag's Mechanic allies had discovered that the air recycling nanoparticles gave residents who had lived in these environments for years acquired immunity to the mind-slaving nanites that overrode their brethren's normal neurological function. It was a gracious wonder that so many of them had survived in these cities and on land, taking to cover and hiding when the Drone-Mechs swept their world, commanded by some unseen Drone-masters to vanquish the free Mechanics.

Two Mechanics strolled next to a freshwater stream gurgling near the pathway. They stopped to talk and eat something with a pungently saccharine odor, far too sweet for Tag. It had the wispiness of cotton candy, and Tag couldn't help but wonder what it was. But when another shadow crossed his path—this one belonging to a two-headed whale-like creature swimming over the dome—his eyes and thoughts turned back to the ocean serving as their sky.

A soft clicking, like someone tiptoeing across the stone pathway, sounded behind Tag. He recognized the easy gait of a familiar Mechanic and crew member: Coren. The alien strode toward him, clad in a formfitting black garment that looked like an undersuit the marines wore beneath their power armor. As Tag had roamed Deep Origin while organizing the repairs and restocking of the *Argo* along with meeting all the right dignitaries and Mechanic bureaucrats to garner support for the upcoming mission, he had seen Mechanics cared very little about fashion. Most wore the same outfit Coren did. In keeping with their no-nonsense nature, the clothes were designed purely for maximum dexterity and environmental protection.

Coren glanced up to watch the enormous creature Tag was looking at. "Don't worry. Of all the bubble cities we've constructed, not one has so much as cracked. You're perfectly safe."

"I know, I know," Tag said, an easy grin breaking across his face. "Mechanic technology is amazing. It's the best gift the gods gave this world."

The edge of Coren's mouth twitched. A subtle gesture—the Mechanic's version of a smile. "The gods didn't give us this technology. We gave it to ourselves." Coren matched pace with Tag. "No, strike that. We *earned* it ourselves."

"As long as that Mechanic technology is good enough to get the *Argo* back into space, you can say whatever you want about it. That is, while we're on your planet. Once we're space-bound, all bets are off."

"Ah, Captain, you've hardly been one to deride Mechanic technology. I fear your insults have no effect on me."

"I don't think you understand the implications here. This moratorium on respect toward Mechanics while we're on Meck'ara will end for Sofia too."

Coren feigned a humanlike expression of shock, his thin lips making an O shape and his single working eye bulging slightly even as his scarred-over eye looked as blank as ever. "You wouldn't dare."

"I would. You know her tongue is sharper than a plasma-scalpel. And those are damn sharp. I would know, I'm a—"

"Doctor," Coren said with a hint of exasperation. A woman with a long, dark ponytail streaming behind her was bounding for them, waving. "As you people are inclined to say, 'speak of the devil.'"

Lieutenant Sofia Vasquez butted between the duo. "Skipper,"

she said to Tag. Then, looking at Coren, "Your majesty, the king of all things mechanical and our honorable, superior scientific overlord."

Tag imagined that if Coren had possessed eyebrows, he would have raised them as he said, "Sharp tongue, eh?"

"What?" Sofia asked. "You don't like the title."

"No, the title is fitting," Coren replied. "Maybe not nuanced enough. A little lackluster in the sarcasm department."

Tag looked behind them. "Where's Alpha? I thought she was with you."

"She *was*," Sofia said, "but she kind of got distracted."

Sofia pointed toward the edge of the park near the Deep Origin Governmental Complex building where they were headed. A gaggle of black-furred, lanky Mechanic children gathered around a silver-bodied, synth-bio droid: Alpha.

Tag checked his wrist terminal to ensure they were still on time for their meeting with the Mechanics and their newfound allies, the Melarrey. *Fifteen minutes to spare.* They approached Alpha and her posse of young Mechanics. Each of the children stared at her with wide, curious golden eyes as she regaled them with the intricacies of human-created artificial intelligence and the biological engineering necessary to make her existence a reality. Tag couldn't tell if the children were more captivated simply by her mere presence as a living, talking synth-bio droid or by the technical challenges she explained to them. Knowing Mechanics, either option was a very real possibility.

Seeing Tag, Sofia, and Coren approach, Alpha looked up. "Captain Brewer, I lost track of time. I see the meeting is about to reconvene."

"That it is," Tag said. A few of the Mechanic children backed up as if afraid of him. Murmurs of his name spread through their ranks. "Have you been telling them ghost stories about me or something?"

Before Alpha could answer, one of the Mechanic children tugged on his sleeve with a six-fingered hand. "You created her!"

"Captain Brewer!" another called. "Tell us about the neuro-silico connections!"

"What about the processing power of a synth-bio brain compared to a traditional computational intelligence?"

Their voices rattled off a litany of questions to rival even the most aggressive of human academics at the galaxy-renowned University of Ganymede.

"Maybe later," Tag replied with an amused laugh.

The group crossed a street—really more of a magnetic railway for the autopods that swerved through pedestrian traffic like water around rocks. Tag still hadn't gotten used to the wind whipping past him from the AI-driven vehicles. They always seemed to be on a collision course with the pedestrians casually crossing through the traffic, but he did his best to follow Coren's lead and confidently continue toward the government building. To do so was to fight a screaming voice inside his head telling him he was going to die each time an autopod careened in his direction and abruptly changed course at the last second.

An energy shield-like door fizzled away as the group approached the government building, and a squad of Mechanic soldiers escorted them through the obsidian halls. A sense of pride swelled in Tag's chest as Mechanics paused what they were doing at their terminal pods to stare at him and his crew. Whispers of his crew and their role in the retaking of Meck'ara accompanied them like the rustling of leaves trails a gentle wind. Not long ago he was a mere scientist and physician aboard a research vessel.

Now he was …

He wasn't quite sure what he was.

Some of the Mechanics' news streams were calling the *Argo's* crew heroes. Tag had a reputation now as a brilliant scientist, leading the technological charge that had deactivated the Drone-Mechs and created Alpha's synth-bio sentience. He'd even been inducted as an honorary member of the Mechanic Enclave.

Still, others speculated the *Argo* and its crew were part of a greater conspiracy, painting them as potential traitors allowed in the midst of the acting and still-reeling Meck'ara planetary government. No matter what the people of the ME called him, no matter what they thought of him or what rumors transpired throughout their crippled empire, Tag paid it little heed.

The only thing that mattered to him right now was determining who the bastards were that the *Argo* was supposed to be after. They had perverted nanite technology into a genocidal, species-enslaving technology.

His thoughts stewed as he entered a conference room filled with alien dignitaries, military officials, and others he didn't know. One of the few he did recognize, Sergeant Ryan "Bull" Buhlman, gave him a curt nod.

Tag sat at the conference table, flanked by the other marines. Alpha, Coren, and Sofia found their seats as well. All the humor they had shared outside, the joy of walking around unhindered by the constraints of EVA suits or the cramped corridors of spaceships and space stations, had vanished. Wandering the city of Deep Origin had made it easy to forget that there was war going on. But as one of the Mechanic commanders, Bracken of the MES *Stalwart*, began to speak, any belief that this was a time of peace was shattered as swiftly as polyglass hit by a Gauss round.

"This is what the rest of Meck'ara looks like," Bracken said. She waved her hand over a terminal, and the holodisplay lit up in an array of colors. It flashed through the cities left on the planet's surface. Each had its own unique environment, whether cradled between mountains, tucked away in lush valleys, or nestled into forests butting up against breathtaking coastlines.

Where their architecture and environment differed, however, they had one thing in common. The holos showed Mechanic bodies left to rot on streets littered with rubble and pocked by craters. Buildings sagged from wounds levied by pulsefire; some no longer existed at all except for the skeletal remains of scaffolding jutting violently from the earth.

"These are the cities that were hit hardest by the Drone-Mechs," Bracken continued. "And we do not yet know when the Drone-Mechs might return."

# TWO

None of the Mechanics gasped or gave away any expression that belied the inner turmoil Tag imagined he would feel had he seen Earth cities in such disarray. One Mechanic stood, and all eyes turned toward her. Tag recognized her as the acting Grand Elector of the Mechanic Enclave. Her black unisuit had three violet bands around each arm, the only symbol of her rank. The blue-gray fur on her snake-like face seemed to stand on end like she was bristling for a fight. Her fingers curled at dozens of joints, making Tag's stomach twist at the inhuman movement, and she let out a deep sigh that resonated from her narrow chest with all the power of a parent immensely disappointed in her children.

"Now is not the time for silly theatrics or, machine be damned, hysterics," Grand Elector L'ndrant began. She waved a six-fingered hand dismissively at the holos of the destroyed cities. "We know they're dead. The great machine will soon reclaim and recycle their matter. They are the past."

Tag couldn't tell whether he admired her brazenness or cursed her utter disregard for the dead. Sofia raised her eyebrows as if to remind him what they had talked about over and over: Mechanics saw life as mere forward progress in time, a constant cartwheel of cogs moving the universe in one direction or another, driven by science and logic. Spirituality didn't fit into the views of most of their religions, if you could call them that.

"I don't care about what has been destroyed. I care about what will be rebuilt, what we still have to explore, and how we will utilize Meck'ara to retake what is ours," L'ndrant said. She gave Bracken a strange look, her dark brow slightly furrowed, and her golden eyes pooled with light. To Tag, it looked almost like she was expressing pity. "Bracken, I do commend you and these aliens"—she gestured widely to Tag and his crew—"for defeating the Drone-Mechs here. Brilliant work. Really, very brilliant. But your job is done. Your task accomplished. What do you hope to achieve by showing me the destruction of our planet over and over? I have seen this firsthand on my tour of the planet."

"I merely present these images as a rallying cry," Bracken said, "for the proposed mission Captain Brewer hopes to lead."

Now all eyes turned to Tag. A slow heat crept into his cheeks as he felt the steel of their gazes.

"Yes," L'ndrant began, "what do our humans have planned for us?"

A lump formed in Tag's throat as L'ndrant sat. He immediately stood as required by Mechanic custom. The floor was his. He tried to swallow, but the annoying lump in his throat didn't clear until he coughed. His eyes swept all those waiting to hear what he had to say, from his crew to the Mechanics. A Melarrey representative, Jaroon, gave him a strangely human smile. The corners of the translucent jellyfish-like alien's mouth remained curled upward as the nerve bundles visible behind its three eyes sparked as though they were live electric wires. Maybe it was a gesture of assurance. Though a bit unsettled, Tag gave him a nod of thanks back.

"We have uncovered intelligence that may lead to the Drone-masters responsible for the nanites and the Drone-Mechs," Tag said. Then he glanced at Jaroon again and added, "And the destruction of the Melarrey." He explained the *Argo*'s original cover story of a scientific mission, and how only Captain Weber and a few of the ship's officers knew their true directive. Somehow the Drone-Mechs had discovered their purpose and their hidden cargo—enough ramjet thermonuclear weapons to raze an entire planet. Then he described the coordinates of the *Argo*'s destination. Several of the Mechanics nodded along, and the nerve bundles behind Jaroon's eyes burned brighter. Confidence swelled in Tag like a T-drive spooling for hyperspace.

"And what is this intelligence you have discovered leading you to this location?" L'ndrant asked.

All the momentum he had gained seemed to slam against an alloy bulkhead. He held up a paper book. Captain Weber's notebook.

A few of the Mechanic government and military officials broke out in whispers. L'ndrant let out a throbbing huff of a laugh. "This intelligence relies on a notebook? An antiquated physical recording of data? I'm sorry, Captain, but Bracken gave me the impression you had more than a flimsy sheet of paper to support your hypothesis."

"It's more than just this notebook," Tag said. "Everything else I told you is evidenced by the rest of the crew, data logs we recovered from the Mechanic casualties and stations we encountered, and, for the gods' sake, your own experience with the Drone-Mechs. What I have here, even if it isn't our end goal, is the first step of the trail that might lead us to the Drone-masters."

Now more of the Mechanics carried on disgruntled conversations until L'ndrant raised a trembling fist.

"Quiet!" she said. The chatter ceased, and her golden eyes narrowed, focused on Tag. "We truly do admire your courage in defending our people and helping us retake Meck'ara. But we have only just retaken this world. Bracken's show demonstrated the work we have to do here, and, machine willing, the Drone-Mechs or their Drone-masters won't be back before we can at least reorganize our forces."

"She's right," a grizzled Mechanic admiral said. "Our fleet is spread thin as it is, and my time would be better spent organizing naval restructuring instead of listening to this factually unsupported thesis."

Tag shook his head, half-admiring the scientific way the admiral spoke. He had never heard such language from an SRE admiral, though it was common enough in his scientific circles.

"This may be true, and I am inclined to dismiss the human's claims outright," L'ndrant said. The fur on her head smoothed, relaxing. "But I do think we at least owe it to him to hear what he's requesting before we turn it down. Give us something we can work with, Brewer."

This earned a few reluctant huffs of agreement.

"Go on," L'ndrant said, motioning to Tag.

"We are asking for your support to travel to these coordinates. My ship expended a great deal of our ordnance on route to Meck'ara. We graciously request a restock. In addition, if the coordinates are, as we suspect, the origin of the nanites and the Drone-masters, we believe it's best if we act immediately. There won't be time to send courier drones back and forth; we want to strike quick and we want to strike hard. I think it would be wise to send a Mechanic strike group with us."

The room erupted into shouts of dismay, and discordant

voices clanged against Tag's eardrums. He stood tall, like a light-house against the storm, and waited for L'ndrant to order them into silence again.

One of the admirals shouted, "We cannot spare a single cruiser, much less a dreadnought and its escort!"

"And what shall we defend ourselves with, the ruins of our planetary defense space stations?" another asked.

L'ndrant held up a fist. "This is quite simply unreasonable."

Tag opened his mouth, ready to protest, but Bracken gave a slight shake of her head.

"They are right, of course," L'ndrant said, addressing Tag. "We cannot spare an entire strike group. It is best that we err on the side of caution, focusing on our defensive efforts at this point. We will, however, allow you to restock your ordnance. That, I believe, we can spare." She looked to an admiral for agreement, and his black fur wrinkled in a furrow before he gave a sigh that Tag took for a yes. "But a strike group I cannot grant you."

Jaroon did not so much stand as float upward, his gelatinous body shifting vertically. "The Melarrey pledge their support. We have only a few dozen ships remaining. That is, as far as we know, the entirety of our species. I believe it's best for my people that we leave most of our ships here to protect our civilians."

"Of course," Tag said.

"But we can commit my ship to your charge."

A Mechanic elected official stood, claiming the floor. "One ship? That's all the Melarrey offer, and the human asks for an entire strike force from us?"

Bracken stood next. "Because we can afford to do more. Even among the remnants of our civilization, Mechanic firepower reigns supreme, and it is only logical that we would shoulder the burdens of attacking those who have done our species wrong." Her golden eyes narrowed. "And I will remind you, it is *us* who the Drone-masters insult. It is *us* who they enslave. Would it not be the pragmatic thing to do—to destroy them when they do not expect it?"

Her chest swelled. "If I may borrow a phrase I have come to admire dearly from these humans: Let us catch these Drone-masters with their pants down. That is when they will be most unprepared. That is why we should support Captain Brewer's mission."

Before the room could devolve into chaos once again, L'ndrant raised a preemptive fist. "Your argument isn't without merit." She stroked the mussed fur along her cheek. "But still, it would be most inconvenient—I think you'd agree—if the Drone-masters caught *us* with our pants down once again."

Bracken's gaze drooped, and Tag felt something slide through him. Defeat. He and his crew would have to carry out their mission alone, with only the escort of a single Melarrey ship. As enthusiastic as Jaroon was to help them, he imagined their chances of success would be greatly improved with a squadron of Mechanic vessels to support them.

"All that being said," L'ndrant said, "it might be beneficial to offer *some* Mechanic support on this mission. If for nothing else, it may be a worthwhile intelligence-gathering exercise, as foolish as the odds of your little paper document yielding valuable information may be." She looked around the room, searching the audience, before her eyes landed on Bracken. "Bracken, I believe you and your crew will be best suited for this mission."

Before Bracken or Tag could appeal for more reinforcements, L'ndrant continued, "Now go. We'll have your ships restocked and prepared shortly. Go catch the Drone-masters with their pants down, and prove us wrong."

# THREE

Tag marched beside Sofia as they walked toward the *Argo*. They dodged a Mechanic-driven exo-suit carrying an armful of cargo destined for the *Stalwart*. Other exos moved about the Deep Origin's dockyard, loading and unloading a host of Mechanic vessels.

"L'ndrant is a real peach," Sofia said.

"Sure is," Tag said. "Definitely not the type of a leader I'd expect from the Mechanics."

"What did you think she'd be like?"

"I figured an accountant or something. Not someone as fiery as that."

"And, dare I say it, emotional?"

"Yeah," Tag agreed. "Very strange coming from the elected leader of the most robotic flesh-and-blood race I've ever met."

They merged with the stream of Mechanic technicians and droids resupplying the *Argo*, following the others into the cargo bay. The air car Tag had thought was beyond repair had indeed been repaired, much to his relief, and Coren had been sure to tell him it had everything to do with the Mechanics' technical acumen. Alpha checked in new cargo and ordnance on her wrist terminal. She paused long enough in her inventory to spare Tag a perfunctory nod.

"Captain Brewer, can you show us where to unload the torpedoes?" a Mechanic asked him.

"Alpha, mind doing that for me?" Tag asked.

She nodded again and led the Mechanic workers deeper into the ship. Tag almost smiled to himself. Never in the three hells could he have imagined a scenario where he was on an alien planet telling others where to drop off warheads on his ship. The medical bay and the laboratory still called to him, and he felt a little uncomfortable sitting in the captain's crash couch. But more and more, he realized he was becoming accustomed to his new role.

After all, this is what he had joined the SRE to do—to command a ship. It wasn't the circumstances he thought he'd be doing it in. But when had the gods ever done anything according to a human's plan?

Sofia whistled, drawing Tag from his distracted thoughts. "Look at those torpedoes."

She pointed to the warheads that looked strikingly similar to the design of the Mechanics' navy vessels. Each torpedo resembled a jet-black shark with sleek curves that would make it practically invisible in the depths of space.

Bull sauntered over from where he'd been helping the marines load supplies into the bay. "Hell of a lot more compact than the stuff Starinski Labs makes," he said.

"How does it compare in terms of power?" Tag asked.

"Not much of a payload specialist," Bull said, "but from what

I gathered from Coren, these things are four or five times as powerful as the top-of-the-line Starinski ramjet warhead."

"So in other words, this will more than compensate for the ones the Drone-Mechs stole from us," Tag said.

"Abso-fucking-lutely."

"Starinski or Mechanic-made, that's all that matters," Tag said.

"You got that right, Captain." Bull slapped his hands together, rubbing his palms. "We're going to blow these damned Dronemaster xenos to the high heavens."

The redheaded marine gave Sofia and Tag a shit-eating grin before sauntering off to where the rest of his squad was bent over a crate, examining its contents. A dream-like expression crossed Sofia's face. She pinched a bit of the foam-like packing material from one of the crates and crunched it between her fingers.

Without looking up, she said, "You know, there is something I've been wondering."

Tag leaned against the bulkhead, checking the schedule for their launch on his wrist terminal. He didn't have time for what felt like an impending esoteric philosophical or extraterrestrial anthropological conversation with Sofia. "What's on your mind?"

"Alexander the Great."

"Alexander the what?" Tag strained his mind trying to place the name. It evoked a vague memory from pre-interstellar history, but he couldn't quite place it.

"He was a great conqueror." Sofia let the crumbles of the white packing material fall from her fingers. "Conquered most of the ancient world in Old Asia and Africa."

"Look, we've got a lot to do before taking off. Ancient history is certainly interesting, but—"

"You lab scientist types are all alike," Sofia said. "Always thinking about the future, but neglecting history. Where we're going is determined by where we've been."

Tag raised a brow. "Fascinating."

"Okay, okay." Sofia raised her hands defensively. "Here's the deal. Alexander was a tremendous military leader. Had a lasting impact on the dispersion of culture throughout the ancient world. But most importantly, he was a brazen leader and great strategist. His victories weren't purely on the battlefield."

"Okay, Professor Vasquez, where's this going?"

"Spies. He made good use of spies. Sent them to meet with dissidents to sow discord in his enemies' cities and support his campaign. It worked well enough, but eventually he came in with the cavalry, revealing himself and breaking through their city walls."

Tag was a little more interested now. "And you're suggesting we've seen the spies, they've sowed the dissidence, but we haven't seen our Alexander."

"Precisely, Skipper!" Sofia clapped her hands together. "No sign of Alexander. No cavalry. Why is that?"

"I'd say we showed their cavalry what we can do. Maybe we took down their cavalry when we deactivated the grav wave signals controlling the Drone-Mechs."

"Maybe," Sofia said, but her expression showed she didn't believe him. "But what if it wasn't? What if the cavalry is still out there? Why hasn't our Alexander shown himself?"

"The answers to those questions would assume the Drone-masters are trying to unify the intergalactic empires they've conquered."

"Right. And so far, the massacre of the Mechanics and genocide against the Melarrey don't fit the typical conquest goals of most cultures I've studied. Think about it. Why destroy a species and then just leave their stations and planets? What's the goal here?" She shook her head. "Basically, every war in human history centered on conflicts over resources, and occupying nation-states almost always sought some kind of economic advantages after conquering another."

"From what we've seen, the Drone-masters haven't set up mining operations or trade centers or anything like that on any of the Mechanic planets or stations." Tag rubbed the back of neck, leaving his hand there. "They enslaved the Drone-Mechs, which I guess counts for using them as a resource. Even so, they didn't make the Drone-Mechs do anything, just kept them hanging around the Mechanic planets."

"See, Skipper? The Drone-masters had the rest of the Mechanics dead to rights. But they never made any gesture to tell the Mechanics who they were or what they wanted. They never gave them the option to surrender or die. It's all just…odd."

"And why bring this up now?"

"I'm not sure," Sofia said. "It just seems important. Like something we should be thinking about. When we're in the war room with the Mechanics or the Melarrey or the SRE, we can't assume these enemies are like any we've faced. It's imperative we figure out who we're fighting and why they're acting the way they are. We've got to understand them."

"Are you volunteering to go on an anthropological study with these Drone-masters?"

"Fat chance. But—"

"But your point still stands," Tag finished for her. "This might be more than a quest for monopolizing all the galaxy's resources. Something more nefarious might be going on."

"A-plus for you," Sofia said.

Tag felt a shiver snake down his spine. Even the most ferocious of predators killed because it needed to eat. But a creature—or race—that killed and enslaved others for no apparent reason?

That was far more frightening.

# FOUR

The scent of sterile air reminded Tag of the *Argo*'s med bay, the space that had been his home for so long. It evoked images of smooth, contoured surfaces draped in blank whiteness and a uniform cleanliness, a universal tableau in a place of healing and medical research. But the Mechanic version of a hospital looked nothing like what Tag had imagined.

Coren strode, tall and lanky, beside a Mechanic medical scientist named Pradr'n. Pradr'n didn't wear the white lab coat or unisuit typical of human researchers like Tag but instead chose the same formfitting, black garb all the other Mechanics did. His, in contrast to the others, had three white bands on his upper arms; Tag presumed these signified his role as a researcher or doctor.

Pradr'n led them through silver corridors filled with pods in columns like the fingers of dead giants reaching for the heavens. Stacked vertically, each pod contained a slumbering Mechanic. As normal as they looked, Tag knew these were no regular Mechanics.

Each was a Drone-Mech with a self-assembling nanite antenna embedded within their brain. When Tag and Bracken had taken over the Lacklon Institute on Meck'ara, they'd interrupted the normal signaling that led these Drone-Mechs to act like barely sentient zombies, effectively shutting down the entire Drone-Mech fleet within the solar system.

Though the Drone-Mechs weren't dead, they weren't quite alive either. They were like droids without a power source. Their bodies still pumped blood, still functioned on autonomous signals, but their minds had been seemingly erased. Researchers like Pradr'n were working to restore the neurological functions of these Drone-Mechs in hopes they could save the huge portion of their population more or less stuck in suspended animation.

The aliens were visible through a polyglass shield with wires and tubes draping from the tops and into their ear slits, nostrils, and mouths. A few droids, each the size of a sparrow, buzzed around the huge room, scanning the comatose Mechanics, emitting a few beeps and then plugging in new cartridges of glowing solutions into the pods.

"This is how you take care of patients?" Tag asked.

"Similar to your regen chambers," Pradr'n said, "if memory serves me correctly, only we employ far fewer live aids to our patient sectors." He waved a hand around the atrium as his voice echoed against the alloy walls. "I am the sole medical officiant assigned to these chambers."

"All these patients and you still have time for research?" Tag asked.

Coren and Pradr'n both scoffed as if Tag had asked something ridiculous, like whether humans needed oxygen to breathe.

"Most of the actual medical work is handled by the droids." Pradr'n indicated one of the swooping, hovering droids with his gaze. "This frees me up to perform my research."

"With so much free time, have you made any progress?"

The condescension in Pradr'n's demeanor faded. "No, unfortunately our efforts have so far been unsuccessful."

"Their minds are difficult to read?" Coren asked.

"Yes," Pradr'n said. "None of our conscious-recording sensors show any sign of sentient activity within the Drone-Mechs."

Their footsteps clinked against the dark alloy floor, punctuating the momentary silence between them.

"Does that mean their brains have essentially been wiped?" Tag asked, afraid of the implications. If they did find a way to recover them from their neurological stasis, they'd be literal shells of their former selves, nothing more than infants trapped in adult bodies. All traces of their personalities, memories, and knowledge would be swept away like light sucked into a black hole.

"Their minds are, I regret to say, utterly inaccessible," Pradr'n finally replied. "We can't tell whether they are imprisoned somewhere behind the nanites or not. All we get when we probe the remnants of their conscious are wisps of static."

"I see," Tag said. He imagined the scene was like this all across the Mechanic homeworld. Hospitals and research facilities, even warehouses filled with Drone-Mechs in stasis pods. In his mind's eye, he pictured the Mechanics those Drone-Mechs had once been, trapped somewhere behind a proverbial nanite prison cell, yearning to break free of the mind-slaving technology. It brought back memories of his father, stuck on Earth, his own mind lost to neurological disease. There was many a day when he wondered if his father remained somewhere deep within his half-rotted brain, hidden behind the repeated questions and the dull glaze over his eyes.

"What do you think, Captain?" Pradr'n was staring at Tag.

"I'm sorry," Tag said. "Lost in thought. What were you saying?"

"We were just asking if there was any human technology

analogous to the Mechanic conscious miner we could use to determine whether these Drone-Mechs still retain a sense of their old self," Coren said. "Our hypothesis is that human technology has the capability of bypassing the nanites, since, of course, the nanites are based on old human tech."

Tag understood the insinuation behind what Coren had said. Pradr'n would never ask for help because it would imply that human tech might somehow be better than Mechanic tech. "I'm afraid I can't give you a good answer on that," Tag said. "Maybe it's possible, but I don't have any of the SRE's mind-probing tech available. That's all highly secured, highly controlled technology. They didn't want it to get into the wrong hands."

"In case someone abused it, like they did the nanites," Coren said.

"Right," Tag said. He let out a sigh, wondering if there was any tech in the galaxy that could help reverse the Drone-Mechs. But he feared there was very little that could be done.

Their best hope was to find the culprits behind the nanites and force them to deconstruct the technology they had used to enslave an entire race.

———

Tag walked toward the entrance of the Deep Origin dockyards with Coren. Sofia had joined them on their journey back to the *Argo* after having made her final rounds interviewing some of the Mechanic academics for her anthropological reports.

As they approached the gateway leading into the dockyards, Tag stopped and then turned to look at the sprawling infrastructure of the city. He soaked in the sight of the buildings, but most of all, the freshwater rivers winding their ways alongside roadways and the extensive parks. Even the towering skyrisers were draped in greenery, with suspended gardens alive and growing between the tall buildings. Despite their proclivity toward all things mechanical, the Mechanics still seemed to admire the oldest of the universe's technology: the natural engine of evolution and life.

"It is beautiful, isn't it?" Coren asked, catching Tag admiring the artificial landscape beneath the dome.

"I hate to admit it, but yeah, it is," Tag said. He took a deep breath. There was a hint of burning plastic, a reminder that the air had been recycled and purified. Still, the breeze carried scents of otherworldly flowers and vegetation, an aroma that Tag had almost forgotten during his service with the SRE. "I'm going to miss the semi-fresh air."

"Me, too." Sofia gestured to Coren. "Beats the smell of wet dog every time this furry guy sweats."

Coren glowered at her. "At least I am not the one destroying the ship's heads with the foul scents you humans generate."

"That's mostly Alpha," Sofia said.

"Hey, no need to incriminate her when she's not even here," Tag said. "Besides, I think we all know the real culprits."

Sofia and Coren eyed the marines amassed outside the *Argo*. They were in good humor, almost as if they weren't about to embark on a mission that would take them into the unknown, risking their lives and maybe even those of their respective species. Each step they took closer to the *Argo* was another addition to the already overbearing weight settling over Tag's shoulders. The pressure of delving back into the frontiers of human exploration, back into territories that might still be rife with Drone-Mechs and Dreg and whoever the three hells the Drone-masters were, along with whatever else might be out there ready to tear them apart.

Mechanics were milling next to the *Stalwart*, preparing it for flight, and a few of the Melarrey moved in a rolling walk as their gelatinous bodies circled their swan-shaped ship, the *Crucible*, making last minute checks. In an almost dream-like trance, Tag worked his way from the dockyard through the gangway into the cargo bay, finally settling into the captain's station on the bridge of the *Argo*. His crew found their positions and, over the comms, sounded that they were ready for departure.

The *Argo*, the *Stalwart*, and the *Crucible* hovered above their landing pads before rising into an enormous airlock. Huge panels and doors hissed shut behind them, and once they closed, water rushed in around the ships, letting the ocean replace the atmosphere. Soon the chamber's door opened. The *Stalwart* was the first to drift upward, away from Deep Origin and toward the surface, with the *Crucible* close behind.

"Follow 'em up," Tag said.

"Aye, Skipper," Sofia replied, pulling back on the controls and directing the *Argo* skyward.

It wasn't long before all three ships broke the water's surface, accelerating toward the blackness of the star-speckled night sky. They followed the call of the stars. Tag watched through the viewscreen as Meck'ara shrank, becoming nothing more than a marble of blue and green. It reminded him of when he had left Earth, and he felt the longing to revisit his home planet creep back through his torso like a cold wind.

With the reluctance of the Mechanics to support their mission and the threat of the Drone-masters looming ever larger, he wondered if there would be a Meck'ara to return to when their mission ended—especially if they didn't succeed. It was beyond foolish for the Mechanics to ignore his warnings. This might be their only chance at quelling the Drone-master threat.

His thoughts turned back toward the SRE and Earth. Would there be a human homeworld to return to when this was all over?

That question echoed in his mind as he gave Alpha the signal to initiate their jump into hyperspace. Stars and planets blurred across their viewscreen as acceleration pressed his organs to his spine. Soon the inertial dampeners caught up, and the pressure eased. Emerald and violet plasma crackled over the viewscreen as they burst into hyperspace.

# FIVE

The journey to the coordinates designated by Captain Weber's journal would take weeks, even by way of hyperspace. That gave the crew plenty of time to train, take care of the ship, and pursue their independent projects. For Coren, that meant continuously upgrading the *Argo*'s systems to be compatible with Mechanic systems, enabling more precise visualization of hostile and friendly contacts, better power usage from the fusion reactors, and more efficient data transfers between the trio of ships that made up their tiny fleet. The marines made their second home in the gym and the VR sims, where they ran combat drills, while Alpha read everything she could on human psychology, yearning to understand herself as much as her crew by peppering them all with questions when not delving through the *Argo*'s digital libraries.

Tag found himself drifting between crew members, looking for ways he could help. His work in the lab had largely been destroyed during his first run-in with the Drone-Mechs. The only physical evidence of his research on synth-bio AI was Alpha, and he couldn't exactly spend all his time running laboratory experiments when there was nothing but her to experiment on. It was during one of his periods of checking up on the crew that he wandered into the cargo bay.

Stretched between two towers of crates was a hammock. Curious, Tag scaled one of the towers to see who had made the place their home.

His heart thrashed against his rib cage when found Sofia's head—but not her body—nestled on one side of the hammock. A thousand thoughts whirred through his mind, his medical officer training kicking into overdrive, and adrenaline flooded his systems, narrowing his vision on Sofia's strangely serene expression.

Nothing he could think of, however, would help a head with no body.

"What's the matter, Skipper?" Sofia's head asked.

Tag almost fell backward, grasping for the top of the crate to prevent himself from tumbling to the alloy deck. "What... what's..."

"Oh," Sofia's hands appeared first, then the rest of her. She draped what looked like a huge white fur rug over the side of the hammock. "You look like you saw a ghost."

"Gods be damned, I might as well have." Tag willed his racing pulse to settle. "Didn't know you were going around pretending to be invisible."

Sofia laughed, squeezing the white spirit ox hide that the Forinth had given her back on Eta-Five. The hide came from a large, color-shifting mammal on the planet. Spirit oxen's flesh had a unique set of exotic proteins enabling the animal to blend in with its environment like an oversized, furry chameleon.

"I thought those things only worked when the oxen are alive," Tag said.

Sofia sat up, her hammock swinging precariously. "It definitely helps." She pointed to something on her wrist terminal. "But I got to thinking, if the Forinth can practically turn invisible by ingesting their hides, there's got to be some way I could use whatever's in it to, more or less, turn the hide on."

"And you figured it out?"

"Yeah, you could say that," she said. "Very easy to do. I borrowed a couple of the protein preservative solutions from the lab."

"Those are dangerous."

"So is going after the Drone-masters, but you don't see me complaining about that."

Tag raised an eyebrow.

"Anyway, I think I captured the proteins that let this thing change colors. It just needed an electrical current and chromatic input to tell them what to do. Borrowed a couple other parts from the lab, some advice from Alpha, and—voila!" She showed a small button she had clipped to the hide. With a press, the hide turned invisible. With another press, it reappeared.

"Better hope you don't turn that thing on and then forget where you put it."

"Already thought of that," Sofia said. She tapped the button again. "I installed a transponder. This thing is synced to my wrist terminal, so even if it's invisible and for some reason stays that way, I can find it."

"That's all very ingenious," Tag said.

"I know. My intellect is vastly superior," she said, impersonating Coren's accent. She set the hide to dangle off the edge of the hammock again and shifted toward him. "So did you need something?"

"Honestly, I was more curious about what a hammock was

doing in the cargo bay," Tag said. "Right now I'm in between experiments, and the ship's damn near as clean and well-maintained as it's going to get."

"You looking to start a game of Turbo up in here or something?" Sofia asked.

"Gods," Tag said with a laugh. "That's the last thing I'd need. I'm terrible at sports." He brushed a hand through his hair. "No, no games. I've had some time to think."

"Ah, really? Congratulations," Sofia said with a smirk. "I'm proud to hear you can do that, Skipper!"

Tag shook his head. "The Drone-masters. I've been considering your theory about why we haven't seen them, and something else strikes me as odd."

"What's that?"

"Not only did they enslave the Drone-Mechs and massacre the Melarrey, doing who knows what the three hells else to our jellyfish friends, but they left no trace of themselves behind. I had a bit of time to go through the ship's libraries. I mean, Alexander the Great made sure to install some kind of governmental control over every place he conquered. So why didn't the Drone-masters do that?"

Sofia rolled back into her hammock. "I mean, enslaving the Drone-Mechs and using them as an army was kind of installing a defensive network, wouldn't you say?"

"Sure," Tag said. "It looks like that at first glance. But even around Meck'ara, as formidable as their defenses were, that wasn't the whole population of Drone-Mechs from the planet. Plenty of ships and people were gone. Missing." His brow furrowed as thoughts flurried through his brain. "Plus, every space station, every trade or research outpost, even the Mechanic colonies we saw were destroyed or abandoned. We're talking about abundant economic resources lying completely neglected. Undefended. Why?"

Now Sofia's grin faded. Tag could practically see her mind

grinding through the implications. "Yeah, you've got a point. I mean, if the Drone-masters were so goddamned smart, they would surely set up a fail-safe to defend Meck'ara, right? There's no way they would rely on a single layer of defense. If they really, really wanted that planet, they would have stationed some of their own ships there or maybe used another species they were allied with or something."

"Exactly," Tag said. "I don't think the Drone-masters are just killing and enslaving for fun. I suspect you were right before. There's a reason they're acting so different from our expectations." He picked up the spirit ox hide, rubbing the coarse fur between his fingers. "You told me the Forinth treat all life as sacred, but they also appreciate the delicate balance of their ecosystem, that overburdening it would mean death to all of them."

"Which is why they sacrifice one of the elderly Forinth when a new one is born," Sofia said. "You think the Drone-masters are performing some kind of culling to keep the balance in this part of the universe?"

"I don't know, but it seems just as plausible a theory as any." Tag studied Sofia for a moment. Since they had escaped Eta-Five together, he had found it easier and easier to trust her. His thoughts lingered to how one of their marines, Rebecca "Lonestar" Hudson, had been duped into planting a transponder on the *Argo*, alerting Drone-Mechs to the ship's location. Someone in the SRE had tricked Lonestar—someone with evident ties to the Drone-Mechs or Drone-masters. "What still bugs me is why this genocidal species would take the effort to infiltrate SRE military intelligence. Why use an MI official to track the *Argo* down?"

"Damn," Sofia said. "My Alexander the Great metaphor really runs deep, doesn't it? Gods, they already have spies in the SRE sowing confusion."

The icy pinpricks of fear needled Tag's skin. "Which means an attack on humanity is imminent."

# SIX

Tag lay in his bunk, listening to the mechanical whoosh of air pushing through the air recyclers, tasting the subtle plastic flavor of it as it blew over him from the vents in his cabin. Darkness flooded his quarters, and his eyelids sagged, heavy under the weight of anticipation and exhaustion. The longer he spent on the *Argo*, the more capricious and unreliable a companion sleep had become. Sleep continued to evade him, its escape fueled by his conversations with Sofia.

It seemed every time they found an answer to one question, the mystery of the nanites and the Drone-masters gave them two more questions. They were in a never-ending race to solve a conspiracy fast spiraling out of his control. He hoped Captain Weber's journal held the answers he sought, and that when they finally reached the coordinates they'd at last come face-to-face with their enigmatic enemy. Tag was ready for an end to the mysteries, an end the massacres and subterfuge once and for all.

A seed of worry planted itself in his mind, ensnaring his brain like a weed. He feared there was far more to the nanites, far more to the Drone-masters than he could ever hope to understand from one bombing run his former captain never had the chance to complete.

He turned in his berth, trying to find a more comfortable position. Soon he gave up and swung his legs over the side. Donning his uniform, he treaded into the corridors with their lights dimmed to simulate night. Long shadows loomed from the stanchions, accompanying his walk to the mess. His footsteps clanged noisily along the passageway, and he worried about disturbing his crew until he heard the growling murmurs of voices.

Expecting to have the ship to himself, he was surprised when he nudged open the hatch to the mess, greeted by the boom of cheering voices hitting with an unforgiving force, shattering the quiet of the simulated late night.

"Damn, that was a textbook powerplay!" Marvin "Gorenado" Goreham said, slamming his palms against a table.

"Told you my Bucs are smarter than they look," Lonestar said, jabbing Bull playfully with an elbow to his ribs.

Bull let out a long sigh, his face flaming crimson and his arms folded over his chest.

"Captain!" Fatima "Sumo" Kajimi said, the first to notice him. "Come to watch the game?"

Instead of the normal view of space, a game of Turbo filled the mess's viewscreen. Players from two teams rushed each other at the start of a new round as flashes of lasers and holos played across the field. Tag tried to make sense of what was going on but quickly gave up.

"Want to sit?" Sumo asked, motioning to an open seat near her. "You're from Old Houston, right? The Texas Ridgewings are playing. You a fan?"

"Should I be?" Tag asked, settling into the seat.

"They're from your hometown," Lonestar said. She leaned across the table. "What's Texas like nowadays? My great-grandpop always told me about the cowboy ranch franchises everywhere."

Tag laughed. "When I was last there, Texas was as much as an urban sprawl as any other SRE state. You're from an actual frontier colony. You lived the real thing, so why are you so concerned about a fake experience at a franchise?"

Lonestar shrugged. "Fake or not, Texas is where my ancestors came from. Would be nice to visit the motherland someday."

"When this is all over, I'll gladly visit it with you," Tag said, "but don't blame me when your romantic view of your ancestral lands is tarnished."

Lonestar shrugged and knocked back her drink. The odor stung his eyes, reminiscent of homebrewed gutfire. When Lonestar caught Tag eyeing the glass, she wrapped her fingers around it and gave him a sheepish smile.

Again, Tag laughed. "Go ahead and enjoy yourselves now. I don't blame you. Might as well live it up these last few days in hyperspace before the real work begins." He looked at Bull, the only marine without a cup of the contraband alcoholic drink. "You already finish yours?"

Bull's forehead furrowed in gorges of wrinkles. "Promised these jarheads we're getting up at 0500 for calisthenics. I'm not hankering for a hangover like them."

"Probably a good call," Tag said. "Just in case, I'll have Alpha prep a few painkillers."

Sumo looked at him with a hint of surprise. "Really? If the officers on the *Montenegro* caught us drinking, they'd hang us out to dry."

"I trust Bull will take care of that for me," Tag said. As long as they were around to do their jobs when the time came, what they did in their moments off didn't concern him so much. Might as well relish it while they could. The dark clouds he had been trying to ignore seemed to be rapidly forming a funnel cloud, precipitating into a tornado of pessimism. Whatever madness they found themselves in on the other side of their hyperspace jump, he didn't mind if the marines spent the moments of this last calm before the storm enjoying themselves.

"Something bothering you?" Bull asked. "Not usual for you to drop in and join us for a Turbo match."

Tag opened his mouth to respond when Gorenado and Lonestar jumped up in unison, yelling victoriously about something that had happened on the viewscreen. They hugged each other as Sumo's expression grew dour. Once they'd settled into their seats again, Tag turned back to Bull.

"Nothing in particular," Tag said. "Just revisiting my old friend insomnia."

"Good friend of mine, too." For the first time, Tag noticed the dark bags hanging under Bull's eyes, offset by the smattering of boyish freckles that contrasted with his muscled frame.

"Does it worry you to think what we might find on the other side?" Tag asked.

"Maybe a little bit," Bull said. "Dreg, Melarrey, Mechanics, Drone-Mechs, Forinth, ice gods. I've had enough surprises for a goddamned career and it's only been a few months since we set sail from the *Montenegro*." He spoke in a hushed voice, leaning across the table as the other marines argued about MVP picks for the ongoing Turbo match. "Whatever is waiting for us, we're ready. I promise you that."

"I don't doubt it," Tag said, but he wasn't sure he meant it. The marine's stare remained fixed and sincere as if he was waiting for something. He realized Bull wasn't looking to Tag for a technical assessment of their chances of success. Rather, he wanted to see that same confidence radiating from the captain of this ship, the leader of the mission he and his squad had been assigned to.

In the lab, it was acceptable—even encouraged—for Tag to express his doubts about their experiments and research. That was how science worked, how intelligent conversations started. But as captain of the *Argo*, sharing too many of those doubts depleted the crew's morale.

The marines weren't stupid. He knew that much from his short time spent with them. What they wanted now, what they didn't talk about, was assurance that they were doing the right thing. That they were being led against seemingly insurmountable odds by a captain who believed in his crew and their mission.

That success might even be a thing they could achieve, however unlikely their gut told them it was. And right now, Tag was supposed to be that person.

He forced a grin and grabbed one of the empty cups on the table. "Lonestar, fill me up."

She gave him a nonplussed look before he gestured to the cup, and she obliged, pulling a bottle from beside her chair.

"I propose a toast," Tag said, holding the cup. He could already taste the unforgiving drink, its aroma practically burning his nostrils. "To the best goddamned marines in the SRE navy."

"Here, here," Sumo said.

"Yippee-cay-yay," Lonestar said in an exaggerated ancient Texas accent.

Gorenado growled in agreement. They all turned to Bull. At first, he held up his hands in a defensive gesture, but it didn't take him long to relent.

"As the sergeant would say," Tag said, glancing at Bull, "when we transition, whatever monsters we meet, let's kick some xeno ass!"

The marines cheered, and even Bull offered a half grin as they clinked their cups together and then drank. Tag's throat lit up in flames as the gutfire drizzled into his gullet, and a sheet of water formed over his eyes as he did his best not to cough. It had been ages since he'd touched the stuff, and now he remembered why.

But when Sumo clapped his back, wrapping a hand around his shoulder and hooting with laughter, he joined in. The alcohol burned away the tendrils of worry that had taken root in his mind. He knew they would be back later, but at least for now, he was thankful for the momentary reprieve.

Maybe he'd even find some solace in sleep.

He pushed himself up from the table, and Sumo gave him a disappointed look.

"You leaving us so soon, Captain?" she asked.

Tag nodded. "Like Bull said, tomorrow's an early morning, and I'll leave the hangovers to you all."

He strode to the hatch, feeling the warmth of the gutfire in his stomach, already hinting at the regret he might feel later. But for now, as he looked back at the marines, even Bull seemed to be sitting up straighter, joining in with the cheers and groans of disappointment as the Turbo game continued. It was against protocol for a captain to share a drink with his subordinates, especially while on a mission. But gods be damned, he couldn't help but feel proud of the difference that small gesture had made to the marines.

As he walked back to his quarters, the same place he'd had since he first stepped aboard the *Argo* as the Chief Medical Officer, something scratched at the back of his skull.

Something didn't feel right.

It wasn't that he'd ignored SRE protocols and had a drink; three hells, Captain Weber had been known to throw back a glass of gutfire or two with the crew.

No, there was something else. And as he entered his cabin,

his eyes roving over the desk in one corner and the tidy bed in another, he realized what that was. He had assumed the role of captain after being promoted by Admiral Doran and had initiated this mission into the unknown. He was *playing* the part of captain—but that was just it. Up until now, he'd been playing the part.

He needed to own it. To become what he had tried to be for the marines tonight. The lynchpin holding this crew together, the keystone of the *Argo*'s leadership.

Playing the part was no longer going to be enough. He needed to *be* the part. That meant thinking like Captain Weber had and studying what he had planned for the *Argo* before his untimely end.

Instead of settling in for sleep, Tag resolved that tomorrow would be a new dawn for his stewardship over the *Argo* and its crew. He left his familiar quarters and climbed the ladders toward another, larger cabin that had been vacant since the Drone-Mechs' first attack on the *Argo*.

It was time for Tag to finally acknowledge his role on the ship, to finally accept that the ghosts of the past did not determine the threads of their future. He was the captain now.

He stepped into the cabin.

His cabin.

# SEVEN

Tag tightened the straps on his crash couch and buckled into the captain's station for their imminent transition into normal space. Alpha situated herself in ops, preparing the holomap for when they reached their destination, and Sofia cracked her knuckles at the pilot controls. Coren warmed the weapon systems with a few taps on his terminal.

"All systems prepped?" Tag asked his crew.

"Energy shields and navigation systems online, ready for deployment," Alpha said.

"Ready to fly this bad boy like our lives depend on it," Sofia said.

"Good, because they do," Tag responded.

"Weapons are fully loaded and countermeasures are prepared should they be required," Coren said.

"Excellent." Tag glanced at the viewscreen. Through the sheets of crackling plasma, he could see the *Crucible* gliding on one side and the *Stalwart* on the other.

"Bracken, Jaroon, ready for transition?"

"We're ready," Jaroon called back through the comms.

"Affirmative," Bracken said.

"Initiate transition," Tag said. He felt the familiar brace of momentum yanking at his insides, pushing him forward against his restraints even as the ship put on its gravitational deforming "brakes." The inertial dampeners caught up and relieved him from the temporary nausea grappling with his guts.

He expected to see the usual quilt of sporadic spots of light betraying the distant location of the stars as the plasma gave way to the silent void of dark space. Instead his stomach plummeted when he saw the enormous asteroid careening straight toward the viewscreen.

"Sofia!" he managed to shout.

"On it!" She pulled hard on the controls, and the *Argo* veered out of the path of the asteroid. But they weren't safe yet.

All around, huge gobs of rock and ice tumbled through space, some as small as a wrist terminal, others as large as a Mechanic skyriser. An asteroid no bigger than an air car slammed into another roughly the size of the *Argo*, and shards of the larger asteroid split off, shedding ice and minerals in a cloudy shower.

"Shields up," Tag said. "Get us the hell out of this asteroid belt."

Alpha tapped on her terminal, and the green glow of the energy shields shimmered as they went up, then disappeared when they stabilized. Sofia rocked the *Argo* side-to-side, looking for a way to escape between the silent, deadly giants in their path. Tinier asteroids pinged against the *Argo*. The impacts resonated through the ship like the sounds of a violent hailstorm.

"Captain!" Bull called from below deck. "Are we under attack?"

"Asteroids," was all Tag offered as a response. "Bracken, Jaroon, what's your situation?"

"Caught in the asteroid field," Jaroon reported back.

"This is what happens when we trust human technology," Bracken said drolly. "We, too, are trying to find our way out of this mess."

All across the holomap, ropes of asteroids streamed in glaring red dots. Tag peered at the viewscreen to locate the *Crucible* and the *Stalwart* amid the rocky chaos.

"Alpha, find us the nearest escape trajectory," Tag said.

"Yes, Captain," she said calmly.

Something slammed against the energy shields, and the viewscreen burned with a brilliant glow as the asteroid melted, smaller chunks peppering the hull.

"I believe we are at risk of a hull breach if we collide with more asteroids like that," Alpha said.

Before Tag could respond, Sofia snapped, "I know that, Alpha, which is why I'm trying to avoid the damned things!"

"I'm highlighting the best route now," Alpha said.

A trajectory appeared on the holomap that traced waypoints between the mass of red dots. The same images appeared on Sofia's holoscreen.

"You good with that, Sofia?" Tag asked.

"I'll have to be."

Another echoing roar shook the bulkhead as an asteroid collided with their starboard side. It rattled Tag's teeth, and his fingers curled around the ends of his armrest. He could sense the frustration building up in Sofia, radiating off her like a thermonuclear warhead, and he didn't bother issuing any more commands. He trusted her to know how to best fly this damn ship through the insane obstacles ahead of them, but even so, he was worried her skills as a pilot wouldn't be enough.

"Coren," Tag said, "activate the point-defense-cannons. I want any large asteroids headed our way shredded before they hit us."

"Of course," Coren said. His fingers danced across his terminal, and strands of pearly orange fire lanced into the nearest asteroids, blasting through them like a mag train through a snow bank. The asteroids were reduced to pebbles as Sofia jockeyed the ship, but she was unable to completely avoid the smaller rocks, which burned up in the energy shields.

"Captain Brewer," Bracken called over the comms. "Aren't you afraid too much fire will attract the attention of any Drone-masters or Drone-Mechs in the area?"

She sounded like a mother chiding an insolent child, and her tone grated on Tag's already frayed nerves as another storm of debris pelted their hull. "Doesn't matter whether they see us or not if we don't make it out of here alive, does it?"

"This is true," Jaroon said. "We too are having a hard time evading all the incoming asteroids."

Translucent bubbles jetted from the *Crucible*'s strange weapons, accumulating and expanding around asteroids, crushing them until they were nothing but space dust.

"Fine," Bracken said. Orange pulsefire lanced from her ship to impale a skyriser-sized asteroid. The impact shredded a hole through the middle of it, and the *Stalwart* passed through the freshly made tunnel before turning its cannons on another target.

The asteroids seemed to be swarming more aggressively than a squadron of Drone-Mech fighters. Sweat coursed down Tag's forehead, dripping into his eyes. He wanted to wipe the beads of sweat away, but he couldn't risk removing his EVA suit's helmet just in case something went wrong and they lost atmosphere on the bridge.

Then an enormous asteroid damn-near the size of the entire city of Deep Origin loomed in their path. Cannon fire and pulse rounds from the *Stalwart* joined the odd bubble cannons of the

Melarrey ship, but their fire left nothing but craters on the asteroid's surface.

"We've got to get around that thing!" Tag said.

Even as the words tumbled from his mouth, he saw the tidal wave of other asteroids crashing toward them, descending in a maelstrom of ship-crushing sizes, blocking their routes of escape. There was no running. He briefly considered trying to perform a hyperspace transition, but it was too risky. As gravity shifted around them, the effects of their T-drive would be overwhelmed by the influx of nearby mass, leaving them and the asteroids equally crushed.

"Should I use torpedoes, Captain?" Coren asked, his normally level voice pitched with a hint of nervousness.

Tag hated to expend the torpedoes on a target like this. For one thing, the asteroid would probably shatter into smaller but equally deadly fragments. And even if they survived, they might later find themselves in desperate need of those weapons when they confronted the Drone-masters. Going up against unknown enemies with their ordnance already partially depleted wasn't optimal—but neither was being smashed to bits before you could face them.

"Bracken, Jaroon, one of you please tell me you can do something about this damn thing."

Bubbles still jutted from the *Crucible*, and glaring orange beams cut through space from the *Stalwart*.

"Torpedoes?" Bracken asked. She, like Tag, sounded unconvinced that it was their best option.

"I think I have an idea," Jaroon said. "I will need your ships to follow very closely behind mine. Close enough that you can feel the heat from our impellers."

"You heard him," Tag said to Sofia.

She pulled back on the controls, and the *Argo* fell in behind the *Crucible*. The *Stalwart* disappeared from their periphery, weapons still firing on the asteroids, and Tag watched on the holomap as the blip representing the *Stalwart* cinched up to their stern.

"Now I'll need you to trust me," Jaroon said. "Full thrust ahead!"

The *Crucible* accelerated, glowing a brighter blue as it careened toward the asteroid's surface. Tag barely had time to unclench his jaw, bracing for what seemed to be an inevitable impact, as Sofia took the *Argo* straight after him with the *Stalwart* close in their wake. There was no time to ask Jaroon what he had planned as the asteroids around them began colliding. The violent shockwaves would have torn apart the ship if they weren't in vacuum. There was only time to pray the jellyfish-like alien knew what he was doing.

Tag tried to gulp, finding it difficult to even swallow as they accelerated toward the murky brown surface of the asteroid. The white patches of ice on it expanded until they clotted his view, and he choked on a scream right before it seemed they would crash into one. The *Crucible* hit first, and a blinding flash of blue light overwhelmed the viewscreen.

# EIGHT

The flashes of blue light settled. Tag's stomach did not.

He had expected to see a tunnel drilled through the center of the asteroid, leading them to the other side, taking them to safety. There was no tunnel, yet at the same time, according to the holomap, they were inside the asteroid.

"What in the three hells?" Sofia asked. She leaned over the controls.

All around them, the rock seemed to shimmer and give way as if they were traveling through fluid rather than an enormous chunk of minerals and metals. Sofia kept the *Argo* close to the *Crucible*, and the *Stalwart* remained right on their tail. Everything in the viewscreen reflected a faint blue glow, reminiscent of the sapphire alloy encompassing Jaroon's ship.

"This is…this is amazing," Coren managed, his working eye wide.

"Jaroon," Tag called over the comms. "What did you do?"

"I've extended our ship's energy shields to encompass yours and Bracken's," Jaroon said.

Alpha cocked her head in a quizzical manner, and Tag asked the question that was no doubt on her synth-bio mind.

"How exactly does that work? Our shields couldn't drill through rock like this."

Jaroon emitted a burbling noise that must've been a Melarrey laugh. "We are not drilling through the rock. Our shields work slightly differently than yours. Instead of absorbing and dispersing energy, they proactively emit energy to alter the state of matter. We're effectively liquefying the asteroid around us, but we're using an enormous amount of power to do that. We won't be able to sustain this field for very long, and the rock outside of the field quickly solidifies."

"So if Sofia doesn't keep us close to you," Tag said, "we'll get stuck in the rock."

"And likely crushed," Jaroon said. "So as I mentioned before, please stay close."

Sofia hunched over her station. "You got it."

Soon the *Crucible* slipped out of the asteroid, followed shortly by the *Argo* and *Stalwart*. The asteroid solidified again with no hole or crater to evidence their journey through the thing. Tag heard his crew breathe a collective sigh of relief as they sailed once again in open space, with only a few lingering asteroids to contend with.

"Captain," Alpha said, "we should be approaching Captain Weber's prescribed coordinates shortly."

"Initiate all long-range sensor arrays," Tag said. "Full power. If anything's out here, I want to see it."

Bracken and Jaroon both appeared on Tag's holoscreen in a joint comm link.

"Brewer, you did say your former captain was supposed to

raze a whole planet," Bracken said. "You don't think those aster-oids were what remained of it, do you?"

"Hard to tell," Tag said. "Sofia and I figured the SRE would've sent a few different vessels to these coordinates in case Weber failed. They do like to plan for redundancies. Still, I don't know what the SRE has that could obliterate a planet into crumbs like that."

"True," Bracken said. "I can't imagine humans possess the weapons technology to cause such destruction."

"And Mechanics do?" Tag asked with a raised brow.

"Not exactly," Bracken said.

Her face remained as stoic as ever, but Tag took a slightly guilty pleasure in her admission of the Mechanics' inadequacies.

"What about the Melarrey?" Tag asked. "That material phase transfer tech is pretty impressive. Could that destroy a whole planet?"

"Theoretically," Jaroon said. "But it would take a concerted effort by an entire fleet, and I'm afraid we simply do not have the resources to do something like that after what the Drone-Mechs did to us."

"Either way," Alpha piped up, "that asteroid field is several hundred thousand klicks from our target destination. If the target was a planet, tremendous forces would've been involved to move it this far out of orbit."

"It would be nice if our work was done for us," Tag said, "but even if our target is destroyed, it wouldn't give us any clues about the Drone-masters or if they're actually gone. Let's keep on our current trajectory."

For several tense minutes they continued through the void until the speckles of red signifying the asteroid field disappeared from their holomap. They glided through the monotony of space with only the three ships' impeller drive signatures pinging on their sensors.

Each second that passed without detecting anything worried Tag. What if he had misunderstood the coordinates Weber had written in his book? What if Grand Elector L'ndrant was right that they were wasting their time? This might all be a fool's errand, a wonderful distraction, something to throw the SRE and Mechanics off the Drone-masters' trail. Maybe Captain Weber had been duped just like Lonestar had.

All those anxieties crashed against the inside of Tag's skull like gale-driven waves against a rocky cliff.

And then a ping broke the crew's silence. A new red dot appeared on the holomap.

"Contact," Alpha muttered. "Maybe a small planet…or a large space station."

"Bracken? Jaroon? Are you reading this?" Tag asked.

They both responded in the affirmative, and Tag's pulse quickened as they narrowed the distance between themselves and the mysterious object.

"Slow the approach," Tag said. "Spool up the T-Drive."

Alpha and Sofia both nodded, carrying out their respective orders.

"If things go south," Tag said, "we're jumping to coordinates B."

"Copy," Jaroon said.

"Understood," Bracken replied.

As they got closer to the object, the red dot on the holomap split off into smaller fragments. There was still a central dot that loomed much larger than the others, but several dozen more swarmed around it like bees around a hive.

"Bring all weapons systems online," Tag said.

"Yes, Captain," Coren said as he tapped on his terminal. The hum of the Gauss cannons magnetizing their rails and the pulse cannon charging filled the bridge.

A speck appeared on their viewscreen, the source of the ho-lomap indicators finally visible by outward cams. Sofia brought the *Argo* in closer until the speck became a larger blob. It became more and more clear that this wasn't a small planet at all. Instead the object seemed to be a space station—but was like none Tag had ever seen.

Huge masts jutted from its central bulk, and there was very little geometric organization. It reminded him of an electromag-net that had been turned on and randomly attracted all the metal objects in its vicinity to it. Except instead of tacks and nails and screws, there were spaceships that had been secured together with a latticework of alloy frames and patchwork welds and tunnels made of sheet metal.

Bracken gasped over the comm line, and Tag quickly spot-ted the origin of her surprise. One of the ships attached to this gigantic relic was a sleekly contoured battlecruiser of ebon al-loy. It was undoubtedly a Mechanic craft. As Tag's eyes roved the structure, he identified other ships adhered to the framework. Some appeared to be made of glass so clear he could see the stars on the other side of the station. Others were boxy and pocked with rust, like old Earth container ships that had learned to fly through space. There were ships as small as an air car with wings for atmospheric flight, and others larger than even the Mechanic dreadnoughts, bristling with cannons and ports and torpedo bays that Tag hoped were as nonfunctional as they looked. One sap-phire-colored craft, shaped vaguely like a bird of prey, reminded him of Melarrey tech.

"Is that..." Tag began.

"That's one of ours," Jaroon confirmed.

All told, there were hundreds of different ships joined togeth-er by a patchwork of tubes and wires and corridors.

"What is this?" Tag asked.

Judging by the silence coming from the *Stalwart* and the *Crucible*, his compatriots were just as mystified.

"Hostile contacts identified," Alpha said. The holomap glared with the scarlet markings of the smaller ships they had detected earlier. Now those smaller ships blazed across the viewscreen. Tag immediately recognized them by their muddy, organic appearance.

"Dreg," Tag said. A few dozen of the insectoid ships were headed toward the trio. Inside them were the ugly, flying slug-like creatures he had come to dread. Each was no larger than his head, but if they got aboard the ship and swarmed through the passages, their diminutive size would hardly matter. "Open fire."

Pulse and PDC fire exploded from the *Argo*, cutting into the approaching Dreg. The parasitic little bastards loved scavenging other aliens' scraps. Tag didn't want to give the putrid aliens a chance to attach their ships to his hull and cut their way into the *Argo*. As the first few Dreg ships were battered and broke apart under the fusillade of combined Mechanic, Melarrey, and SRE efforts, something else caught Tag's attention.

His heart stopped, and his blood froze for an instant. It wasn't the impending interspecies conflict that frightened him. Rather, it was a strangely familiar sight, something he had never expected to see all the way out here, that caused his nerves to dance with violent electricity. As more Dreg ships unlatched from the station and sped toward the *Argo*, they revealed the shape of the hulking spaceship at the heart of the station.

Its bulbous shape had been transformed by the pylons and scaffolding extending from its hull, but Tag recognized it despite the additions. It had clusters of cannon batteries and torpedo ports, but the main purpose of this ship wasn't war. It was an exploratory vessel, one meant to identify distant planets and initiate colonization efforts.

As the station slowly rotated, Tag saw huge white letters painted across the hull. He let out a sharp breath as he read what had been written there long ago.

It was an old script, but Tag knew how to read it. The ship was human: the UNS *Hope*.

# NINE

"What is that doing out here?" Sofia exclaimed.

"I thought...the United Nations...we lost contact with it hundreds of years ago," Tag said in disbelief. The *Argo* had originally been dispatched to follow the trail of the missing generation ship. Their primary mission had been to uncover the mystery of what had happened to the *Hope* and the thousands upon thousands of humans who had lived on it.

They didn't have long to wonder why the giant ship had made this desolate part of space its home, nor how it had evolved into the monstrosity they saw now. The Dreg opened fire on the fleet, expelling organic spikes that trailed oozing lines of brown goo. Most of the spikes were intercepted by the PDC fire and chaff pluming from the *Argo*, but a few made it through the screen of countermeasures, piercing the *Argo*'s shields and crashing against its hull. The ship quivered with each impact.

"Take them out!" Tag shouted.

The pulse cannon charged and launched a spear of intense cobalt fire into the nearest Dreg ship. As the ship disintegrated, the Gauss cannons chugged away, levying kinetic slugs into the Dreg's ranks. Each time a round passed through the carapace-like vessels, more goo streamed out in long tendrils along with wires that looked like blood vessels and the writhing bodies of the slug-like Dreg.

The Dreg didn't stand a chance. Not in open space like this. Not when Tag, Bracken, and Jaroon had come prepared for much, much worse. Streams of pulsefire and PDC rounds spiraled through space, pounding the Dreg ranks as the Melarrey bubble weapons crushed the attackers. Soon all that remained of the attacking fleet were chunks of ships and corpses frozen in the vacuum. A few more Dreg ships were scattered across the station, but no others ventured out to repeat the ill-fated assault of their brethren.

"That all they got?" Sofia asked.

"This is too easy," Tag said. "I don't like it."

Again Jaroon and Bracken joined Tag on the comms.

"That ship—the UNS *Hope*—that's the one you told us about," Bracken said.

"It is," Tag said. "I had no idea *this* was our target. It doesn't make sense. Alpha, we are at the correct coordinates, right?"

"We are, Captain," Alpha said. "There is a small margin for error, but other than the asteroid belt, I do not detect any other significant masses that would indicate an alternative target."

"Strange," Tag said as much to himself as to the others. "Maybe you were right. Maybe the *Hope* had discovered something out here—something the SRE wanted to disappear. Maybe that debris field really was the planet."

He wanted to believe that their mission had already been done for them. Perhaps this war had ended without their realizing it. The lump in the back of his throat told him it couldn't be true.

Still…

"The presence of the Dreg would indicate that this station has likely been abandoned," Bracken said. "Whether there were Drone-masters or humans or something else here, the fact that so many Dreg have tried to establish residence makes me think whoever was here before is gone."

Sofia stared at Tag, her gaze burning through his visor. He knew what she wanted. This was an archaeological mystery. Whether this structure had started with the humans aboard the UNS *Hope* or the *Hope* had simply been the seed of a station assembled by another species, this was a curiosity far too intriguing to pass up.

"We have to investigate, of course," Tag said. "I want to know what happened to the *Hope*'s crew and who created this station. If this was Captain Weber's target, if he was supposed to destroy this…this *thing*…then I want to know why."

"I agree," Bracken said. "I didn't come all the way out here to torpedo this mess and leave. I'd like to know *why* you dragged us out here, too."

Tag sensed a bit of good humor in her statement amid the dripping derision.

"We are agreed as well," Jaroon said. "This is far too curious. I would very much like to join any boarding crew investigating the station."

"Excellent," Tag said. He studied the huge relic rotating in front of them. It would take days, even weeks to walk through the maze-like structure if they explored each ship and corridor. There would no doubt be enough to keep them occupied for months if they dug deep into the data stored in the individual computer systems. The vast knowledge and technology they might uncover was tempting.

But if the Drone-masters were still out there, if this was just the first breadcrumb on their trail, they couldn't afford that luxury. They needed to find out what they were supposed to do here—or where they were supposed to go next.

"We should split up," Tag said. "Jaroon, start at the Melarrey ship we spotted. Bracken, investigate the Mechanic battlecruiser. Find out why those ships are here. We'll start out at the *Hope*."

"Sounds logical," Bracken said.

"Very good," Jaroon said.

The two alien ships took off, heading toward the nested vessels respective to each species. Sofia eased the *Argo* forward, past the floating remains of the Dreg ships, and skirted between the tentacles of other spaceships-turned-space-station chambers. The UNS *Hope* filled the viewscreen as they approached. It was larger than Tag had even imagined. Generation ships like this had been built to support entire human cities, civilizations shooting into the stars without the support of resupply ships or trade networks. That meant they had everything from squadrons of fighters to agricultural sectors and manufacturing facilities. In essence, the generation ship could maintain and repair itself like a living, breathing creature.

Docking ports appeared on the viewscreen, lining the one side of the UNS *Hope* not covered by the makeshift add-ons. The luer lock docking apparatus of the *Hope* was antiquated compared to the more advanced grav tether connections favored by the SRE now, but Alpha assured them they would be able to make do.

"Bull, better make ready down there," Tag said.

"'Bout time," he said. "I hate missing out on all the fun."

"Well if this expedition is like our others," Sofia said, "there will be plenty for you to enjoy."

The *Argo* connected to the *Hope* with a jolt that rattled through the bridge.

"Connection secure," Alpha said.

Tag undid his restraints and stepped out of his crash couch. "Everyone to the docking port. Alpha, put the ship on lockdown. Coren, maintain remote weapons controls just in case any Dreg decide to board while we're gone."

The group rushed down the ladders to gear up in the armory and then join the marines already waiting at the docking port. They were armed with a menagerie of weapons. Tag had ensured Coren, Sofia, and Alpha were also equipped with all manner of sample and data collection equipment, too, as they prepared to embark on what Tag hoped would be a fruitful treasure hunt. The marines marched into the airlock first, and the others followed. The crew was unusually silent, wrought with anticipation.

Tag clicked on the terminal, and the airlock began pressurizing to the atmosphere on the other side of the *Hope*'s docking hatch. It didn't take long for the air to hiss out. Tag's HUD indicated that the pressure was not off by much—less than a tenth of an atmosphere difference between the *Argo* and the station. The *Argo*'s computer systems overrode the *Hope*'s dormant airlock and forced the hatch to open. Dim red lights wavered along the interior as Bull led them in, his rifle pressed firmly against his shoulder. Grime covered the bulkhead, and a few loose wires hung haphazardly from rusted-out holes in the ceiling. Metallic groans resonated through the alloy like the howls of distant, mechanical wolves.

By all signs, it appeared this was the first instance in a very long time that a human had set foot inside the *Hope*.

Tag planned to find out exactly why that was by the time they were off this gods-forsaken ghost ship.

# TEN

The emergency lights glowing along the empty corridors cast eerie pools of red over the stanchions and deck, giving the place a decidedly blood-soaked appearance. Bull signaled the marines to fan out, securing both directions of the corridor. Each marine bristled with weapons and battle-hardened stares, determined to bring down any threat that dared challenge their entrance. Tag bent to examine the deck and wiped a glove in a centimeters-thick layer of dust. His finger came away coated in a substance that he couldn't be sure was organic or something else entirely. He shivered before standing straight.

"This mission is one of science and research first and foremost," he said to the crew. He fought against the urge to whisper. Their voices were mostly contained within their suits, anyway. Though his HUD reported the atmosphere had appropriate oxygen levels, pressure, and even bearable temperatures, he didn't want to risk encountering some kind of toxin or contaminant. If the Drone-masters had been here and found the humans, they might have left some present behind—perhaps even a human version of the mind-enslaving nanites.

"Any active terminals we find, Alpha and Coren will tap into them. Sofia and I will take care of any biological samples."

The group affirmed the orders with a flurry of nods.

"Alpha, call up our schematics of the *Hope*," Tag said. "I don't know how much of this thing has changed since it was built, but they might still be helpful. We've got two main targets. First, the *Hope*'s labs. Second, the bridge. Got to be something in those places to clue us in to whatever happened here. Any questions?"

Lonestar raised a hand. "When do I get to shoot something?"

"*Hope*fully never," Tag said. He tapped on his wrist terminal to transfer a three-dimensional map of the *Hope* to each of the crewmembers' wrist terminals. On his helmet's HUD, the map loaded and showed their current position in the docking station. He used his wrist terminal again to mark a waypoint to the labs, which were closer than the bridge. With a hand signal, he directed Bull to lead them out of the docking bay and into the rest of the gargantuan ship.

Gorenado and Sumo dropped into rearguard behind Tag. Sumo gave him a wink. "I won't let any boogeymen get to you, Captain."

"It's not the boogeymen I'm afraid of," Tag replied.

Their steps resounded through the metal corridors. Streaks of grime dripped along the bulkhead and covered the debris on the deck. Each step they took left a clear footprint. Tag scanned the floor, looking to see if any other lifeforms had left a trail through this corridor, but other than the tracks of his crew, he didn't see anything.

Creaks moaned through the bulkheads as they arrived at a large chamber where wire-framed scaffolding led to three additional decks above their position. Each level was marked by a bevy of other corridors. A pungent odor reminiscent of decay permeated the place, even through the suit's air filters. Tag's hand moved toward his holstered pulse pistol.

The whistle of air blowing through ventilation shafts seemed more pronounced here. Somehow the life-support systems were still functioning, still humming with a shred of life. That surprised him. Something must've been maintaining these ships; something that hadn't left too long ago, or else the *Hope* would've fallen apart due to neglect.

If Tag strained his ears, he thought he could hear the buzz of Dreg wings beating the air underneath the current flowing through the corridors. The sound was permanently ingrained in his memory since their time at Nycho station, back when they'd been searching for any signs of free Mechanics. He half-expected the sickening creatures to come pouring out of one of the corridors or draining down a vent to assault the *Argo*'s crew at any moment.

"Lab's up that way," Bull said, gesturing with his rifle.

Tag's gaze followed where he indicated. Three decks up.

"Shit," Gorenado said.

"Anyone a good climber?" Sofia asked the group.

The ladders and scaffolding leading up to the lab deck had, at some point in the ship's vacancy, collapsed. Skeletal remains of a few support columns jutted up toward the high ceilings, and part of a ladder swung from the top deck.

Sofia pointed to the ladder. "Give me a running start and I can make it."

"Too bad the grav generators are still running," Coren said.

"As much as I like floating around," Lonestar said, "I like being able to plant my feet firmly on something better. Lot harder to dodge a charging bull when you can't do anything but float."

Alpha turned to Tag. "Should I calculate an alternate route?"

"Do it," Tag said. He pulled up the map of the *Hope* on his wrist terminal. Undoubtedly, the quickest route was through here; the top deck included a corridor straight to the lab. All the other routes seemed to skirt the perimeter of the ship, drawing them farther and farther away from their goal.

"By my calculations and the current state of the ship, I estimate two alternative routes that would add another half hour to three hours," Alpha said. She tapped on her wrist-terminal, and a holo appeared in front of the small group. Their faces reflected the ephemeral blue glow of the holo as they examined the green lines Alpha had traced through the *Hope*'s schematics.

"This is the fastest route?" Bull asked gruffly, pointing to one of the lines. "Looks like it starts straight through that hatch."

He sauntered over to the hatch the route indicated. The other marines joined him, and Sumo tried pulling on the release. The door groaned when Gorenado put his hefty weight into it, but it still didn't budge.

"Looks like an emergency hatch," Sofia said, indicating the scarred red lines crisscrossing the doorway. "Not going to be easy to open."

"Any other way to get through?" Tag asked.

Coren strode forward and clicked on his wrist-mounted weapons. A blue tongue of plasma leapt from the end of one of the barrels. "I can take care of it." He guided the plasma cutter around the edge of the doorway, making slow progress. Sparks jumped from red-hot metal and bounced across the deck.

Some of the detritus on the floor caught fire, and Lonestar yelped, stomping it out. It took Coren another five minutes to cut halfway around the hatch.

"Might've been faster just to take that other route," Sofia said.

"I can do this," Coren said, his voice echoing over the comms with a hint of exasperation.

"Looks like we're committed now," Sumo said.

Coren finished cutting, but still the emergency hatch didn't move.

"My turn," Gorenado said. He braced himself against the deck, bending at his knees. With a yell, he grabbed the handles on the hatch and pulled.

"Don't throw your damn back out!" Sofia yelped.

"The probability of injury is rather high," Alpha added.

Gorenado paid them no heed as he yanked the freshly shorn door away and dropped it at his feet. It hit the deck with a clang, sending up a cloud of brown and black dust. As the dust settled, a new smell permeated the air filters in Tag's suit, and he gagged. Plumes of black fog shifted out from the newly opened passageway, carrying the distinct odor of carrion.

"Uh, I suppose we're supposed to go that way now, huh?" Lonestar said, standing at the entrance with her rifle barrel staring down the dimly lit corridor.

Sofia coughed. "I'm beginning to think there was a reason this hatch was closed."

# ELEVEN

L et's move out," Tag said. "Bull, take us in."

"Lonestar, you're on point," the marine sergeant barked. "Gorenado, rearguard. Sumo, stick close to the captain."

"Don't trust me to handle myself?" Tag asked.

"I'd like to keep you alive," Bull said with no indication of humor.

Dull-red emergency lights continued to guide their passage through the dormant generation ship. Gunk clung to every surface, seeping from the joints in the walls and out from rivet holes. Every several meters, Tag thought he heard the scuttle of the Dreg's insectile legs scratching against the bulkheads or the ventilation shafts tracing the hallways.

"Is all this filth from the Dreg?" Tag asked Coren.

"I don't believe so," Coren said. "The Dreg typically do not leave this type of mess behind while scavenging."

"But from everything you told me, they usually don't stick

around those places for long," Sofia said. "Maybe the Dreg are living here. Maybe this is a hive."

"It has been almost impossible for us Mechanics to avoid the Dreg in space, but I personally didn't deal much with them," Coren said. "I'm no expert on their culture or homesteading. Maybe our resident anthropologist would care to spend some more time aboard the *Hope* if it does turn out to be a hive."

"It would be greatly beneficial to my threat assessment algorithms if we had more data on this species," Alpha added, looking hopefully at Sofia.

"Et tu, Alpha?" Sofia asked.

Alpha looked at her quizzically, then her eyes brightened. "Ah, this is a human historical *and* literary reference. Shakespeare's *The Tragedy of Julius Caesar*, correct?"

"Perfect marks," Tag said. "But I'd prefer if we didn't become part of history just yet. We're getting close. Keep your guard up."

Lonestar stopped at a corner and motioned for silence. With a quick hand signal, she summoned Bull to her side, and they peered around the corner. Tag pressed himself flat against the bulkhead beside Coren. Sumo gazed fiercely around, placing herself slightly in front of Tag.

Tag half-expected them to unleash a torrent of fire into whatever they had spotted, but after a few seconds, the marines waved the rest of the group to join them. Lonestar and Bull marched along either side of their corridor, creeping forward in slow, steady steps. Sumo remained in front of him like a walking shield. As his eyes followed the line of scarlet emergency lights down the passageway toward the hatch at the end, he saw what had alarmed Lonestar. Long gouges marred the bulkhead. They were torn deep enough through the layers of grime to reach the shining silver beneath. The lights reflected off the alloy, giving the bulkhead the eerie appearance of a wounded animal. Another crisscross of gouges tattooed the hatch, and underneath it lay a particularly lumpy mound of the brownish-black grime that covered the decks and bulkhead. Something protruded from the mound, and as they crept nearer, Tag could see the sheen of white bones.

"I'm guessing this isn't the Dreg's doing," Sofia whispered through the comms.

"My probability analysis suggests it is unlikely," Alpha said.

"I won't disagree," Coren said.

The scratching behind the bulkheads seemed louder now, competing for attention with Tag's pulse pounding through his eardrums. Maybe the Dreg—or whatever had been scratching the walls—were actually louder here, or maybe it was just the effects of adrenaline heightening his senses in anticipation.

"I'm not one to back down from a fight," Lonestar said, "but whatever did this is wilder than a mountain lion." She kicked at one of the bones. "And damn hungry to boot."

Bull pressed a palm against the hatch. "First chamber of the laboratory sector should be through this door."

"Coren," Tag said. "Get us through." He could feel the hairs rising on the back of his neck. "And let's hurry."

"You got it," Coren said. He activated his wrist-mounted weapons, and the plasma torch lit up again. It cast a flickering blue glow that melded with the red emergency lights. Orange and yellow slag dripped and sparks danced from the torch as it cut into the hatch with a hiss that snaked down the corridor.

Bull and the other marines stood sentinel. Sofia gazed nervously between Coren and the other end of the passage. Though the crimson lights illuminated swatches of the intersection from which they had last turned, they still allowed enough shadows to make Tag shiver. The tension stretching between the crew was almost as thick as the grime under their boots. He saw the shadows flicker and dance, as if something liquid flowed through them, and he shook his head, convinced it was his nerves playing tricks on him.

Alpha remained statuesque, her expression betraying no emotion. But when she opened a private channel to Tag, she said, "I believe I am experiencing fear."

"Understandable," Tag whispered back.

"Did y'all see that?" Lonestar asked, her faux Texan accent coming in strong.

"Negative," Bull said.

Then Tag heard something like the patter of feet through sludge. It was strikingly different than the gentle scritch-scratch of what he thought had been the Dreg.

"Anyone else hearing what I'm hearing?" Tag asked.

Sumo leaned forward as if straining her ears. "Yeah, I think so."

More distant slaps of something against the goo.

"Coren, any chance you can hurry up?" Sofia asked.

"I'm doing this as fast as I damn well can," he shot back.

A howl exploded down the hall. More howls erupted in response, reverberating through the corridors in a hellish cacophony. Scraping claws and a chorus of aggressive barks joined the sonic storm.

"Okay, we've definitely got incoming contacts," Lonestar said. Her finger hovered on the trigger guard, and Bull kneeled next to her, his rifle playing across the openings at the end of the corridor.

Movement caught Tag's eye. His hand twitched around his pulse pistol. He pulled it from his holster, leveling it toward the shadows and red lights where the marines were training their aim. Maybe it was a silly gesture. If the marines couldn't bring down whatever was headed this way with their rifles, then he doubted his pulse pistol would have any significant effect. But it felt better to hold a weapon. Better to do something other than wait in terror.

"How much longer, Coren?" Tag asked.

"Give me ten seconds."

"That's not up to me."

Now Tag knew for sure he saw movement. Shadows loomed, cast by light streaming from the other passages. Distorted by the emergency lights, it was difficult to make sense of the shapes other than to know that they were headed toward Tag and his crew.

"I'm through!" Coren said.

"Gorenado!" Tag yelled. "Get that door out of our way!"

Instead of positioning himself to heft the door out like last time, Gorenado charged. He hit the door like a rhino, throwing his shoulder into it and knocking the panel backward. With a ringing thud, the door crashed beyond the opening into a new chamber filled with amber light.

"Clear!" Gorenado bellowed.

Alpha and Sofia ran in first. Sumo covered Tag as they retreated through the doorway. Bull and Lonestar backed up slowly, their rifles still trained on the shadows that were growing ever larger down the passage. When Bull glanced back to confirm everyone had made it, they both sprinted through.

"Alpha! Gorenado! Get that door back up!" Tag yelled.

Gorenado grunted as he picked up one side, and Alpha latched her silver fingers under the other. They started to lift, but it slipped from Gorenado's grip. He jumped back, cursing. Bull positioned himself to help. At the same time, Lonestar and Sumo sent a fusillade of rounds careening down the passage, flashing and ricocheting against the bulkheads. Tag never got a good look at the monster, but he heard more desperate howls as Gorenado, Bull, and Alpha managed to lift the hatch. They secured it into place.

"Coren, weld that thing now!" Tag said.

The others pressed against the hatch, holding it place as Coren began welding. Through the hiss of the plasma welder, the shrill cries of the creatures on the other side of the hatch continued, piercing the din. Tag motioned to Sofia, Sumo, and Lonestar, and they began heaving lab benches and other unsecured, heavy pieces of equipment toward the hatch to barricade it just before the first creature slammed against the door.

*Definitely too big to be a Dreg,* Tag thought.

Gorenado dug his boots into the grime, pressing his back against the hatch. He shuddered as the hatch shook with more exploding bangs. Sweat trickled down Tag's brow as he shoved another lab bench into place, its legs leaving long, scraping canyons in the filth on the deck.

"Come on, Coren," Gorenado managed, his breath coming in ragged gasps. "Can't...hold...this..."

The hatch jolted, almost buckling under the impact as another creature slammed the door. Gorenado stumbled forward, but Sumo caught him before he face-planted on the deck. Coren finished welding and stepped to admire his handiwork, while Alpha and Bull let go of the door.

"It's not perfect, but it should hold for a while," Coren said.

Sofia and Lonestar slammed another heavy shelf full of coils of wire and microscopy equipment against the hatch. The equipment rattled as the creatures pounded on the other side.

"What were those things?" Sofia asked, her hands on her knees as she caught her breath.

"Didn't get a good look," Lonestar said. "But I don't think they're very friendly."

"That appears to be an accurate assessment," Alpha said.

"What happened here?" Sumo asked, already looking away from the hatch.

Tag nodded, then finally took the opportunity to study the room they had found themselves in. Unlike the corridors, they didn't need to contend with emergency lights. Golden light spilled from light banks. There were heaps of ancient medical equipment piled against crash couches that looked like precursors to those found on the *Argo*. Shelves and lockers hung open, spilling boxes of pharmaceutical supplies. A terminal screen with busted glass decorated an auto-pharmacy that was almost as big as a regen chamber. Against another bulkhead stood a smattering of terminals. Most were attached to broken holoscreens with piles of the fragmented shards accumulated around them. But two were still functional, emitting a faint blue light.

Tag strode toward the nearest terminal, trying to ignore the sounds of the creatures outside the lab. "Whatever happened here, maybe we can find some answers."

He traced his hand over one of the terminals, and the holoscreen lit up. His eyes grew wide. Two short sentences appeared on the holo in English.

"WELCOME TO THE UNS *HOPE* BIOLOGICAL LABORATORIES. GESTURE HERE FOR ACCESS."

# TWELVE

Tag waved his hand over the terminal. His mind whirled at what they might discover. All the secrets of the experiments carried out on the *Hope*, what had become of the crew, and what those creatures were and why were they trying to run them down—by the three hells, they might even contain information about the Drone-masters.

But the holoscreen merely glared at him with a dull-red message: USER NOT RECOGNIZED.

"Alpha, can you get into this?"

"These are highly antiquated systems. I am certain that I can," Alpha said. She stood staring at him blankly for a moment. "I'm sorry, have I not satisfactorily answered your question?"

"That was more of a request for you to access them, not an assessment of your abilities," Tag said.

"Oh, I understand. Thank you for the clarification." Again she stood in front of the terminal like a statue, as the jarring scrape of claws against metal sounded from the hatchway.

"Well, go on," Tag said. "Do it."

"Of course, Captain."

A data collection wire from her EVA suit adhered to the terminal, and she froze as if meditating. While Alpha probed whatever artificial intelligence and security systems existed in the lab terminals, the marines trained their rifles on the barricaded hatch as if it might give way at any moment.

"I think that one is going to hold for a while," Tag said to Bull, "but what about other passages? Can you guys make sure all other entrances are secure while we probe the data?"

"Will do, Captain," Bull said. "Sumo, you watch the eggheads. Gorenado, Lonestar, on me."

Their bootsteps clacked away down another corridor stretching from the main chamber.

"I have successfully interfaced with the system," Alpha said, retracting the data cord from the terminal.

The holoscreen blinked, showing a virtual shelf of data cubes and packets. With a wave of Alpha's hand, the second terminal fizzled off for a moment and then rebooted, allowing another access point.

"Both systems should be available to you and Sofia," Alpha said. Coren shot her a glance, and she asked, "Would you like a terminal, too?"

"Please," Coren said. "As much fun as it is to watch you three do all the work, I would like to do something."

"Then, as Sofia might say, be my guest." Alpha waved her hand over another terminal. Its holoscreen crackled on. The colors were slightly distorted, and the images on it stretched like they were made of melting taffy.

"Great," Coren said. "Give the non-human the junk terminal."

"Aren't all these terminals junk compared to your amazing Mechanic technology?" Sofia asked.

"Good point," Coren said, sidling into his open station.

"So quit your bitching," Sofia said.

Coren shook his head as he began delving into the files. "What exactly should I be looking for?"

"Anything to do with science projects," Tag said. "Maybe we can find nanite research. If we've got Net access, ship's logs would be helpful, too. I want to know what happened to the crew."

For a few moments, they each sifted through the data in silence punctuated only by the shrieks of the creatures outside. Sumo watched the barricade nervously, pacing back and forth between the terminals and the hatch. Tag soon lost himself in the search within the lab's Net systems. A bevy of different projects scrolled over the holoscreen, ranging from basic cell biology experiments to more advanced tissue regeneration techniques, similar to those used in modern-day regen chambers. The pounding against the hatch reminded him they couldn't peruse all this data now. Best to download as much as they could find and give it a more thorough investigation later. He used his wrist terminal's connection to the *Argo* to begin transferring data packets from the *Hope*'s lab.

They could easily take most of this data with them, but he still wanted to make sure they didn't miss any physical clues to what had happened to the *Hope*'s crew—or any connections with the nanites.

"Any luck?" Sumo asked, looking over Tag's shoulder at the names of various data packets. "Oh, hey, I recognize that one!"

She pointed to a list of packet names, and Tag began reading them aloud. "Organotherapeutics. Intuitive Nanotechnologies. Biorecog Technologies. Asimov Cybertech. General AI. Starinski Labs. Bonner-Spice Defense."

"Yeah, those last two," Sumo said. "Weapons and warship manufacturers."

"Weird," Tag said. "I thought we were just looking at bio research, but this is a whole list of companies that contracted work with the *Hope*. Some of them still exist."

Sofia looked up from her research. "Whether it's the UN or the SRE, companies who know how to make money keep making money, right? They don't care who's running the solar system."

"True," Tag said. While the SRE sponsored most of his synth-bio research projects on the *Argo*, there had been some internal debate within the government suggesting that the SRE take contractor-funded projects instead. Tag had vehemently disagreed. He preferred to maintain control over his work and ensure there were no conflicts of interest as he developed it into what later became Alpha. But he imagined that a generation ship like the *Hope* would've been an expensive proposition, so subsidizing government funding through corporation-directed research projects might have helped make possible what would have otherwise been an unaffordable endeavor.

"Too bad none of these companies benefited from this research," Tag said. "Must've lost a boatload of money."

"I wouldn't be too sure about that," Coren said. "Looks like the *Hope* sent a stream of courier drones back to Earth over the decades of its journey. I'm sure *something* in there was valuable."

"That's strange," Tag said, looking at what Coren had found. "Some of these courier drones date past when the *Hope* was considered lost. Supposedly, no one on Earth was receiving contact from them at that point."

"Might be true," Sofia said. "Maybe they were sending the drones, but none of them were getting home."

"It is unfortunate that we do not know what happened

to those drones," Alpha said. "Captain, many of these corporate-funded projects are encrypted with high-priority security systems. I will be unable to breach them without considerable effort and time."

"Can you still transfer them back to our ship?" Tag asked.

The banging and clawing on the hatch still hadn't let up, and Alpha had to speak up to be heard over the din. "Yes, Captain. That is possible."

"Good," Tag said. He recalled their earlier conversation and clarified, "Please transfer those files to the ship. Anyone find anything mentioning nanites?"

"Nothing yet," Coren said.

"Afraid not," Sofia added. "Would've expected the bio labs would be the right place to start looking for it, too."

"Hmm," Tag mused, "I wouldn't be surprised if that information was encrypted. Those kinds of weapons were still pretty controversial in UN times." He thumbed through the classified projects again. "Start unlocking the Intuitive Nanotechnologies packets. See if we find something there."

"You might be interested in what else I found in the drone records," Coren said. "Apparently, the ship logs continue past the alleged disappearance of the *Hope* three hundred years ago. Here's the final entry."

Coren gestured over the terminal to expand the text, and Tag peered at the slightly warped letters on Coren's terminal. The log read:

*We have encountered a grave threat. Unlike any species we have come across, this poses perhaps the greatest danger to our mission, maybe our existence. We've—*

Tag tried to scroll to continue the log, but there was nothing else. "Does it really just cut off here?"

"Unfortunately, I cannot find anything else," Coren said.

"Damn," Tag said. "So close..."

Coren tapped on the screen. "What's even stranger is that there was a ship-wide evacuation ordered."

"Doesn't sound so weird if they came across some kind of crazy dangerous threat," Sofia said.

"That would be true," Coren said, "if the order to evacuate hadn't come almost two hundred and fifty years after that last ship log."

# THIRTEEN

S ofia pointed to her holoscreen. "Found something else we might be interested in."

A long, skinny figure rotated on the screen with a snake-like face and serpentine limbs that Tag had grown all too familiar with.

"That's a Mechanic," Coren said, sounding irritatingly unimpressed.

"It is," Sofia said. "They have an amazing amount of data on your species. Stuff here about the politics and customs of Meck'ara, along with individual bios on a few Mechanics."

Tag leaned over Sofia's shoulder. "And all that biological data on the genetic transcription and translation processes." An image appeared next to the rotating Mechanic showing a labyrinth of cells and tissues making up one of the alien's organs. "They really did a full workup here."

"Enough reading material to keep us scientists and anthropologists occupied for a few months," Sofia said.

"I'm pleased that you're so captivated by the clear exploitation of my species, but is there anything there to implicate these humans in the nanites?" Coren asked.

"I'm not sure yet," Sofia said. "But Mechanics weren't the only subjects of interest to the *Hope*'s crew."

"What else did you find?" Tag asked.

"In scientific terms: a shit ton."

As Tag stared at the holoscreen, the sounds of the creatures banging against the hatch seemed to fade away, as did the rest of the laboratory. All he saw were the lists of other alien races scrolling across the screen. The reports oozed with information documenting civilizations and physiologies of races Tag couldn't have conjured in his wildest dreams.

"Our other friends are in here, too," Sofia said. She stopped at one point in the list.

An amorphous creature with a translucent body and visible nerve and blood vessels spiderwebbing through it appeared.

"The Melarrey," Tag said. "This is insane. How did the crew of the *Hope* discover all this on their own?"

"Maybe they did not, Captain," Alpha said from her perch at her own station. "While much of this data is corrupted, I believe most of these files originated prior to the final ship's log. However, these studies began after they reported seeing something that frightened them all."

"Are you suggesting another species intervened here? Maybe took over the ship and uploaded all their data to the *Hope*?"

"Probability analysis suggests that the dominant sentient species aboard the *Hope* in the years after the final ship log were indeed different from the original crew," Alpha said. "In summary, yes, it is unlikely humans were responsible for these research reports."

"I don't know," Tag said. "Still seems odd a race with that much knowledge would want an old human ship like this."

"I could buy it," Sumo said. "My aunt was one of those—what do you call 'em?" Her eyebrows scrunched together for a moment as she tapped her rifle. "Ah, a hoarder. She collected Star Frontier toys and holo cartoons. You know space station apartments are already cramped to begin with. Imagine what one looks like when you've got bundles of 3D fabricators printing out new action figures of Romulus Martin and his friends with all their gadgets and spaceships. I don't know how she lived there, but she loved collecting that stuff. Maybe these aliens were collectors or something."

"I find this hypothesis reasonable," Alpha said.

"Me, too," Coren added. "This whole space station is one big collection of various species ships."

"Gods, do you think that's the threat the ship log mentioned?" Tag asked. The ramifications of an entire alien race who abused their superior technologies merely to "collect" information and ships from other races staggered him. "These Collectors, or whatever you want to call them, capture anything that comes their way and add it to this space station."

"So what, we're some of Aunt Sumo's collectibles now?" Sofia asked. "Let me guess, your aunt was a bit crazy, too."

"Yeah, that's definitely fair," Sumo said.

"Wonder how crazy these Collectors are," Sofia asked.

"I just hope they're not around anymore," Tag said. "We can't let the *Argo* become a permanent fixture in this collection. Download all that data. We'll sift through the corrupted stuff and repair it later if we can." He turned to Alpha. "Have you found anything related to nanites?"

"No, I am afraid my answer remains unchanged."

"Damn," Tag said. Once again, he found himself facing more questions than answers. Maybe Grand Elector L'ndrant had been right.

A wave of anger flushed those doubts from his mind. No,

Captain Weber must have been ordered to take out these coordinates for a reason. Maybe it was the Collectors that Weber had been after, not the source of the nanites. Either way, something evil was going on here.

Sofia was frowning. "Maybe the Collectors are actually more like me. They employ a bunch of anthropologists to study the worlds around them."

"That's an awfully optimistic way of looking at it," Coren said. "Why do you say that?"

Before Sofia could answer, the sound of footsteps pounding along a corridor drew their attention. Sumo raised her rifle slightly, settling in front of the others in a defensive position. She lowered her weapon when Bull stormed from the shadows with Lonestar and Gorenado behind him. The dim light glimmered over long streams of sweat beneath his visor. Tag thought the marine seemed even paler than usual.

"Captain, you're going to want to see this," Bull said gruffly. The banging on the hatch continued, and he eyed the barricade. "Maybe it's best everyone comes along."

"Alpha, how's the data coming along?" Tag asked.

"I believe I have all the data I can access from these terminals."

"Good," Tag said. "Bull, lead the way."

Leaving the wan yellow lights of the laboratory behind, they followed another corridor swallowed by dark shadows. A glimmer of light blinked at the end of the corridor. It led them into another chamber, cavernous as the belly of an ice god. Fluid of some sort dripped from the high ceiling and pinged against brown puddles covering the deck. The emergency lights didn't seem to work as well here. Some of the banks provided an unenthusiastic glow over a few bulkheads, while other light banks switched on and off, the cause of the blinking they had seen before. Most remained dark. A putrid, rotten smell like a spaceship trash compactor that hadn't been emptied in decades wafted through the air, piercing the filters in Tag's suit. His eyes watered at the stench as they slowly adjusted to the poor lighting.

His stomach churned as he gazed around, nausea twisting it into an agonizing knot. "Good gods," Tag said. "This is how the Collectors knew so much about these species."

# FOURTEEN

It was like a zoo. The most revolting, twisted zoo Tag had ever seen.

Jutting from the ground were rows of cages and tanks, all of various sizes. Many sat in disrepair, cracks leaking fluid or merely rings of broken polyglass demarcating where a tank had once been. Suspended from the ceiling were other enclosures, equally abused or neglected as those lining the deck.

Tag stepped forward slowly, cautiously. His nerves tingled, telling him to be prepared to run, to fight. To do *something*. But the pull of curiosity was too great. He was an iron filing to the magnetism of the unknown, and he couldn't stop the urge—the need—to investigate this place.

Pressing a palm to the nearest tank, he peered inside. The fluid in it was a murky green. Something bobbed at the surface. A creature. It had long trailing fins, feathered like a bird's wing that attached to a decayed torso with protruding bones. Dozens of what appeared to be empty eye sockets dotted the creature's skull.

"What is it?" Sofia asked, sidling next to him.

The marines kept their rifles trained on the shadows, ever watchful, but even they were stealing the occasional glances at the atrocities around them.

"I...I don't know," Tag said. "Coren? Alpha?"

Coren shook his head. Even his scarred, white eye seemed to fill with sorrow as he gazed at the rows of tanks.

"According to the downloaded files from the laboratory, I believe it is a Dullaquetzl," Alpha offered. "But it appears to be long dead."

There were no smart replies from any of the crew members telling Alpha she was stating something that was painfully obvious to all of them, scientific training or no. This was not a place for humor.

When no one spoke, she continued. "The Dullaquetzl are an aquatic species from the planet Quetzlaquenta. They are a space-faring species that only just—"

"They're sentient?" Sofia asked, turning to Alpha. There was a wet sheen in her eyes.

"Yes," Alpha said. "Very much so."

Several more Dullaquetzl floated in various stages of decay in the nearby tanks. Scratches marred the inside of one, and another had been cracked, emptied of all fluid, with the alien lying desiccated on the bottom.

"Were they prisoners?" Tag asked. Not that it would justify their treatment, but at least it would be a more palatable explanation than what he feared.

"No," Alpha said. "Nothing in the ship's records indicates the taking of prisoners. I believe I have located a reference to this room in the databases. It was labeled Specimen Storage."

The twisting in Tag's guts tightened painfully. "This is terrible."

They walked to another set of cages that barely gave the alien inside room to stand. Long-dead brown skin was stretched over a skeletal structure that resembled a three-legged, humanoid bird. The alien's stubby fingers were wrapped around the cage's bars in rigor mortis. What was left of the being's face looked like it had been frozen in a perpetual state of anguish, its features pulled downward as if it had been resigned to defeat.

Next to the three-legged bird alien was an enclosure whose inhabitants had been packed in like popcorn, each of them roughly the size of Tag's hand. They looked almost plant-like, their skin bark and their feet roots. But they had no soil to take root in, nor any sun to offer their dried-up, leafy appendages light. Another cage contained a puddle of gelatinous goo with cartilaginous spikes poking through a sheer membrane.

As they passed other enclosures, Tag's senses grew numb, his thoughts clouded by a dark smog of sadness and anger. All of these sentient beings imprisoned for no other purpose than to serve as experimental subjects to the Collectors. Yanked from their homes, their ships, their friends, their families, and kept here in this room, each distraught and angry and horrified and depressed and...

Tag pounded his fist against one of the broken polyglass tanks. There were no creatures in this one. Missing shards spoke of a possible escape. Other cages and enclosures showed signs of distress, sitting empty between those habitats in which their mummified inhabitants had languished. Maybe some of these beings had found freedom. Maybe they had wreaked havoc on the Collectors, seeking their revenge. Tag could imagine a punishment no more fitting or just.

Coren seemed entranced by one cage in particular. He approached it slowly, almost reverently, his hands held in front of him with fingers splayed. When his fingers touched the polyglass reinforced by alloy bars, he pressed his palms against it and muttered softly, "The machine remembers. The machine remembers."

Tag joined the Mechanic. Huddled in a tangled mass at the floor of the enclosure was a corpse with leathery black skin and obsidian fur that had fallen out in large patches. It took no leap of imagination for Tag to imagine the snake-like face and golden eyes the alien had once possessed.

"Bastards," Coren said, his six-fingered hands curling into shaking fists. His nostrils flared as he swiveled, taking in the whole specimen complex. "I cannot imagine the suffering these poor people endured."

"If there are still Collectors on this ship, we will bring them to justice," Tag said.

"Count me in on that," Bull added, patting the side of his rifle.

Sofia knelt beside another cage. An alien no taller than her knee had perished there, one of its arms stretched out from between the bars, eternally reaching for help that had come far, far too late. "Why would they do this? There are so many better ways to learn ..."

Something began to tingle down Tag's neck as his crew explored the chamber. Something was wrong here—besides the obvious—but he couldn't quite place where this feeling was coming from. It was as if they were missing a piece of the greater puzzle, and once he figured out what it was, everything would become clear. It felt like it should have been obvious... He looked around at the cages one more time, trying to catalogue all the inhabitants. He would have holo recordings from his suit along with the memories that would forever be scorched into his mind.

"Alpha, I want you to try to match up all these cages with the list of races you found in the other lab," he said.

"Yes, Captain," Alpha said. Even her droid features belied a hint of shock. For a fleeting moment, Tag wished he could have shielded her from what some sentient forms were capable of when they disregarded the value of other races and other lives.

He was reminded of his time in the Forest of Light when the Forinth watched him from the woods or of his missions onto other stations where the Dreg crept after them from the shadows. Searching the room, he shone his helmet-mounted lights onto a suspicious patch of darkness. Green eyes reflected the light back at him. He swept the beams over a cat-like creature with six legs. It vanished, hissing, into the shadows before Tag could pull out his pulse pistol.

"Was that one of those things that attacked us earlier?" Sofia asked, concern in her voice.

"No," Lonestar said, "those bastards were three times bigger. That cat-thing just looked like one of the scared strays that wanders onto my family's ranch."

"Still," Tag said, "be cautious. We don't know what that thing is. If it's survived when everything else is pretty well dead, then the creature might be more dangerous than it looks."

"Got a point, Cap," Gorenado said. "It's got to be damn smart, damn deadly, or damn lucky."

The marines formed a circle around Tag and the others, searching for potential threats.

"I still want to take samples from all the prisoners here," Tag said. "I don't know if it will be helpful or not, but maybe it'll tell us why the Collectors were so interested in them."

The others nodded, and Alpha, Coren, and Sofia pulled their bio-collection vials from the packs secured to their shoulders. Tag followed suit, bending over the nearest alien. He used a pair of forceps to secure several pieces of its flaking skin and secured them in a vial before moving onto a rat-sized alien covered in what looked like snail shells.

As they continued collecting samples, Tag tried not to think about the horror surrounding him. He focused instead on the task at hand. Collect a sample. Deposit it. Secure the vial. Repeat. Over and over. Lonestar shadowed Tag, keeping watch over him like a bodyguard. "You ever have a dog, Captain?" she asked.

"Sorry, what?"

"Ever had a pet?"

Tag shook his head as he bent over another creature who looked more fungus than animal. "Nah, I didn't. Why?"

"Maybe you wouldn't understand," she said, "but when I was maybe six or seven, the whole colony experienced a huge power outage—a complete blackout. And when things got dark on the ranch, they got real dark. There were always rumors floating around about the aliens who used to live on our planet before we arrived. That maybe they still haunted the place, their spirits wondering who these strangers were taking their ancestral ground."

Tag shivered. "Does this story have a point?" he asked, more sharply than he intended.

"I never really believed in that hocus-pocus mumbo-jumbo," she said. "But anyway, night of that outage, my parents were at some dance hosted by my uncle. I was all alone in this rickety wooden house that creaked when the wind tickled it. So there I am, my house whispering to me, sitting in the darkness, and my dog, Casey, sleeping in bed with me."

Tag deposited another sample into a vial.

"All of a sudden, Casey jumped down from my bed," Lonestar continued. "The door to my room—never was real secure to begin with—creaked open. Maybe it was just the wind, maybe it was something else. But all I saw was pitch-black nothingness outside that door. And Casey. Oh, boy. Casey just stared out that door. His fur stood on end, his haunches tight. He started growling, but I couldn't see what was spooking him. He just kept snarling at the shadows.

"Then he yelped and started whimpering. Jumped right back into bed with me, and I pulled the covers over my head, snuggled up with that dog, shivering and crying the both of us. Not a proud moment."

Tag paused from taking another sample and looked up at Lonestar. Her eyes were transfixed by some spot in the darkness he couldn't see.

"Guess the point of that whole story is: that's how I feel right now."

Again, a shiver passed through Tag. "That makes two of us."

# FIFTEEN

While they explored the specimen chamber, Tag kept searching for the green eyes of that cat-like creature he had seen before, wondering if it was biding its time before it would descend on him in a flurry of claws.

But the cat never appeared again. Unfortunately, that didn't mean they were safe.

He heard distant shrieks but didn't react, uncertain if they were in his imagination or real. Nearby, Lonestar froze; it wasn't just in his mind. He followed the angle of her rifle barrel toward another corridor. The shrieks seemed to be emanating from there, their ghastly calls booming against the bulkhead, amplified by the specimen chamber.

"It's those damn creatures again," Lonestar said. She knelt, peering down her rifle as the shrieks grew louder.

"Everyone form up on me!" Tag said. "Bull, Alpha, I want you to get us out of here. Now!"

The scrape of claws on metal pierced the cries of the scream-ing aliens. Alpha held her wrist terminal out, and a holo of the *Hope* projected from it. The image zoomed in on their location.

"The route we took here is blocked off by our barricade," Alpha said.

"And those monsters, whatever they are," Sumo added.

"But we should be able to take the path toward the bridge."

"Excellent," Tag said. "Priority number one is making sure everyone is safe. If we can lose these things and make it to the bridge, all the better. Understood?"

"Yes, Captain," came the chorus of replies.

The faint, flickering emergency lights at the far end of the specimen chamber briefly illuminated the first of the creatures. Long talons raked from skinny, sinewy arms. The beast ran on four legs, not unlike a centaur, except instead of a horse-like body, its lower half looked more similar to a reptile. A tail tipped with spikes trailed behind it. The creature's face sported obsidian tusks that protruded from a massive underbite, and beady black eyes met Tag's from the end of long, lobster-esque stalks. Three more of the creatures burst from the end of the corridor, scrambling over the remains of the specimen enclosures toward Tag and his crew.

"Looks like some goddamn overgrown scorpions," Lonestar murmured.

"Go!" Tag yelled.

The aliens shrieked, their tails flicking behind their heads. At first, Tag wasn't sure if their tails were keeping them in balance or somehow used for locomotion. The needle-sharp spines pinging and embedding into the gunk around him answered his question.

"Look out for their projectiles!" Alpha said. One of the spines pierced her suit as she warned the others, embedding itself in her arm.

"Alpha!" Tag yelled, reaching out to help her, his stomach

churning at the sight of the finger-sized spine buried in her synthetic flesh.

"Do not be alarmed," Alpha said. "It has hit nothing vital. My biosensors detect a discrete neurotoxin within the spines, however."

Tag knew the only living cells within her chassis were located within her head as part of her synth-bio brain, and the neurotoxin would be unable to make its way there. Still he felt the anxiety of a parent seeing a child hurt. "Be careful, Alpha!"

The group sprinted from the chamber toward another corridor with Bull leading them. Lonestar and Gorenado took potshots at the creatures. Each of the scorpioids was no taller than Tag's waist, but what they lacked in size, they made up for in ferocity. Pulsefire and kinetic slugs slammed into their bodies, and blue liquid oozed out, tinted violet by the crimson emergency lights. A few lucky shots found fatal targets, piercing heads or gouging holes through chests, but most of the beasts continued onward even when their eyestalks were scythed by gunfire. Dozens of them spilled into the specimen chamber, and more were still emerging from the hall.

"Faster!" Lonestar said. "These things are angrier than a bull after a branding!"

They rounded a corner, losing sight of their pursuers. The cries and shrieks assured Tag the beasts were not far behind. He found himself wondering, between gasps of breath, if these things were creatures the Collectors had brought aboard and left forgotten, resigned to live in the relic of a station forever. Maybe they had escaped from the specimen room. Three hells, maybe they had killed the Collectors.

Bull charged ahead, leading the group onward. Lonestar and Gorenado fired another wall of slugs at the creatures before they turned a corner.

"You do know where you're going, don't you, Bull?" Sofia asked, her voice raspy.

"Bull is still taking us along the correct route," Alpha said.

Tag gasped for air as he ran at a near-sprint. He tasted something metallic, and his lungs began to burn even as his suit reacted to his increased pulse and air intake, pumping extra oxygen into its atmosphere. The adrenaline surging through his veins provided some relief as his muscles strained, pulling and stretching, taking him further from the alien scorpioids still shrieking with wild yells.

A beast rounded a corner, dangerously close, and leapt. Lonestar's shots missed, and Tag fired wildly with his pulse pistol, but it was Gorenado who saved her by butting the creature with his rifle. When the scorpioid was knocked off balance, Lonestar fired into it with abandon, and rounds burst through the creature's rib cage.

Two more scorpioids followed, accelerating toward them, their voices raised in high-pitched shrieks that threatened to burst Tag's eardrums. The first cocked its tail back, ready to strike. He braced himself for the monster's attack, preparing to fire, but a sudden hissing sounded from behind Tag instead. He didn't have time to turn before a shape blasted past him and jumped at the first scorpioid.

It was the cat-thing they had seen earlier in the specimen chamber. The little devil scratched at the scorpioid's eye stalks, and Tag squeezed his pistol's trigger. Orange rounds lanced from the weapon, impaling the scorpioid over and over. Its mission evidently complete, the cat-thing dashed off to disappear in the shadows once more.

"Thanks, buddy," Tag called after it.

A twinge of regret tickled through him as he watched the other creature mowed down by Sumo's fire. It probably wasn't the scorpioids' fault that they were stuck on this hellscape of a space station. Maybe they were once peaceful—friendly, even— but their time spent imprisoned here had warped their minds, bent them toward sociopathy. Maybe they were just desperate for food. A thousand reasons whirled through Tag's head as to why these things were after him and his crew.

None of those reasons really mattered right now.

All that mattered was his crew's survival.

"We're almost there!" Bull boomed. "Just a little farther. Marines, hold it together back there!"

The marines answered with a hail of gunfire that brought down the next wave of pursuers. Several of the scorpioids went down, but their comrades paid them no heed as they trampled their bleeding corpses, saliva dripping in long ropes from their tusks. Their tails continued to whip, flinging spikes against the bulkhead in response to the marines' fire.

"Captain! Look out!" Sumo yelled.

Tag swiveled as he ran, trying to figure out what Sumo was warning him about. Understanding came too slow. He saw the scorpioid's tail flick forward, the spike shooting out from it faster than he could blink. With barely any time to move, he tried to duck.

He wasn't going to make it—he'd reacted too slowly.

Then something blocked his view. Blocked the spike. It took him an adrenaline-fueled moment to realize Sumo had thrown herself in front of him.

His vision tunneled as she fell backward, her body crashing into his. Even in his own EVA suit, her power armor was too heavy, knocking them both to the deck. Alpha turned with Sofia, standing over them and firing into the scorpioids.

"Sumo!" Tag said, turning her over, his eyes tracing over her chest where he expected to see the spike sticking out.

Instead, she jumped out of his grip. "I'm fine! I'm fine!" She kneeled and fired at their attackers before Tag could say anything else. "Mag shields work against pulsefire and projectiles."

"But not against claws," Bull said.

They continued running and lobbing the occasional volley back into the scorpioids until Bull and Lonestar halted. Sumo and Gorenado paused and fired into the corridor, using it as a chokepoint against the monsters.

"What's going on?" Tag asked, trying to see around Bull's hulking form. His stomach plummeted when he saw what had stopped the marines.

An enormous cylindrical room stretched twenty decks tall. A central pillar with the diameter of an air car ran through the middle of the chamber. Crooked, brown vines snaked up around the pillar, rising from the abyss toward the ceiling.

"The bridge is up there," Alpha said nonchalantly, pointing at the top of the pillar.

Catwalks connected to the central pillar, and ladders to other corridors were arranged around the circumference of the vast room. Several of the catwalks appeared to have rusted out and fallen away, lost to the void below. The catwalk connecting their corridor to the central column was one of those missing, and they were currently on deck eleven.

The unfettered shrieks of the scorpioids resounded louder and louder against the bulkhead as the monsters spilled through the corridor. Their feet scrabbled in the brown gunk covering the deck as they charged.

For every scorpioid they brought down, two more seemed to emerge, clotting the corridor with their corpses yet continuously pushing forward, centimeter by centimeter. Tag glanced back at the pillar, then back at the growing mound of scorpioids. There was nowhere for them to run.

"We've got to jump!" Tag said.

He could sense Sofia's unease as she stood next to them. The marines were equipped with power armor suits that would help them make their jump with ease. Coren was the most agile of the group; his lanky limbs made him a powerful long jumper. Alpha had the advantage of a mechanical body that Tag had seen carry her distances longer than the leap to the nearest ladder spiraling around the pillar. Only Sofia and Tag were limited by their relatively fragile, clumsy human bodies inside lightweight EVA suits.

The scorpioids were just meters from their position. There was no more time to delay, to find an alternative escape. It was either do or die.

"Bull! Lonestar! Get your asses to the ladder on the other side and cover us!"

Bull looked about to hesitate but then sprinted, jumping the chasm to the ladder. He reached out with one hand and grabbed a rung, quickly climbing to the nearest landing. Lonestar joined him. They laid down a wall of mini-Gauss fire to ward off the scorpioids. Alpha and Coren soared over the abyss next, making the jump look effortless.

Sofia looked at Tag. A glimmer of fear showed in her eyes. "I don't think I can make it."

"Then don't think," Gorenado said. "Jump with me!"

He held her hand, and together they jumped. Sofia never would've made it if it weren't for Gorenado's help. When his body slammed against the ladder, he gripped her wrist with his free hand, holding Sofia as she dangled, then pulled her toward safety. Her chest heaved as she cemented her grip around the rung.

Tag mentally prepared himself for the jump. In his mind's eye, he saw his hands connecting with the ladder. As if thinking it would make it so.

"I got this," he said under his breath. He was taller than Sofia. He could make it.

"Cap, let me help," Sumo said.

The calls of the scorpioids grew louder, and they charged more brazenly than before, scrambling over the ranks of their dead.

"Now or never," Tag said. Sumo grasped his hand. Together they sprinted toward the edge. With his muscles straining from the effort, he pushed himself off, flying over the darkness below. Sumo hit the ladder first, sending a tremor up the tubular rungs. Her grip tightened around Tag's fingers, helping him to swing toward the ladder. He crashed into it, carried by his own momentum.

She smiled at him through her visor. "Told you—"

She didn't have a chance to finish. The impact resonated upward, shaking Sofia's already precarious grip on the slime-covered rungs. She fell past Gorenado's reaching hands. Tag reached out for Sofia as she fell toward him. Her arm slid through his grip until his fingers interlocked with hers.

For a fraction of a second, Tag thought he had saved her. His relief was swamped by a rush of adrenaline as Sofia pulled him downward, toward the darkness, toward the unknown ten decks below them. Sumo reached for him, but it was already too late. Tag saw a look of sorrow and regret on her face as she yelled his name, red emergency lights flickering over her as the blackness swallowed Tag and Sofia.

# SIXTEEN

Tag held Sofia's hand as they dropped, as if doing so would somehow save them both. Suddenly, they hit something soft. After a moment of resistance, it gave way, slowing their descent. His helmet-mounted lights flickered over dark vines that stretched like a gargantuan spiderweb. He groped blindly for the vines as he and Sofia broke through the first layer, but he couldn't gain purchase. The vines seemed to retract from his grip. Still he fell against them, each consecutive layer receding and breaking slower than the last. Their fall slowed until they were hanging in a tangle of vines less than a foot from the floor. They wriggled free and planted their boots on solid ground, both of them panting and laughing.

"Captain!" Sumo's voice called through the comms.

"We're okay!" he boomed back. "We're okay!"

Sofia grinned, wrapping her arms around him. "Oh my gods, we're alive! We're actually alive!"

Bull's voice growled, "Glad to hear it, Captain. But a bunch of those things fell down there with you. If you're alive, so are they."

Even as he spoke, Tag heard the swish of talons scything through the vines. Growls and shrieks surrounded them, but he couldn't see the scorpioids through the mess of strange foliage.

"This way!" Sofia said. She yanked on Tag's wrist, and they began sprinting through a narrow clearing in the vines.

Rustling sounded from ahead. At first, he thought it was more scorpioids. Nothing pounced at them. Instead the vines moved as if blown by a wind he could not feel. They quivered. Any other time, Tag might be alarmed by such movement. With the scorpioids moving fast behind him, there was no time for luxuries like caution. Onward he and Sofia ran. More brown gunk covered the floor, threatening to make them slip. Several of the scorpioids followed the curve of the clearing after Sofia and Tag.

They fired as they ran. Orange rounds of pulsefire streamed from Tag's pistol. His shots connected with one of the scorpioids. Another leapt over the fresh corpse and flicked its tail in one fluid motion. A spike flew straight at Sofia, but Tag tackled her. The spike flew over her head and disappeared in the darkness.

Tag stood, helping Sofia to her feet, and they kept moving. The clearing led into another corridor, where the brown vines traced the bulkhead and decks. A few hatches offered potential routes of escape, but all were clogged with vegetation. The vines there were thick enough that Tag didn't bother trying to cut them away. The vines seemed to part just a little wider, beckoning him. There was only one path forward. The uncanny thought that the vines were guiding them somewhere passed through his mind. He forced it out just as quickly; no use ruminating on things like that with the scorpioids in dogged pursuit.

They cleared another corridor with only a single red emergency light at the end to guide them. Dim amber lights summoned them from the end of a side passage illuminating a much larger space. Maybe they would find ladders that weren't rusted out there. They needed to reach higher ground and reunite with the rest of the crew.

"How are things going up there?" Tag asked over the comms.

"Captain," Bull said, "we're trying to find a way down to you, but we're getting blocked off."

"The vines stretch meters deep," Coren added. "We're having trouble cutting through."

Alpha spoke up. "You may be forced to engage the hostile aliens, Captain, in which case your probabilities of success are—"

"No need for probabilities," Sofia said. "Just get your asses down here!"

"But be careful," Tag said. "I don't want anyone to do anything reckless!"

"You mean like fall ten stories off a ladder?" Sumo asked.

A scorpioid pounced at Tag, preventing him from making a smart reply. He caught it in the chest with pulsefire, and it somersaulted to the deck, yowling as blood bubbled out of its mouth.

Tag and Sofia burst out of the corridor and into the chamber with the dim amber light. Brown vines, some as thick as the trees in the Forest of Light, crisscrossed the room.

"Where are we now?" Tag asked, searching for an exit. A quick glance at his wrist terminal showed they were in what once was the *Hope*'s central computing and comm center. He didn't see any readily accessible terminals, much less a hatch other than the one at their backs.

Just more vines. Vines every gods-damned direction he looked.

Once again, they were cornered. This time there wasn't a ten-story plummet for a desperate escape, and there were no marines to hold back the scorpioids with gunfire. Sofia aimed her pulse pistol at the corridor, standing shoulder to shoulder with Tag. The first misshapen silhouettes of the scorpioids appeared, clambering against each other as they rushed toward their prize.

"It was a valiant effort," she said. "The others will carry on without us."

"But I hate to miss out on the fun," Tag said, acting braver than he felt.

The scorpioids poured out of the corridor like water from a faucet. His fingers shook slightly as he aimed at the scorpioids. He squeezed the trigger as fast as possible, trying to bring down as many of those spike-throwing bastards as he could. He and Sofia backed up until they were pressed against a thick wall of vines. There was no chance to say anything else to her as they faced death. It was all Tag could do to shoot and duck as spikes and scorpioids came at them in a relentless tide.

Then something tapped his shoulder.

As he turned, he saw brown vines wrapping around his arm and Sofia's ankles.

"Sofia!" he yelled.

She looked down at her feet, firing at the vines until they retracted.

"Oh, gods," she muttered. More vines shot from the walls.

Tag tried to help, but the vines wrapped around their wrists and ankles, holding their limbs in place. A larger vine enveloped around Tag like a boa constrictor, covering his body from toe to neck. He struggled, but the vines only pulled tighter.

They were stuck, imprisoned by the living foliage so that they could not fight back against the scorpioids. But then more vines wrapped around the scorpioids, dragging them by tail and limb before slamming the aliens into the bulkhead. The creatures hit the walls with such force that their flesh burst open. Their insides spilled in a foul mess.

Each time one of the scorpioids charged into the huge atrium, another vine wrapped around the creature. Struggle as they might, desperately scything at the vines with talons and tusks or impaling them with spikes, the vines grabbed the monsters and dashed them against the walls. Soon the scorpioids began pausing at the edge of the corridor, and at last, the remaining creatures retreated. But the vines pursued them like an octopus's deft tentacles, grabbing them, hoisting them in the air, and sending them to a fate just like the rest of their brethren's.

"No more scorpioids," Sofia said softly.

Tag heard the words she hadn't said because he was thinking, too: *We're next.*

They were lifted into the air. Tag struggled to breathe as the vines tightened around his chest. He opened his mouth, gasping, desperate for the little bit of air he could still choke down. His fingers wriggled, itching to reach the pulse pistol, but he couldn't move his hand far enough.

He closed his eyes, ready to be splattered against a bulkhead.

And then it stopped. The vines loosened slightly. Not enough for him to use his pistol to escape but enough for him to breathe. He opened his eyes again and saw Sofia suspended next to him. They were at the top of the atrium, maybe four or five decks up from where they'd entered.

"Bull," Tag managed, his voice coming out in rasps. "We're… about to be killed by some…some…plant. Go on without me. Coren, you've got command of the ship."

"No, Captain!" Bull replied, his voice filled with fierce determination. "We're on our way."

"I'm afraid…it's going to be too late."

Tag stared at the deck below, prepared to find himself plummeting in freefall for the second time in mere minutes. It was as if fate meant for him to die smashed against the filthy, grime-smeared deck, and it was now seeking revenge for him cheating death before.

"Skipper, it's been a pleasure," Sofia said.

"We're looking at death, and you're going to give me clichés," Tag said.

"It's a bit hard to be creative when I think about my brains splattered against the deck." She inhaled sharply as she slid half a meter out of her viny cocoon, then stopped. "Right now, I'm missing the Forinths and that colorful jungle of theirs more than you can imagine."

"My only regret is that we didn't all settle down there," Tag said. "I was learning to like their singing. And the plants there were ten times friendlier than here."

The vines around his ankles slithered as if they were readjusting and loosening. He had to remind himself to breathe as apprehension crept under his skin, still waiting to fall, waiting for the deck to rise up and meet him.

"It really was nice knowing you," Tag said. "I only wish we had more time."

"Now who's the one with clichés?"

Tag opened his mouth to respond. Something moved in his periphery. He fought to twist his neck just enough to see what it was. He expected to see the talons of a scorpioid descending upon them.

It wasn't a scorpioid.

It was something much stranger and more terrifying.

# SEVENTEEN

The vines parted to reveal what looked like an enormous beak. It took Tag a moment to realize the beak was part of a much larger plant, rippling with scaly, flaking flesh from which all the vines seemed to originate. The vine-creature opened its maw, revealing an unexpected set of crooked, hooking teeth that appeared well-suited for tearing apart meat. A long series of grunts and other guttural sounds rolled over the thing's whipping tongue. Spittle flew from the mouth, covering Tag's visor and dripping down his suit. It was as brown and murky as the gunk coating the decks and bulkheads around the station.

"What in the name of the gods is that thing?" Tag asked.

"Wish I knew," Sofia said. "But I'm guessing it's carnivorous."

Once again the cat-thing appeared, tearing out of the curtains of vines. It arched its back and hissed at the monstrosity inching toward Tag and Sofia. A quick thwack with a vine made it duck, and it sprinted from the chamber before the other vines could snatch it.

"Thanks for trying," Sofia muttered.

The beak opened as if ready to swallow Tag and Sofia whole. It let out a cacophonous growling cough. Then it began, for lack of a better word, to speak.

It was speaking in English, the old United Nations standard language, but it still sounded horribly mangled by the creature's beak. Tag tuned in his universal translator, which made short work of the creature's strange accent.

"Are you as dumb as you are puny, humans?" the vine-creature asked. "Or are you choosing not to respond out of insolence?"

The vine-creature shook them. Tag's joints popped. His muscles and tendons struggled to hold his limbs together.

"What...what do you want?" Tag asked.

"Oh, the little primate speaks!" the vine-creature boomed, its voice rattling Tag's bones. "We should be asking you the same question. You come in here, bringing those vile little monsters in tow. Although, we suppose we should thank you. Most of them had learned not to bother me, which had prevented me from killing the rest of them. Until today. So, thank you for that. Most kind of you."

"You're...welcome?" Tag said. The vine-creature was rambling like some poor soul left in a nursing home finally receiving a guest after weeks of solitude. It evoked painful images of seeing his dad wandering lost and confused, missing the son he could barely remember.

"But that is such a little thing, really," the vine-creature continued. "You also shot me up quite good. That was an unkind thing." It held up two roping vines like fingers in front of Tag and Sofia. "One thing kind, bringing those monsters to me. Another thing unkind, shooting at me. But we should expect nothing less from you humans. Vile, selfish creatures, the whole lot of you."

"What do you know about humans?" Tag asked. This was the

first time since his departure from the *Argo* that another race he encountered actually recognized his species.

"What a silly, stupid, trite question." The vine-creature let out an ear-splitting honking that might have been laughter. "We find it odd that you think you can ask us questions here. This is *our* home now. Not yours. Not for humans. No, no, no. And you have done one kind thing and may think you have earned favor with us, but you have not. Your kind thing and your unkind thing cancel each other out. You do understand the math, don't you?"

"We didn't—" Tag began.

"And if you think about it—which we know you humans like to do—we have done you a kind thing." The beak paused, tilting slightly as if the vine-creature was lost in thought. "Actually, two kind things. We saved you from a fall, and we saved you from those pestering little monsters. That is two kind things, and by my math, you have canceled out your only kind thing and therefore have done us zero kind things."

"What do you want from us?" Sofia asked.

"We want to know why you have returned. Why the *humans* are here again."

"This is the first time we've ever been aboard this ship," Sofia protested.

"We're not that stupid, human. We know how short your lifespans are. We are asking why the humans are here again. We thought you had left us alone, left us at peace in our home."

"We're looking for the crew of this ship," Sofia said.

"You mean the ship that is now the *Hope* Station?"

"Yes," Tag said. "We want to know what happened to the people here."

"Ah, we can certainly tell you that. We can tell you when they left and where they went and why they abandoned us."

Tag's heart beat in anticipation. All the answers they had been searching for, resting in the vine-creature's mind—or whatever it had instead of a brain.

"Please," Tag said, "what can you tell us about them?"

The vine-creature undulated with that eardrum-piercing honking again, and Tag winced.

"That would be another kind thing you ask of us. *Another* kind thing. The math does not please us. That would be an imbalance, a preposterous request. Most unfair!"

Vines moved around Tag, some slipping and others tightening. He wasn't sure if the thing was about to drop him or squeeze him until his ribs cracked and his organs burst.

"All right," Sofia said. "All right. I understand. That would be a kind thing from you. A very, very kind thing."

The vines relaxed, letting Tag and Sofia dangle once again, just secure enough to prevent them from falling.

"Yes, you understand," the vine-creature said. "This one understands." It shook Sofia slightly. "We want to talk to her, to this one. She seems smart, intelligent, bright. All the things we remember liking about the humans, though there were so many humans we did not like at all. So many that were not smart or intelligent or bright and who preferred to do the unkind things. Not the kind things that Raktor likes."

"Raktor?" Sofia asked, almost cooingly. "Is that your name?"

"Yes, that is our name. That is the name the humans called us. Names are such a peculiarly human thing. We never bothered with them before. Nor did my forbearers. Names are a distraction, an identity. Meant to discriminate one from the forest, the collection—"

"Raktor?" Sofia tried, interrupting its soliloquy.

Tag cringed and waited for Raktor to explode at being interrupted. Much to his surprise the beak closed, and saliva dripped from the corners of the giant mouth as it seemed to wait for Sofia.

"I am Sofia," she said. "This is Tag. We prefer to do the kind things. That's why we were searching for the humans who once lived in the *Hope*."

"Yes, the kind things. That is good you say you prefer to do them, but we haven't seen proof yet of this claim. We do not know that you are deserving of more kind things to be done for you."

"Then," Sofia said, "let us do a kind thing for you. Then you would owe us one kind thing. That is how the math works, isn't it?"

"A deal. A negotiation. A barter for services," Raktor said. "Raktor has made deals with humans before. Once we believed humans were the bringers of kind things, but we learned."

Tag tried to keep track of Raktor's constantly switching references to itself from third to first person. He wanted to shake the damn thing, to tell it to slow down, to talk like a normal being. But Sofia seemed to be having a calming effect on it. Best to let her do the talking.

"What can we do for you, Raktor?" Sofia asked. "What would be the best, biggest, kindest thing we could do?"

Raktor's beak retracted into the vines, tilting and twisting as it hummed. Then, without warning, the beak burst forward again, and Raktor began speaking, spittle spraying from its mouth anew, splattering against Tag and Sofia, the decks and the bulkhead, and even dripping over its own vines.

"This is Raktor's home now," the strange creature said. "After everyone has abandoned it and left us to fend for ourselves, this is our home. Raktor's home."

The beak drew close to Tag, and the stench of carrion drifted from its mouth, pungent enough to permeate his suit and make him long for a shower. When he signed up for this mission, he'd had no idea it would involve a schizophrenic talking plant with bad breath.

"New people that have started tearing apart this station, our home," Raktor said. "They have stolen from us and tried to hurt us and tried to take what is now ours. They want only to take and take and take and do all the unkind things."

"The Dreg," Tag muttered.

"The Dreg?" Raktor asked. "We do not know that name. They look like human excrement and they fly around and we want to squash them, but they are so many. So many little pests. So many out of our reach." Raktor's beak aimed toward the deck. "This makes us sad. Makes all of us here sad. The station is still functional because Raktor takes care of it as we can. As we have learned from the humans. We keep things running and working because without the air and the heat, Raktor would freeze. We would die. All our seedlings, everything we have built here would die. Our forbearers knew winter, and so we remember it. We fear the cold.

"We do not want death. We do not want it at all. And you can do a kind thing by stopping the unkind Dreg."

Raktor shook Tag and Sofia, its beak clacking in anger once again.

"Kill the Dreg. Remove the little pests from our home, and we will tell you what you want to know."

# EIGHTEEN

Raktor lowered Tag and Sofia to the deck, and its vines slowly unraveled from around them. Tag stretched his fingers; his skin prickled as the blood flowed back into his limbs.

"May the rest of our crew join us?" Tag asked. "They can help us fight the Dreg."

"No, no, that will not be possible," Raktor said. "We do not trust them, and they are much too far away. We will only permit you two. Humans Tag and Sofia. You two. You two must do this, the kind thing."

"Where are the Dreg?" Tag asked.

"This is the sad thing," Raktor said. "They have closed themselves off in the life-support and power facilities. This is why we cannot get rid of them. They are smart in the way they do these unkind things, so you will need to root them out."

"The rest of the crew could help us, though," Sofia said.

Raktor's beak lowered toward them, booming its single-word reply: *"NO!"*

"Okay," Tag said, holding up his hands defensively. "We'll do it. Just Sofia and I. And when we do, you'll tell us what happened to the humans here. You'll answer all our questions, right?"

"It would be our kind thing for your kind thing. That is pleasing math."

Raktor's beak withdrew and disappeared into the shroud of vines draping through the atrium. More vines shifted, seeming to guide Sofia and Tag down a corridor.

"Bull, Coren," Tag said. "We encountered…an interesting alien. It promised to give us information."

"The way you say that makes it sound like there's a very big 'but' at the end of that sentence," Bull said.

"Yeah, you could say that," Tag said. "The alien wants us to get rid of the Dreg on the station. Sounds like there might be a hive or something."

"What can we do to assist you?" Coren asked.

"If there's any chance you can join us in the power plant," Tag said. "But I have a feeling your routes here are going to be limited."

"Funny you say that," Coren said. "Every time we've tried following a corridor to reach you, we end up running into a wall of vegetation."

"Yeah," Sofia said. "The vine-monster that sent us on this little errand doesn't want you all to help. He has some issues."

"And I bet you'd love to study him," Tag said.

Sofia gave him a noncommittal shrug. "Might be interesting. At least he's more talkative than the Dreg."

They plodded on as the vines guided them to their destination. Soon the hum of distant motors reverberated through the bulkhead. Tag also heard the familiar scratch and flutter along with a persistent droning, like flies buzzing next to his ear. The droning grew louder as they entered a wide corridor three decks tall. The corridor was curved around a central facility. The air shimmered with heat.

"The Dreg are overheating the system," Sofia said.

"Must be how they're keeping Raktor out," Tag said. "Too hot for his vines."

Sofia knelt on the deck and picked up a shriveled twig. More desiccated branches covered the deck.

It didn't take long for the intense heat emanating out of the central facility to overwhelm Tag's EVA suit. Streams of sweat trickled down his forehead and stung his eyes.

"Those damn Dreg can put up with a lot," Sofia said. "Surviving near vacuum in temperatures that would freeze us solid to living in a place hotter than the three hells. I'm really beginning to dislike these little assholes."

"They do seem to get in our way at the most inopportune of moments," Tag said.

A faded sign, hanging off the wall by one rusted rivet, pointed toward the Fusion Reactor Containment facility. He figured that way would be as good as any to infiltrate the alleged hive. A Turbo-ball-sized Dreg suddenly popped out of a vent and started flying their direction. Tag looked for somewhere to hide, but it was already too late. The Dreg shrieked and made a beeline back for the vent. Tag reached for his pistol, but firing right now would alert the whole hive. Then again, letting that thing run shrieking back to its friends would be just as bad.

"There goes the element of surprise," Sofia lamented.

Before Tag could pull the trigger, something shot from the shadows in a flurry of claws and hisses. It was the cat-thing again. It soared toward the Dreg and hit the slug-like alien with a solid thump. Their bodies rolled over the deck. Muscles rippled under the scaled cat-like creature's skin and long claws jutted from its six legs, piercing the Dreg over and over until the alien's wings stopped twitching.

Then the cat-thing arched its back, its tails whipping about behind it, and sauntered toward Tag and Sofia. Tag tightened the grip on his pistol.

"Think it's dangerous?" Tag asked.

"Don't know," Sofia said. "The damn thing has been following us." She kneeled before it and held out a hand. The creature rubbed its neck against her fingers. "You like that?"

The cat-thing let out a sound halfway between a purr and growl.

"Okay, little guy, you're really lucky you popped out now, because things are about to get a lot more dangerous down here, you understand that?" Tag asked it.

It cocked its head at him as its glinting green eyes surveyed him.

"Seriously," Tag said. "You're not going to want to be around here in a few minutes. Things might get crazy."

The cat-thing rubbed against Tag's legs, bounded through the corridor, jumped from wall to wall, and then disappeared into an open duct.

They crept past maintenance bots covered in grime. Careful not to step on one of the dormant machines, they took each step slowly until they reached a hatch. Tag gingerly wrapped his fingers around the handle, half-expecting the superheated alloy to burn through his gloves and melt his fingers. The EVA suit managed to ward off most of the heat, however, and he gently pushed the hatch inward. The droning of the Dreg grew into a roar as he inched the door open, trying to make the gap just large enough for him and Sofia to slip inside.

The hatch groaned on its hinges, and Tag froze. He locked eyes with Sofia as they waited for the Dreg to descend on them, latching their razor-sharp teeth onto their suits to dig into their flesh. But the sounds continued no louder than before. The Dreg hadn't noticed them—yet.

Tag slipped inside. Sofia followed, and they pressed themselves into the dark recesses of a new hallway. Heat rolled over them like a blast of air from the three hells. Tag looked around, almost expecting to see the orange light of a fire flickering against the bulkheads, but the huge room was bathed in shadows and darkness, with only a few red emergency lights glaring from overhead like the eyes of a demon.

Tag spotted a bank of terminals at the edge of a catwalk which seemed to stretch the circumference of the enormous facility. Four huge drums stood in the center of the chamber, reaching from the deck to the ceiling. The reactors thrummed with life, still seeming fully functional, even after their abandonment.

"I wish Coren was here," Sofia said. "Human tech: still functional even when facing the gods-damned Dreg."

All around them the droning ebbed and flowed. The Dreg had built their hive in the spaces between the reactors, and the aliens crawled over them, disappearing into honeycomb-like tunnels and reappearing. Hundreds more flew through the chamber, jumping into ventilation shafts. Others came from the ducts and various passages carrying pieces of equipment. Tag watched twenty Dreg carrying a surgical bed from one of the *Hope*'s medical suites through one of several dozen holes that had been bored into the floor.

He pointed at one, whispering to Sofia, "That must be where their ships docked. Chewed through the hull, straight into here."

"Brazen little suckers," Sofia said. "Not sure I'd want to tunnel into a power plant."

A Dreg zoomed their direction, and Tag ducked behind the terminals, pulling Sofia down with him. The Dreg's wings buzzed louder, and Tag held his breath, waiting for it to discover them. The Dreg careened into another corridor and disappeared into the darkness.

"This would be a lot easier if we had the rest of the crew," Sofia whispered.

"And the Melarrey and Mechanics, too," Tag said, "but I'm not sure even with all that extra firepower we'd be able to exterminate the hive."

"You're probably right," Sofia said, miming two pistols and pretending to fire into the Dreg. "Going all Lonestar on these guys ain't going to cut it."

"Right," Tag said. "We need to think of some way to wipe them out in one fell swoop. We've got one chance to do this, so I want to do it right."

Sofia looked around the facility, a crafty look on her face. "I've got an idea."

"I'm all ears."

"We're all wearing EVA suits, but the Dreg aren't. We don't need the atmosphere in here. We could shut down the life-support systems. Turn this place into a freezer."

"I like where you're headed," Tag said. "It's efficient. But our plant friend is fragile. He was trying to keep the life-support systems online, so if we shut them off and freeze his leafy ass, he'd probably count that as an unkind thing."

Sofia crouched, her hands on her knees. "True. Very true. I'm getting a little ahead of myself because I hate those damn Dreg so much."

"Harsh words for an ET anthropologist."

"They're always trying to mess up my ship. Ever drove an air car down a flyway and have bugs splatter all over your windshield? I hate that. Hate it with a passion. When these guys stuck themselves to the *Argo*, it was like that but a thousand times worse."

"All right," Tag said, holding his hands up in a placating gesture. "I get it. We've got to get rid of them for our own sake as much as Raktor's. If those things break up this station, we lose the chance to learn what he knows. Raktor might have information leading to the crew of the *Hope*, the Collectors—maybe even the Drone-masters. I don't want those flying slugs to ruin our chances of saving humanity."

"So you got a better idea?"

Tag thought for a moment. Sofia was right; something quick, unexpected, and ambitious would be a surefire way of catching all the Dreg off guard. It was absolutely necessary to ensure they rid the power plant and life-support facilities of the slimy bastards, but they couldn't do it at the sacrifice of the whole station, much less Raktor. Sofia's plan evolved in his mind, taking shape into something new. Something risky. Something he hoped would be even more effective.

With a grin on his face, he finally said, "I got it."

# NINETEEN

Tag motioned to one of the containment drums around a fusion reactor. "When those things go into overload, they're jettisoned so they don't explode on the ship."

"So what, you want to turn that into a bomb?" Sofia asked. "Doesn't sound particularly safe."

"No," Tag said. "I'm thinking we simulate an overload. At least on the *Argo*, there's an override to jettison a fusion reactor in case the AI's censors malfunction."

"And when we dump the reactor, we just keep the dump-hatch open to suck all these bastards out!"

"Exactly," Tag said.

"Can we jettison the reactor from these terminals?" Sofia asked.

"No," Tag said, his grin fading. "It's got to be a manual override."

"Don't tell me the manual override is by the reactor."

"That's exactly where it is." He pointed to a lever shielded by a protective polyglass shell. The nearest manual override was next to one of the Dreg hives, and the slug-like aliens were crawling all over it and the reactor it controlled.

"How do we get past them?" Sofia asked.

"Hadn't quite thought that far ahead."

For a few moments they both sat in silence, gazing about their surroundings as if some clue would appear telling them how to proceed. The heat was getting to Tag. His shirt clung to his chest and back, and sweat saturated his gloves. The rising temperatures were making him impatient, and he silently willed himself to ignore his extreme discomfort.

*Just focus on a solution*, he thought.

"How about I cause a distraction?" Sofia offered.

"What are you thinking?"

"Those repair bots we saw on the way here. I could manually program one to go clanging down a ventilation duct."

"Should be noisy enough to attract the Dreg."

"No doubt," Sofia said. "Might give us a few seconds for you to reach the lever and activate it. And that's it, right? It should be pretty instantaneous."

"Should be," Tag agreed. "If we can actually make that happen that quickly, we should be home free."

Sofia gave him a look that seemed to say, *Please don't jinx this.* Every time they had thought something was going to be easy, it usually proved to be anything but. He had no delusions that their plan was sure to succeed. But what choice did they have? If they wanted Raktor to help them, they had to help the leafy monster first.

"Sooner we get this over with, the sooner we're out of here," Tag said.

"That I can agree with."

"Ready?"

"Ready."

"I'll wait for your signal," Tag said.

Sofia crept back down the corridor and grabbed a slumbering repair bot, then disappeared into the shadows. Tag waited several minutes, listening to the cacophonous droning of the Dreg. His vision wavered as the intense heat and exhaustion took their toll. He shook his head and tried to stay alert behind the bank of terminals.

Eventually, the comms in his suit buzzed on. "I'm in position," Sofia said. "I'm going to set the bot loose."

"Go for it," Tag said. He braced himself, ready to sprint to the manual jettison controls.

"Ready...here we go!"

A loud clanging sounded from one of the ventilation ducts, and green and blue lights flashed from within it. The buzzing of the Dreg crescendoed into a high-pitched fit, and the little beasts descended on the duct like a living cyclone. They funneled into it, leaving only a few scrambling around the hives.

Tag heaved himself forward, opting for speed over stealth. His footsteps clanked down a stairway to the bottom of the reactor facility. A lingering Dreg fluttered after him, trying to land on his suit, but Tag backhanded it away. The alien smacked against a bulkhead, its wings crumpling, and it plopped onto the deck.

The manual release was within reach now. Drawn by the commotion, more Dreg threw themselves at him, and he unholstered his pistol. Orange pulsefire scorched their skin, and they flew like they were drunk on gutfire until they crashed into a jumble of broken insectile limbs. Tag holstered his pistol again as a tsunami of Dreg filtered out of one of the hives. Their beady eyes searched the room for the disturbance. Spotting him, they took off like a living cloud of smog.

Digging his fingers under the edge of the polyglass cover, Tag tried to pry the shield loose from over the manual jettison control. The damn thing wouldn't budge. It was adhered to its pedestal by the same sludge that covered the rest of the facility. The first few Dreg slammed into Tag, and several attached to the back of his suit. He reached around to peel them off, but he only managed to remove two. The sounds of the others grinding their teeth into his suit reverberated up into his ears. There was no time to waste trying to stop the Dreg. He battered the polyglass shield, hammering it with the grip of his pulse pistol.

"Tag!" Sofia yelled. "The swarm is coming back!"

Dreg poured out of the ventilation ducts. As if they were a single entity, the swarm was headed straight at Tag.

The polyglass fractured at last, and Tag brought his pistol back down, summoning all the strength he could muster. Shards of polyglass flew. He grabbed the lever, then yanked it back.

Nothing happened.

His heart thrashed against his ribs. Panic flooded his chest, rising up into his throat. Then he saw it. The key.

He twisted the little key beside the lever—the failsafe mechanism to confirm he actually wanted to jettison the reactor.

A computer-generated voice boomed across the facility. "Thirty seconds until complete core ejection."

Thirty seconds to escape the imminent depressurization before he would be sucked into a vacuum. Thirty seconds to survive against the flood of Dreg. Thirty seconds seemed simultaneously much too short and much too long.

Tag sprinted toward the stairs, took them three at a time. He rounded the catwalk and he spotted Sofia further down from where they'd entered. Pulsefire exploded from her gun, shredding the Dreg who ventured too close to Tag. It wasn't enough to defeat the swarm, but it gave him a few extra seconds.

It would have to be enough.

"Fifteen seconds remaining," the voice boomed, much too calmly for Tag's liking.

Together, he and Sofia tried to outrun the Dreg. One of them latched onto his shoulder, and another clung to his leg. The smack of their grotesquely soft, slimy bodies flopping against him and Sofia accompanied the pounding of their feet against the deck.

Sofia gestured to a corridor that offered them an escape. "There!"

They were close. Meters away. A Dreg wrapped its twig-like limbs around Sofia's foot, and she tripped, falling face-first to the deck. The other Dreg took advantage of her spill, and they fell over her like a crashing wave.

"Sofia!" Tag yelled, sliding to a stop. He scrambled over the gunk threatening to slip him up and fought through the torrent of Dreg. Their bodies hit him like a flurry of punches, but he persevered. He'd come too far, seen too much, to be defeated here by a bunch of ugly flying slugs. He reached down, straining to grasp Sofia's outstretched fingers.

Dreg covered her body. She looked like a monster ascending from the swamp.

"Five seconds," the voice said.

They had to make it to the hatch at the end of the corridor. Outside that hatch, and they would be fine. The weight of the Dreg dragged on him, and he staggered as he ran. It was like trying to march up a mountain with a boulder tied to his back. More and more Dreg joined the pile on his back, and their weight pushed him onto his knees. He tried to crawl forward, pulling himself across the deck.

But he couldn't do it.

"Full core ejection initiated."

There was a second of silence as all Tag's senses tuned out the buzzing of the Dreg. Then he felt their weight lifted from him. Air rushed past his body, grasping at his suit, and he was blasted backward by the depressurization of the facility.

# TWENTY

The vacuum of space lifted Tag and Sofia into the air. All around him, the Dreg tumbled end-over-end. The frantic fluttering of their diminutive wings was no match for the pull of the void.

Through the mass of Dreg, Tag saw the fusion core reactor get sucked out of the open hatch in the deck. As soon as it cleared the opening, the Dreg followed like water swirling down a drain. Several of the little aliens still clung to his suit as his fingers scratched along the floor, desperately seeking purchase. He grabbed a stanchion protruding from the bulkhead, and his muscles strained as he held on to Sofia's hand with his other. She whipped behind him, trying to find something to grab onto.

Hordes of Dreg poured from the ducts and their hives. Their bodies tumbled against each other, bouncing against terminals and other pieces of equipment. One of Tag's fingers loosened from the stanchion. He tried to pull himself up and secure his grip, clinging to Sofia with his other hand.

One by one his fingers popped free. He and Sofia were sucked down the corridor, straight back to the facility. They were going to be condemned to the same fate as the Dreg. In his mind's eye, he saw the frozen corpses of the aliens littering the void around the *Hope*.

He wanted to believe that he and Sofia would be okay. Even if they couldn't find a handhold and were pulled into space, at least they had their EVA suits. They could survive until the rest of the crew came to their aid. But then air started rushing out of the pinpricks in his suit where the Dreg had punctured it in their attack, and the depressurization was quickly draining his oxygen supply. Judging by the sheer number of Dreg clinging to Sofia's suit, he doubted she was in any better condition.

Once they hit the open space over the hatch, Tag knew there would be no chance to save themselves. All that stood between them and the hatch now was the catwalk.

"Get ready!" Tag said, as they zoomed toward it.

He braced himself just before he slammed against the railing. The wind was knocked out of him with the impact, but he managed to spread his body flat against the railing. Sofia pulled herself next to him, hand-over-hand. Several more Dreg that had been crawling over their suits fluttered away, disappearing into the black.

It felt like half an hour had passed since the hatch opened. It might've only been a few seconds, but Tag's mind raced as he tried to calculate when the ejection hatch would shut. His muscles burned as he maintained his grip, desperately trying not to let himself fall over either side of the rail. His limbs began shaking, and his fingers grew numb. But he could do it. He could hold on for a little longer.

But Sofia couldn't.

She started to slip. He reached for her.

It was too late.

Her body tumbled toward the open hatch with the last of the Dreg.

Tag yelled her name as she plummeted toward the hatch. He stretched as far as he could, reaching for her outstretched hand. She was only a few meters away, but it might as well have been lightyears.

The hatch closed just before she reached it. Her body hit it hard with an echoing thud, crushing the Dreg beneath her.

She didn't get up.

Tag dropped the last meter toward the deck. He ignored the burning lactic acid buildup in his muscles and ran to Sofia. The few Dreg that had survived were still trying to bore their way into her suit. He yanked them off, throwing them at the bulkhead. He rolled Sofia over. Her visor was cracked, and dark rivulets of blood traced down her forehead and over her nose. With his wrist terminal, he checked the biosensors embedded within her suit. Her heartbeat was weak.

But she was still alive. Still breathing.

Something scratched across the deck to his right. One of the Dreg he had thrown off her suit was dragging itself toward her. *Relentless little bastards.* He drew his pulse pistol and fired at it until smoke wafted from its crisped body.

"Bull," Tag called over the comm. "You there?"

"I read you," Bull said. "What's with all the commotion? Heard a boom down there."

"We jettisoned one of the core reactors," Tag said.

"Damn," Bull said. "You've been busy."

"We have," Tag said. "Sofia's hurt. Can you reach me?"

"Afraid not," Bull said. "We're still locked out of every damn passage by those vines."

"Gods be damned," Tag said. He needed to get Sofia back to

the med bay aboard the *Argo*. There he would at least have the equipment he needed to help her. Although her heart was beating, there was no question she had suffered a concussion, but it might be worse than that. If her brain was swelling or her skull was fractured, he wouldn't see any outward sign of it until she slipped into unconsciousness—or death.

Tag scooped Sofia into his arms. He loped over the deck, nearly slipping on the bodies of the dead Dreg and the disgusting gunk they'd left behind. Tag made himself slow down and pay attention to where he placed his feet. Sofia couldn't endure another fall. Back down the catwalk and through the corridor he went. Each step seemed harder than the last. At least, thanks to the core ejection, the temperature had cooled considerably. Without the Dreg swarm, Raktor could send his vines back into the life-support systems and manipulate the *Hope* to his heart's content.

Meter by meter, Tag pushed himself onward, following the tunnel that Raktor had made for them. His lungs heaved as he struggled to carry Sofia. There was no choice but to take her back the way they'd come. Until Raktor decided to let them return to their ship, they were essentially the plant-creature's captives. He hated Raktor in that moment, hated having to obey the thing like it was his captain and he was dutifully fulfilling orders. He wanted only to bring Sofia back to the *Argo*. Back to where she would be safe.

But they needed answers. For this trip to be worth something, they had to find out what Raktor knew. The only information about the *Hope*'s crew, the last humans who had ever been aboard this nightmare of a space station, was held by that overgrown, psychotic plant.

Finally, Tag made it to Raktor's chamber.

"I'm here!" he yelled.

Vines unfurled around the black beak of Raktor. "Very good. You have done the kind thing we asked."

"Yes," Tag said. "I have. Now tell me what happened to the humans as quickly as possible."

"You are a very nosey human. I like the other better."

"She's hurt, thanks to you," Tag said. He knew he should be treating this situation like a leaky fusion reactor, but as he held Sofia's limp form in his arms, Tag found that he had run out of patience. "I need to get her back to our ship."

The beak twisted from side to side. For a moment Tag thought Raktor had played them. It seemed ready to rescind its offer, and a soul-crushing realization swamped Tag: what could he do if it did?

He had no real recourse. Raktor could fling his body into the bulkhead and be done with him.

"It is true that you have done a kind thing," Raktor said. "But we have done two for you, and you have done just one for us. I think you must do two more kind things to make this worth our time. We must have an even trade. You humans only call an even trade an even trade when it is not even at all. You call it an even trade only when it is better for you. More kind things, or you do not get the answers you want."

Heat flooded Tag's face, and his fingers trembled. A lone Dreg continued to gnaw on the back of his suit, churning on his anger even more.

"There will be no more kind things," Tag said. "We have done enough. We saved your life. Saved your seedlings. You can't get a better gods-damned deal than that."

The beak opened, and Raktor began its honking laughing again. "Angry human."

"That's right," Tag said. "I need to know what happened to those other humans. I need to know where they went and when they went there. You must uphold your end of the deal."

"Must we?" Raktor asked. "We have learned from the humans. They do not keep their word. They lie—an unkind thing—and cheat. They cheat each other. Other beings. Raktor. It isn't right. But we will treat the humans as they treated us, because that is what they deserve. That is the nature of kind things and unkind things and balance. It's only mathematics, you understand?"

Tag shook with rage. He wanted to jab his pulse pistol straight into Raktor's beak and let loose, showing it exactly how unkind humans could be.

"Two more kind things, that is all we ask," Raktor said, continuing as though it hadn't noticed Tag's anger. "There is still the matter of removing the Dreg ships and their ugly hives from the *Hope*. Surely you have noticed the buildup of waste and decay in the corridors that must be cleaned, and a human would be most useful at doing that. Even we are growing weary of the smell of corpses from the Specimen Storage chamber. The humans should clean that, too."

Tag's world turned red with frustration.

"Listen here, you overgrown—I've had enough of this," Tag said. "You will give me what I want, or I will do a most unkind thing. The unkindest thing ever."

# TWENTY-ONE

Tag tried to stand straighter even as he felt like his spine was about to give out. Raktor's beak leaned down, and a multitude of vines descended with it, whipping about like angry snakes.

"What would you do, human?" Raktor asked. A glob of spittle stuck to Tag's visor and began dripping down.

"Sofia and I had a choice when we were exterminating the Dreg," Tag said. "We could've shut off the life-support systems instead of venting the reactors. That would've killed the Dreg."

"And us!" Raktor roared.

"Exactly," Tag said. "It would be a shame if we shut the life-support systems down."

A vine tremored next to Tag's face.

"That is too unkind," Raktor said. "We will kill you before you can do this terribly unkind thing."

The vine whipped around Tag's neck, slowly squeezing. He could still breathe.

For the moment.

"I wouldn't do that if I were you," Tag said.

"And why not?"

"My crew is aboard this ship," Tag said.

"We are aware of this information," Raktor said. "They are within the reach of our vines. We could kill them, too."

"You told me earlier that you knew about the other aliens on this ship—the ones we call the Mechanics and the Melarrey," Tag said. "But you don't have vines up where they are. You can connect to the computer systems on this station, can't you? That's why you made your home in the central computing core of the *Hope*."

Raktor said nothing, and the silence all but confirmed Tag's suspicions.

"You might know where they are, but you can't touch them," Tag said. He chinned his comms. "Jaroon, Bracken, if you don't hear from me or my crew in twenty minutes, blow the *Hope* to bits."

"Why?" Jaroon asked. "Are you okay?"

"Understood," Bracken said, and for once Tag felt grateful for her Mechanic pragmatism.

"Just trust me on this one," Tag said. He turned off the comms. "Now do you see what danger you're in, Raktor?"

"This is an unkind thing," the plant replied.

"On the contrary. It is a very kind thing. If you help me, if you answer my questions, I will tell the crews of two different alien warships to *not* kill you. That is *two* kind things. Is that an even enough trade for you?"

"HUMAN TREACHERY!" Raktor bellowed. The force of the word threatened to knock Tag and Sofia over.

"Is it a deal? Two kind things. Just like you asked."

Raktor let out a guttural roar that shook through Tag's bones. The vines quivered, closing in as if to imprison him. Vines wrapped around him and Sofia, but he protected her as best he could, trying to shield her.

Just before they were completed cocooned, the vines abruptly began to retreat.

"Fine, human Tag," Raktor said. "You will do these two kind things that you promised. Tell these other aliens to leave us be."

"I will," Tag said, "after you give me what *I* want."

Raktor did not respond, but nor did he attack again. Tag took a moment to regain his breath.

"First, tell me when the humans left and where they went," Tag said.

The vines around Raktor's beak shifted. Something behind them cracked, and a shower of sparks descended. Tag gently laid Sofia on the deck and reached for his pulse pistol, determined to be ready for whatever surprises Raktor had in store for him. Sofia groaned and tried to sit up.

"Sofia," Tag whispered. "You okay?"

"Head...hurts...," Sofia said. She pressed one hand to her helmet. "What happened? I feel like I was run over by a Death Walker."

"We jettisoned the fusion reactor, but I *think* Raktor is finding us some answers," Tag said.

Sofia staggered to her feet. She spread her arms out as though dizzied by the movement, and Tag placed a hand on her shoulder to steady her.

"Careful," he said.

"Damn thing's going to betray us," Sofia said. "I know it."

More sparks exploded overhead. Something tickled at the back of his neck, and he didn't think it was just the cool air wafting into his suit from where the Dreg had punctured it.

"I made a deal," Tag said. "He tried to trick us, but I told him the Mechanics and Melarrey would blast him to the three hells if he didn't give us the information we came for."

Sofia pursed her lips, dried blood cracking around her mouth. "I have a feeling he didn't go for it."

Klaxons bleated and red emergency lights flashed like bloody lightning over Raktor's vines. Distant sounds of metal slamming against metal reverberated throughout the *Hope*, echoing and building into a din like the footsteps of a thousand charging giants.

"What is going on?" Tag asked, drawing his pulse pistol. He aimed it first at Raktor's beak, then at each of the vines threatening to draw near him, pivoting wildly.

Sofia held up her hands. "Raktor, stop this madness!"

Raktor's beak shot toward her, stopping centimeters from her face. Sofia didn't flinch. A hot wall of anger fired through at the thought of this bastard of a plant harming her, and he leveled his pistol at the center of Raktor's vines where he imagined its heart would be.

Sofia said calmly, "What are you doing, Raktor?"

"We may not be able to reach those Mechanics and Melarrey," it said, "but we can reach your human friends. We have activated the *Hope*'s emergency lockdown. They will be stuck in the bridge, no way out, and my vines are growing ever nearer to them. We are ready to do a most unkind thing."

"Then I'll have the Melarrey and Mechanics burn this whole place up from their ships," Tag countered.

"The Melarrey and Mechanics are trapped now, too." Raktor let out a brief, honking laugh. "We have learned something about your species. You do not like other lifeforms all that much. You do not care for them. You do not value them. Humans value only their own species, their own lives. They hold themselves more sacred than any kind or unkind thing any other lifeform might do for them."

The beak twisted, its slithering tongue playing over the individual ragged teeth that lined its mouth like so many knives.

"We know that you do not care for these Melarrey or Mechanics. You care only for other humans," Raktor said. "We will kill your human friends. Perhaps we have already killed them!"

"Bull?" Tag asked, trying to calm the shaking of his voice. "Bull, you there?"

"For now, Captain," Bull answered back. "We're...tied up... the vines...."

Each word sounded like it had struggled to escape Bull's lips. Like the sergeant was already choking, desperate for air.

"You might think you can threaten us with your alien friends," Raktor said. "But we know that you will do whatever we say if these humans' lives are at stake. We can snap them like dried twigs. We will do the unkind thing if you force us to do it, because we know, above all else, humans do not want to be held responsible for the loss of another human life."

Tag's finger trembled above the trigger of his pistol. He wanted to smash the pistol straight into Raktor's gullet and burn him from the inside of that ugly, bird-like maw.

"Don't kill them," Tag said, lowering his gun.

"See?" Raktor said. "We knew it. You fold so easily. You are so predictable. Everything we have learned is true."

"Is it?" Sofia asked, taking out her pistol. She pressed it to the side of her head, her finger finding the trigger. "Because then you know I am not afraid to lose my life to protect the others. Human, Mechanic, or Melarrey—I will stop you to save them."

# TWENTY-TWO

Tag watched in horror as she jabbed the muzzle of the pulse pistol against her head again. "Sofia…"

"Check the computers," Sofia said. "You'll see a slight power discrepancy in your life-support systems."

Vines along one of the walls moved, snaking into the ports of the terminals. Sparks flew from a cracked screen as the vines twisted and coursed.

"You said it yourself," Sofia said. "A human will do anything to save another human."

"Don't do this," Tag said, grabbing Sofia's shoulder. She shrugged him off.

"That power problem you're seeing in the life-support systems is because I modified them," she continued, ignoring Tag. "Right before I brought one of those repair bots back online to distract the Dreg, I set up an explosive charge."

Tag racked his mind, trying to figure out how she had set it up. When had she pilfered the explosives from the armory? But now wasn't the time to ask.

"That bomb is transmitting a signal to my suit," she said. "Go ahead and tap into the communication arrays on the *Hope*. You can confirm the power leak yourself."

The vines continued squirming at the terminals, but Raktor said nothing.

"See?" Sofia asked. "The bomb is set to go off when my heartbeat ceases. I knew you would play us, Raktor. I needed some assurance you would tell us what we want to know without trying a double-cross. Unfortunately, I was knocked out a bit too early for that, but hey, now we're making up for lost time."

Blood still dribbled down her forehead, and her face was rapidly going white. He moved in to steady her.

"I got this," she hissed.

"You are an unkind human," Raktor said.

"On the contrary," Sofia said. "I knew *you* would be unkind. This was just a precaution."

"Your friends will die if you set off this bomb," Raktor said.

"They have their EVA suits. They can survive if the temperature goes haywire, if the atmosphere is sucked out by vacuum, and if all the life-support systems are completely destroyed. But you can't, can you?"

Again, Raktor was silent.

Sofia's knees shook. She stumbled forward, catching herself. This time, Tag didn't try to intervene; he didn't understand her strategy, but he respected her.

"I don't know if you noticed," Sofia said. "But I also suffered a nasty head trauma. I'm getting weaker as we speak. Can barely keep myself upright. It would be a real shame if I dropped dead right here."

The vines suddenly sped from the ceiling. For a wild moment,

Tag thought they were going to tear him and Sofia to pieces, but instead they carried a handful of silver objects: data cubes.

"This is what you want," Raktor said. "All the information we have gleaned on the humans here. They left fifty years ago. The coordinates are on these devices. We give you our word on this, though you have done a most unkind thing. Please, just leave us be. Leave us to live; leave us to spread our seedlings in peace. We have had enough of you humans."

The klaxons' wailing ceased, and the flashing lights returned to their steady glow throughout the atrium. Vines parted along a corridor, and Tag started walking toward it. Suddenly, he was lifted off his feet as a large vine scooped him up. Another grabbed Sofia and shoved them along, carrying them back to the passageway leading to the labs. Coren, Alpha, and the marines soon arrived on other vines, each looking bemused by their unconventional mode of transport.

"What just happened?" Bull asked. "I could barely breathe one minute, then the next I'm here."

"Like riding a bronco," Lonestar said, grinning, "only a lot less fun."

"Let's get out of here," Tag said. "Then we can debrief."

To his surprise, Bull saluted and then jerked his chin at the rest of the marines. "You heard the captain—move out!"

"Bracken, Jaroon," Tag said. "We're getting back to the ships. Had a bit of a run-in with the natives."

"Affirmative," Bracken said. "We have recovered all the data from the Mechanic portion of this station that we could."

"Same with us," Jaroon said. "We believe we may have some information that will be of interest to you."

"Great," Tag said. "We'll arrange a conference once we're all safe."

They continued past the specimen chamber, where the odor

of death chased them through the laboratories. With their previous route blocked, they were forced to use an alternative passage that took them back to the chamber where they had first run into the broken stairs and ladders.

"At least going down is easier than up," Sofia said. She leaned over the precipice, placing her hands on the busted rungs of a ladder.

"Can I help you now, or are you going to give me the evil eye again?" Tag asked.

"Help now is fine," she said.

They made it to a catwalk. Sofia started to slip herself over the side, and Tag leaned over, gently easing her. She still had to drop a few meters to reach the deck, but at least she had let him do *something*.

"What a gentleman," Sumo said. "How about I help you now, Captain?"

"Thanks," Tag said. Sumo guided him down, and at his nod, she let him drop the couple meters. He tried to absorb the fall, bending at his knees, but still slipped, covering himself in the gunk along the deck. Soon the others had finished helping each other down. Alpha leapt down last; her droid chassis would have no issue with a drop of a few meters.

They made it back to the docking bay and into the *Argo* without running into more scorpioids or vines. As the airlock hatch closed behind them, something slipped through. Tag turned, pistol drawn, and he realized it was the cat-thing. Its tails flicked lazily behind it, and its green eyes widened as it looked up at him.

"Aw, that thing's kind of cute," Lonestar said.

It rubbed against Tag's legs, then wound between Alpha's.

"Fascinating behavior," Alpha said. "May we keep it for further observation?"

"It's probably dangerous," Tag said reluctantly. "I don't know if that's such a good idea. We don't even know what it is."

"According to the laboratory documents, this creature is a Rizzar. They are domesticated animals that often accompany the Mao-Mao-Go people." Alpha showed them an image of the Mao-Mao-Go on their terminal. The bipedal aliens shared some common traits with humans although they appeared covered in scales and had far more reptilian features. "As loyal companion animals, they are fiercely defensive of their families."

"See?" Gorenado said, bending down to pat the thing's head. "This little guy might not be so bad."

Tag couldn't believe the hulking marine had already been won over by the Rizzar.

"It did try to save us," Sofia said. "A few times, if I remember right."

"Fine," Tag said. "But if that thing tries to attack anyone, I'm giving it back to Raktor."

The Rizzar let out a growling purr again as if to assure Tag that would not happen.

"It needs a name," Sofia said.

Sumo turned to Gorenado. "What did you say when we first saw it? It would only survive in the *Hope* if it was deadly, smart—or lucky."

"Lucky it is then," Sofia said.

Tag turned to Sofia as the airlock hissed open, releasing them into the ship. "How did you sabotage the life-support systems, and when did you bring a bomb aboard?"

Sofia laughed. "I didn't. I had to use a power cable from the life-support systems to jumpstart the repair bot, but I never had a bomb. I'm just glad Raktor believed me."

"Me, too," Tag said.

"See?" Sofia said. "Sometimes it pays to have an anthropologist with ET training around. Understanding aliens can be pretty helpful."

Coren gave her a sideways glance. "You think so, huh?"

"I can read you like a book, Mechanic," Sofia said.

"Really? And what am I thinking now?"

Sofia pressed her fingers to her temple and closed her eyes like she was probing Coren's mind. "You're ready for a meal, and you think humans are stupid."

"Impressive," Coren said in a tone that contradicted his statement.

"I do not think humans are stupid," Alpha said.

"Thanks," Sumo said. "We humans appreciate your confidence."

"Quit your sucking up," Gorenado said, clapping Alpha's shoulder. "You're just saying that to make the captain happy."

"Either way," Tag said, smiling as he looked at his crew, "there's plenty of work to do. Grab some food and rest, and then let's start parsing that data. We've got some other stupid humans to track down."

# TWENTY-THREE

The hodgepodge of spaceships that made up the space station glimmered through the viewscreen. Tag reclined on the crash couch, lost in his own thoughts now that he was safely aboard his ship. No more scorpioids or Dreg after him. No more plans to outwit a giant sentient carnivorous plant. No more nightmarish tableaus of alien carcasses strewn about a "Specimen Collection Chamber."

No, those images only existed in his mind now, every time he closed his eyes.

He shuddered.

Something truly evil had been going on aboard the *Hope*. What had the Collectors wanted with those species? And what did they do to the humans?

An alarm on his wrist terminal chimed. It was time to debrief with Bracken, Jaroon, and his crew. As he followed the corridors to the captain's conference room, he wondered briefly what it was that Captain Weber had been sent to destroy on that station. Surely it wasn't Raktor. Even the scorpioids—though dangerous—were not a significant threat to humanity. Maybe the SRE had known about the Collectors and wanted to take them out.

Tag entered the conference room and slumped into his seat. He nodded a brief hello to Alpha, Sofia, Bull, and Coren, then hit a button on the terminal in front of him. Jaroon's holo-projected, amorphous form flickered into existence in one of the seats, and Bracken appeared beside him.

"First order of business," Tag said, "I want to construct a timeline for what happened with this station. After scouring through the data we recovered and what we got from Raktor, there's a bit of a discrepancy."

"Discrepancy?" Jaroon asked. "What do you mean?"

"The *Hope* recorded its last log entry approximately three hundred years ago after describing some kind of threat to humankind," Tag said. "The *Hope* continued to send courier drones to Earth and other elements of the UN."

Bracken's lips pursed. "Judging by your human expression, you don't know what was on those drones."

Tag sighed. "Unfortunately, according to the SRE, we never received those messages."

"Or maybe," Sofia said, "no one ever admitted to it."

"Most of the courier drone logs were scrubbed," Alpha said, "and I was unable to complete the restoration of these logs due to poor data integrity."

"When you say *most*," Bracken said, her holo leaning over the table, "does that mean you recovered something?"

"Yes," Alpha said. "There was a final courier drone fleet sent approximately fifty years ago. It was passed along to a set of coordinates where no humans were known to reside. It is unclear to whom the message was sent, but the content of the message is reasonably understandable."

"And what is it?" Jaroon asked.

"It simply said that the station will be abandoned."

"Not very helpful," Bull said, folding his massive arms over his chest.

"No," Tag said. "But this does align with Raktor's claims that the humans left at about that time."

"That is accurate," Alpha said. "I haven't uncovered any evidence that humans remained on the ship after the final ship log."

"Then how do you explain the courier drones?" Coren asked.

"Automation," Alpha said. "The courier drones were all pre-scheduled. They were programmed to be sent at regular intervals to Earth and other human-controlled colonies and space stations with frequent status reports regarding the *Hope*'s conditions, discoveries, and research projects."

Tag steepled his fingers. "I'm guessing this threat that the humans encountered was the Collectors. The specimen chamber data logs suggest the experiments began after the *Hope*'s crew reported that grave threat."

"That hypothesis is certainly upheld by our own findings," Bracken said. "The data we recovered from the Mechanic battlecruiser described being conquered by an unknown race. The ship was subsequently boarded, and the captain had only a few minutes to describe the invaders. He mentioned they had blue skin, were bipedal, and were two-point-five to three meters in height. Their technology was able to overcome the battlecruiser's systems, somehow shutting down their AI systems and the energy shields."

"When did that happen?" Tag asked.

"Approximately one hundred fifty years ago," she replied. "I do not think the technological capabilities or the descriptions match humans in the slightest."

Tag caught the implied jibe that human tech couldn't possibly disrupt Mechanic tech like that, but he had to admit it made sense. "Maybe these blue beings were the Collectors."

"The Melarrey ship we investigated recorded an encounter very similar to what Bracken described," Jaroon said. "And I don't mean to be condescending, but I've seen your human technology, and we've seen what the *Hope* looks like. I doubt humans took over the Melarrey vessel and added it to the station like that. It just doesn't feel right to me."

"Here's what bothers me," Sofia said. "Raktor absolutely knew what humans looked like. I'm guessing our ugly plant friend was one of the aliens that escaped the specimen chamber at some point."

"What are you implying?" Tag asked.

"Raktor must have seen humans aboard the vessel, which meant they were still there *after* the Collectors took over."

"That's debatable," Coren said. "Whatever it is, plant or something else, it was able to access the station's computer systems. It probably knew what a human looked like based on the data available to it. In all likelihood, it was just lying to get you off the station."

"I'm not buying it." Sofia drummed her fingers on the table. "It had at least some comprehension of human value systems and ethics. I don't think it was just making that stuff up, and I doubt it got that understanding from the ship's systems."

"What if there were humans still aboard the *Hope*?" Bull said, curling his fingers into fists. "Maybe they were enslaved by the Collectors. Three hells, maybe they were just biding their time, resisting the Collectors and inciting rebellion."

Tag frowned. "If these Collectors were as technologically advanced as Jaroon and Bracken said, I doubt any human resistance would've lasted against them." Bull's cheeks started to turn red as if Tag had just insulted him. "Look, I want to believe humans would've fought them and might've even inflicted some damage, but we need to look at facts and probabilities."

"You sound like a Mechanic," Bull grumbled.

"What do we know?" Bracken asked, ignoring Bull. "Most of the data has been corrupted. We have files documenting the physiology and cultures of the species that were imprisoned on the station. From the ships, we have evidence that the Collectors are more technologically advanced than we feared."

"And evidence that they are exceedingly strange," Jaroon added. "Hobbling together a station like that from scrap ships is not something we have seen before."

Tag's eyes went wide. "Yes, plenty of scrap ships from the races they captured. But no Collector ships."

Bracken's expression didn't change, but the nerve bundles behind Jaroon's eyes sparked with electricity.

"Look," Tag said excitedly as a theory took shape in his mind. "That last courier drone was sent to coordinates where no humans had ever lived, but it might've been a report to a Collector space station or ship or colony or something. The last Collector ship probably left then, too. They abandoned this place for whatever reason. I'm willing to bet that Captain Weber was supposed to nuke the station because the SRE thought the Collectors were still there?"

Coren and Sofia were nodding. The area of Jaroon's jelly-fish-like body where his head was bobbed, expanding and deflating. Bracken merely stared at him.

"You think we'll find the Collectors at those coordinates?" Sofia asked.

"Or at least another clue to their trail. And if we find them, we've got the weapons to end them."

Tag looked around the conference table. Even Bracken's

golden eyes glowed as if she was imagining the Collectors exploding into a million irradiated pieces.

"These Collectors possess technology beyond what we're capable of," Tag said. "They may have stolen the nanite technology from the humans aboard the *Hope* and perverted that to enslave the Drone-Mechs. They might be our culprits."

"Captain," Alpha said. "If I may interject, we still haven't found definitive proof that nanite research was being performed aboard the *Hope.*"

"I understand," Tag said. "But this is the simplest explanation. Most of the data was scrubbed, so I have no doubt that they'd scrub that, too."

"I have to agree," Jaroon said. "This all certainly sounds plausible."

Bull punched into the open palm of his left hand. "I say we take the fight to them. Let's finish Captain Weber's mission."

Bracken's brow furrowed, her fur crinkling. "I suppose if we concoct a reasonable countermeasure strategy—or a feasible method of escape—I could be convinced to pursue these Collectors."

"Yes," Coren said, his sole working eye glaring with a hint of anger. "And if they are responsible for the nanites, we will have our revenge."

"Based on our current assumptions and the data analyses I have run, I give Captain Brewer's hypothesis an eighty-seven-point-three percent chance of proving true," Alpha said.

Only Sofia looked unconvinced. "I'm sorry, but I'm not sure I buy this whole explanation. Raktor said he last saw humans fifty years ago."

"He lied to us, Sofia," Tag said. "He tried to trick us—he tried to *murder* us. It stands to reason he was lying to save his own viny ass."

Sofia brushed a hand through her long brown hair and left it on the back of her neck. "Fine. Let's go find your Collectors."

# TWENTY-FOUR

Tag gasped for air but didn't let the pain stitching his sides slow him down. He nodded at the terminal, ramping up the speed on the treadmill, and he forced himself to run faster, telling himself that he enjoyed the sensation of sweat dripping and muscles cramping. If his time aboard the mutant station that had once been the UNS *Hope* had taught him anything, it was that maintaining some semblance of physical fitness was going to be useful if he wanted to stay alive against whatever the universe threw at them next.

Nearby, Sumo was pulling on the bands of a resistance training machine. She wore a thin workout one-piece that showed off her ropey muscles.

She winked at him. "There's a few genies involved, but I keep it mostly natural."

"Got it," Tag managed between breaths. It made him feel slightly less inadequate to know most of the marines had dabbled in genetic enhancements—or genies—to bolster their physical aptitude. As a medical officer, he had never felt the need to do so. But with the abrupt change in his career trajectory, maybe it was time to rethink that.

"You've been hitting the gym more than usual," Sumo said, somewhere halfway between a statement and a question. She racked another set of weights onto the band, her lean biceps bulging. "Just trying to stay busy while we sit out here?"

"Damn scorpioids," Tag said. "Figured I need to focus a bit more on my cardio."

"Ah, makes sense," Sumo said, increasing her weights once again.

"I used to tell all my patients the best thing they can do…" Tag paused, slowing the machine down a bit so he could actually talk. "The best thing they can do when confined to a ship is get some exercise." The muscles in his chest seemed to loosen, the pain fading as he jogged at a more comfortable pace.

"You got that right," Sumo said. She did a last set of curls then dropped the bands. With the back of her hand, she wiped the sweat from her forehead. "Best thing you can do for the body *and* the mind." She tapped her temple with one finger.

Running had certainly served a dual purpose for him. Over the last few days, every time he hit a dead end in the lab, he had come down here to let his mind wander while he ran. His thoughts had often drifted between the data on the species they had uncovered to the classified projects the *Hope* had been working on as he tried to piece together the puzzle.

"You know," Sumo said, adjusting the resistance bands to start a set of squats, "you had me worried out there, Captain. Don't know if you noticed, but we've gotten used to having you around the ship."

"True," Tag said. "You all need a doctor on board."

Sumo laughed. "Eh, we have Alpha now. And besides, you know that's not what I mean." She grunted as she performed her squats. They continued working in silence until she finished her sets. Sumo stood, stretching her arms and cracking her joints. "That's it for me today, Cap." As she walked to the hatch, she called out, "There's another Turbo match on tonight, if you want to join us."

"I might just do that." Tag sped up the treadmill again, pumping his fists, his feet slapping the belt. With each passing day, the marines were feeling more like part of the team. After getting off to such a rocky start, Sumo's words meant a lot to him. It gave him hope that he wasn't doing a completely terrible job as captain. He ran for another fifteen minutes, determined to push himself another kilometer past yesterday's distance.

Light spilled in from the corridor once more as the hatch opened. Two shapes came in, one lunging low and sprinting across the deck. The other stood tall and lanky, striding toward Tag.

"Coren," Tag said. "Why in the three hells did you let Lucky in here?"

The Rizzar jumped on the treadmill beside Tag, her six legs bouncing happily as she ran. She gazed up at him with her green eyes, but when his gaze locked with hers, she hissed, her snout scrunching in a snarl. It wasn't until he looked slightly away that she calmed down.

"Weird little animal," Tag muttered.

"She was mewling out there for the past ten minutes," Coren said. "I could hear her all the way from the lab. If I hadn't let her in, I'm not sure how much longer I could put up with it. Might've spaced her."

Lucky hissed again, her tongue dancing between her yellow fangs.

The treadmill's terminal beeped, announcing that he'd reached his distance goal, and Tag hit a button to slow it to a walking pace. Lucky let out a soft growl as if she was displeased they were already stopping. Tag reached down and scratched behind her ears, and she closed her eyes and moved into his scratching. "I can't decide whether she's more like a dog or a cat."

With a flick of her tails, Lucky smacked his hand.

"I think she's telling you that she's neither," Coren said.

Tag stepped off the treadmill and combed his fingers through his hair, flicking off the sweat. Lucky gave him an offended look when some of it hit her. "Anyway, I'm guessing you didn't come in here just to make Lucky happy."

"No," Coren said. For a second his mouth moved, but no words came out. It was as if he wasn't sure about what he was going to say. Lack of confidence was an unusual trait for Mechanics. "I think I may have discovered something about the Collectors."

# TWENTY-FIVE

Tag followed Coren to the bridge. In actuality, he followed Coren who was following Lucky. The Rizzar acted as if she knew where they wanted to go and trotted in front of them, occasionally pausing to glance back impatiently. She sat on her hind legs when they reached the hatch, and Coren opened it.

Lucky sprinted in first, running ahead to curl up in the middle of the crash couch. Sofia was reclining on her own crash couch, legs draped over the side, while she examined something at her terminal. At their arrival, she faced them, her nose turned up.

"Phew," she said. "Smell what the cat dragged in."

Hissing, Lucky arched her back, evidently offended once again being equated to an Earthborn feline.

"Sorry," Sofia said. "I meant 'smell what the Rizzar brought in.'"

Lucky let out a short, peppy bark before curling back up.

"Just came from a workout," Tag said. "Coren told me this was worth me skipping a shower."

"Let me be the judge of that," Sofia said. "I'm not sure I'm on his side."

Coren ignored her and stood in the center of the bridge, motioning over the ops terminal. Lines of code spilled across the holoscreen.

"What am I looking at?" he asked.

"On this side," Coren began, pointing to the left side of the holoscreen, "we have the virus the Drone-Mechs used to shut the *Argo*'s AI systems down. Modified code from standard Mechanic computational warfare strategies."

"Got it," Tag said. "And this side?" He motioned to the right of the holoscreen.

"These are the bits and pieces Bracken was able to salvage from the Mechanic ship at the *Hope*'s space station. We couldn't find evidence of the virus used to override the battlecruiser's AI systems or its energy shields."

"Then where did this come from?"

"Each of our ships are equipped with a diagnostics log," Coren said. "It records abnormal events in case of accidents, ranging from fusion reactor leakage to enemy attacks to attempts to access our computer systems from unauthorized sources. The logs show the algorithmic software the Collectors were attempting to install on the battlecruiser before the ship's systems were completely overwhelmed."

"And this helps us?"

"Maybe," Coren said with uncharacteristic uncertainty. "There are two major things I noticed about this code." Coren made a sweeping gesture over the holoscreen. Multiple lines lit up in green. "It shares some striking similarities to the virus the Drone-Mechs used on the *Argo* and attempted to use on the free Mechanic fleet."

"Which means we have a way to protect our systems from them," Sofia said, slipping over the side of her crash couch and standing. "We can adapt the program Mr. Genius Engineer over here designed to shield ourselves against the Collectors."

"Excellent," Tag said. "How long do you think that'll take?"

"Not terribly long," Coren said, "especially if I can get Alpha's help on the matter. The engineers and scientists aboard the *Stalwart* will no doubt be."

"This seems to indicate a strong connection between our Drone-masters and Collectors," Tag said, "but besides that, this is the best news we've had since we left the *Hope*."

Sofia beamed, her eyes dancing between Tag and Coren. "Oh, he's got better news than that. This next part is pretty good."

Coren waved his hand over the holoscreen again. This time several lines appeared highlighted in scarlet. "The Collector program does something else interesting that the Drone-Mechs' did not. It requests an identification response from the ship before trying to subvert the vessel."

"Which means?" Tag asked.

"Which means the virus won't activate if it reads the identification code," Coren said.

Sofia still grinned as if she had something to hide.

"There's something else, isn't there?" Tag asked. He looked between them, waiting for an answer. Why would the Collectors need an identification code? Couldn't they simply recognize their own fleet through drive signatures? Wouldn't the system architecture on their ships be similar enough between each ship in their fleet that requesting an identification code would be redundant? Then it came to him. "Three hells, Coren! This is a great find!"

Coren's head bobbed. "Indeed it is."

"If they're stealing ships from all different species, they have to create some kind of ID for those ships so they don't actually shut it down after they have control over it. Their fleet might be comprised of all kinds of ships. We can spoof an ID and pretend to belong to their fleet."

"Exactly what I was thinking," Sofia said. "If it turns out we need to raze these Collectors, we can do it without them even knowing what's coming."

"Hell of a plan," Tag said.

"It is," Coren said hesitantly.

"You don't sound confident."

"I'm not yet sure that we can accurately replicate a Collector ID code."

"Because this data is corrupted?" Tag asked.

"Right," Coren said. "We simply don't have enough data on these ID codes to proceed."

Tag looked at the bridge's viewscreen. The UNS *Hope* was little more than a blurry dot in the distance. "There are ways to get more data."

———

Tag called another meeting with Bracken and Jaroon. He settled into his seat in the conference room outside the captain's quarters—*my quarters*, he internally chided himself. This time the seats around the table were empty. He heard a soft tapping against the hatch, and figuring it was Alpha or Coren with more updates, he opened the door.

When he saw who it was, he shook his head. Lucky wound between his legs and plopped herself onto one of the seats.

"You just couldn't sit this one out, huh?"

One of her claws kicked at a spot behind her ear.

The first holo fizzled on, glowing blue before settling into the black form of Bracken. She sat stoically, clenching her hands together at her simulated spot across from Tag. He nodded his greeting toward her as a holo of Jaroon's gelatinous form appeared next to Bracken.

"Greetings to the both of you," he said.

"I see we have another guest," Bracken said, sending a sideways glance toward Lucky. "Is this a new officer?"

"She certainly acts like one," Tag said.

"I assume you didn't call us here to discuss this specimen joining your already quite diverse crew," Bracken said.

"No," Tag said. "I certainly didn't."

He relayed Coren's discoveries regarding the virus the Collectors had used on the Mechanic battlecruiser. After describing the similarities between that virus and the one used by the Drone-Mechs, he explained the additional ID request nestled within the software.

"These are intriguing findings," Jaroon said. "We've parsed the data we found on the Melarrey ship, and my engineers reported similar results."

"If we are going to pursue the Collectors," Tag said, "I think it would be prudent to do a bit more scavenging. I want to be able to mimic those ID codes so we can get in close to the Collectors and figure out what they're up to."

"You will find no disagreement from me," Bracken said.

"Likewise," Jaroon said. "What exactly did you have in mind?"

"As much as I hate to say it, I suggest we go back to the *Hope* station. Let's explore the other ships. See if we can tap into the computers, draw out any information on the ID codes. Surely, if the Collectors took these ships over, they implanted ID codes on them somewhere. Maybe we can find a pattern or some way to replicate the codes."

"That sounds like a decent plan," Jaroon said. A holo of the space station appeared before them. It looked like a spiral galaxy with all its arms of scavenged spaceships tracing around the central core of the UNS *Hope*. "Shall we split the ships up and each start investigating down a branch or two?"

"That's what I was thinking," Tag said.

Bracken's fur bristled. "It will take days, maybe weeks to work our way through each of the ships."

"Possibly," Tag said. "But at least we'll have the data we need to spoof a Collector ship ID."

"There's no guarantee we'll find the codes," Bracken said. "In fact, there's no guarantee that the Collectors are still to be found at the coordinates provided by Raktor."

"They left years ago," Jaroon said. "What difference does a few days make?"

"Maybe all the difference in the world," Bracken said. "The longer we're here chasing them around, the longer Meck'ara is waiting for the next Drone-Mech attack. Or"—she narrowed her eyes, her holo leaning in toward Tag—"the longer you leave humanity open to an attack from these Collectors, Drone-masters, and whoever else is part of this mad conspiracy."

"I understand," Tag said. "Trust me, I do. The last thing I want is to leave the SRE vulnerable, but that's why I want to do this right."

"Then you would agree it's best to collect this data as efficiently and swiftly as we can," Bracken said.

"I would," Tag said slowly, wondering where Bracken was steering this conversation.

"Then, according to your reports from the *Hope*, I think we already have a surefire method of accessing all the computers aboard the station at once."

Tag swallowed hard as he realized what the Mechanic captain was hinting at. "You mean Raktor."

"Exactly," Bracken said. "It seems like we need to pay our vegetable friend another visit. And by we, I mean you."

"Damn it," Tag said. He wanted to disagree with Bracken, but there was just one problem: she was right. Raktor had access to the entire station network. He could do in minutes what would take them weeks or months. Now he just needed to find a way to make amends with the monster and get it to do just one more favor—one more kind thing.

# TWENTY-SIX

Running wasn't enough. Tag had logged plenty of time on the treadmill, but it hadn't jump-started his mind. How was he supposed to get Raktor's help? He struggled to come up with anything better than taking over the station by force. Threats of violence were unpredictable at best against the strange alien, as Tag and his crew had learned the hard way.

He'd left the gym and now sat at his desk in his quarters, staring at nothing while his mind worked. Several shelves were still empty, waiting for the computational supplies and research files he had yet to move from his old quarters below deck. A single holopainting of the *Argo* was projected on a bulkhead—the only holdover from Captain Weber.

Something scratched his leg, and he looked down to see Lucky pawing at him. In her fanged mouth she held an empty plastic bottle. Tag took it and tossed it across the room. Lucky sprinted after it, pounced, and bounded back to him, holding it in her mouth.

If only making Raktor happy was as easy. He brought up a schematic holo of the *Hope*. He gestured over the glowing image, highlighting the computer core chamber where Raktor's main body dwelled. Maybe there was a way he could infiltrate the place without Raktor knowing and set up a transponder to leech all the data they needed.

There was a knock at his door.

"Come on in," he said, throwing the bottle again.

Sofia and Alpha entered.

Watching Lucky, Sofia leaned against a bulkhead. "Any ideas?"

"Nothing but storming in there with guns blazing and demanding Raktor let us into the computers by force."

"I don't think threats will work. Doesn't seem like it would fall for the same trick twice."

"If I'm being honest, as much as I don't like the plant, I don't relish the idea of exterminating it." Tag cradled his chin in his left hand as he used his right to throw the bottle. "That wouldn't make us much better than the Collectors."

"Maybe we can have Lucky sneak in there and steal the data while Raktor isn't looking," Sofia said.

"Ha, yeah, good luck getting her to do anything we want," Tag replied. "She's on her own schedule."

The Rizzar brought Sofia the plastic bottle and dropped it at her feet. Sofia obligingly resumed the game of fetch.

"Once you start, you don't get to stop," Tag warned. "I'm running into a dead end here. There's got to be some way to convince Raktor to do this last favor for us without threatening it."

"There might be," Sofia said, her eyes starting to brighten. She flipped the bottle across the room again, and Lucky went after it. "Maybe there's a ploy with the seedlings."

"I'm interested," Tag said. "Go on."

When Lucky dropped the bottle at Sofia's feet again, Alpha

took over, picking up the bottle. She threw it inhumanly fast, and it flew like a comet into the corridor. Lucky's claws pattered away, giving them a respite from her game.

"Alpha recovered some data on Raktor that she thought we might find interesting," Sofia said.

"Let's hear it," Tag said.

Alpha tapped on her wrist terminal. "From what the Collectors gathered, Raktor is not the name of the sentient vegetative life-form you encountered, but instead the name of the species as a whole."

"Okay," Tag said. "How does the naming schema help us?"

"Raktor was described by the Collectors as a weed-like species with a collective intelligence, not unlike the Dreg."

"Probably why Raktor was so competitive with the Dreg," Sofia offered. "As different as they seem on the outside, their basic take-all attitude toward resources are similar."

Alpha nodded. The click of Lucky's claws sounded louder, and the Rizzar appeared through the hatch. Alpha sent the bottle rocketing back out into the passageway, and Lucky dashed away.

"Sofia's assessment is accurate," Alpha said. "Raktor are an adaptable, scavenging species. It appears that this particular one escaped a specimen chamber after the Collectors left the *Hope*. As the life-support systems failed, I hypothesize it used the warmth of the terminals in the computer core to stay alive, which simultaneously aided its efforts in understanding the ship's layout, enabling it to tap into the station's systems. In fact, the Raktor have evolved to directly tap into electronic systems in a unique adaptation enabled by the advent of space-faring species. Their vines are capable of confining and transmitting electromagnetic waves through the transport of energy down an organic dielectric material."

"In other words, Raktor and their vines act like an old-fashioned network cable," Sofia said.

"I see," Tag said. "That explains how it's able to interface with ship's systems. I'm still wondering what all this has to do with the seedlings."

"A few things," Sofia said. "The Raktor we know and love realizes that the *Hope* is a defunct station. It isn't stupid, and it knows its life will end aboard the ship in isolation." She held up a finger but waited as Lucky bounded noisily into the room. Alpha took care of the crumpled bottle once more. "If there's one thing I have found in common with every lifeform I've studied, it's the desire to survive and provide more resources for their progeny."

"That is self-evident," Alpha said, "because if a race didn't want to survive, it would go extinct."

Sofia rolled her eyes. "Thanks for the obvious."

"I thought what you were saying was rather obvious," Alpha said, apparently confused.

"Anyway," Sofia continued, "my point is that Raktor's seedlings might never have a chance to propagate. Its lineage will live and die on that station without a chance to spread."

Tag's shoulders sagged as the realization of what Sofia wanted to offer Raktor settled over him. "You want to propose Raktor a trade. All the ID codes from the other ships in return for spreading its seedlings around the galaxy."

"I knew you wouldn't like it," Sofia said. "If Raktor is anything like other races I've studied—and everything Alpha showed me supports that—it will gladly give us the data we want in exchange for ensuring its offspring have a chance to thrive."

"I'm not a fan of spreading weeds," Tag said.

"But what if they could help us?"

Tag stared back at Sofia. A wild look shone in her eyes. He

found it odd that an ET anthropologist would suggest *using* a sentient race like this.

"What if we could use them to take over a Collector ship?" she asked.

"How does that make us any better than the aliens who enslaved the Drone-Mechs?" Tag asked. "I couldn't possibly justify that, even if we're talking about Raktor."

"Trust me," Sofia said. "I understand that. We'd give Raktor and one of its seedlings a choice. I wouldn't force them into anything."

"Why would it choose to help us?"

"There is one more motivating factor besides propagation shared between many species," Alpha said. "I have observed it in humans, as well as with the Mechanics and Melarrey. Sofia and I believe this factor may be shared by Raktor as well."

Tag looked at Sofia. "And that would be?"

She leaned over his desk. "Revenge."

# TWENTY-SEVEN

Aboard the *Hope* station once more, Tag looked over the precipice from which he and Sofia had first fallen into Raktor's waiting vines. Like before, darkness peered back up at him. He flicked on the forward lights from his EVA suit's helmet to cut a swathe from the murky blackness, revealing the latticework of brown vines squirming up the side of the cylindrical chamber. The vines formed a living carpet over the bottom of the deep chasm.

"I'm just glad we're not jumping again," Sofia said, sidling up beside him.

"You're both positive this thing won't smash us against the walls?" Coren asked.

"According to preliminary conversations we conducted with Raktor via the *Hope*'s laboratory computers and my own data analysis," Alpha said, "I believe there is a sixty-five-point-four percent probability that Raktor will not immediately terminate us via that method."

Coren uncoiled a length of climbing rope from his pack. "What's the probability it kills us with some other method?"

"That probability is rather considerable."

"Let's focus on the positive, please," Tag said.

"I believe a common human saying is appropriate in this environment," Alpha said, helping Coren to secure one end of the climbing rope to a stanchion. "*Hope* for the best, prepare for the worst."

Sofia glanced over the edge again. "Yeah, that about sums it up."

"I still say we burn the damn plant," Bull said. "Find all the codes ourselves."

The marines behind him bristled with their weapons. Knowing kinetic slugs and pulsefire would do minimal damage to Raktor's forest of vines, they had brought flamethrowers not unlike the ones in Coren's wrist-mounted weapons.

"I'd prefer not to massacre every living thing the Collectors left here. Dealing with the Dreg and the scorpioids was enough for me," Tag said. "Besides, Raktor isn't the enemy."

"Ain't exactly our friend, either," Lonestar said.

"You know what they say," Tag began. "The enemy of my enemy—"

"Is still a psychotic plant with violent tendencies," Sumo finished.

"All right," Tag said. He motioned to Sofia and himself. "Let us do the talking when we get down there." Then he nodded to Coren.

Coren threw the unsecured end of the rope spooling over the side, and Tag watched it fall among the vines. He grabbed the rope, pulled on it to ensure it was holding tight, and then positioned himself over the edge.

"I, for one, am looking forward to meeting Raktor," Alpha

said. "I believe Raktor and I share a common bond in that we are both lifeforms one would not normally believe to be sentient."

"Better hope you're still sentient after we talk to it," Bull said.

Tag gave the sergeant an ironic salute as he rappelled down the rope and into the embrace of Raktor's vines. The vines seemed to give way, making room for him as he descended. None reached out to him like they had when he and Sofia had fallen here the first time. He wasn't sure if Raktor was being polite, or if it was avoiding so much as touching Tag because it was pissed off. Sofia came down next, landing lightly beside Tag. Rather than have the marines lead with weapons drawn, Tag and Sofia had decided to be the first to approach Raktor as a sign of goodwill.

Not that Tag was foolish enough to think Raktor would be swayed by this small measure of trust. Bracken and Jaroon were watching from their ships, all weapons aimed at the life-support systems of the *Hope* as a final failsafe measure. He figured with Raktor's vines in all the *Hope*'s computer systems and sensor arrays, the posturing by the two warships hadn't gone unnoticed.

The rest of the crew made it down, with Gorenado landing last. His boots hit the deck hard, splashing brown gunk over the others. Everyone seemed too distracted by the moving vines to give the massive marine so much as a fleeting glare. They traveled onward though the corridor, and the vines retreated from their path wherever they went like shadows forced backward by a flashlight.

Tag followed the now familiar passages to the huge chamber where the computational core resided, the synthetic brain of the *Hope*. Raktor's beak snaked out from the curtain of vines and slithered toward Tag, trailing behind it an entourage of gargantuan vines. There was no doubt in Tag's mind that this was a show of force by the alien.

The beak zeroed in on him, opening and closing, teeth

grinding together. Bull and Sumo stepped forward, tension radiating off them, but Tag raised a hand to stay their weapons.

Taking another step closer, Tag stared down Raktor's beak. He found himself wishing Raktor had visible eyes rather than the nebulous pheromone sensor organs Alpha had told him about. The farce of trying to appear confident in the face of an aggressor worked a lot better when he knew which direction he should be looking. The beak would have to suffice as a proxy.

"Raktor," Tag said. "We just want the ID codes the Collectors assigned to all the other ships. You don't even have to do the work for us. Let us use one of your terminals in here."

"Ah, you call them the Collectors?" Raktor said as if thinking aloud. It didn't wait for a response from Tag or his crew. "You will spread our seedlings out into the universe. That is the deal?"

"We will take *one* seedling," Sofia said.

Raktor emitted its grating, honking laugh. "One is hardly a kind thing. It is an enormous gamble. It is better to unleash a brood of seedlings. What if one cannot take root? What if one cannot find nourishment? No, no, the risk of failure is too great. It will not work!"

"You have us," Sofia said, placing a hand over her chest. "We'll ensure it takes root."

"And why should Raktor believe you?" it asked.

"Because we want what you want," Tag said. The beak snapped in front of him, so close that if he moved forward a centimeter, the thing would chomp the front of his EVA suit and take his nose with it. "We want revenge on the Collectors. We want to stop them from enslaving other species and turning them into lab experiments."

The beak opened, and the serpentine tongue curled out, wrapping around Tag's helmet and spreading green-tinged saliva over his visor. Tag willed his fingers to quit trembling and straightened his spine.

"We can do two kind things for you," Tag said. He saw Bull and Sumo take a step toward the beak, raising their flamethrowers slightly. Lonestar and Gorenado followed their lead, while the tongue tightened around Tag. "As we told you before we came down here, as you are well aware, you will die aboard this station. It won't last forever. But one of your seedlings doesn't have to share that fate. It can live free, and"—Tag gulped, both in reflex to the tightening grasp of Raktor's tongue and at what he was about to suggest—"your progeny will command its own ship. It could even help you and the rest of your seedlings escape from this dying relic of a station."

The tongue began to loosen.

"Two kind things," Sofia said. "All you have to do is let us use these terminals."

"What can you do to assure us your word is good?" Raktor asked.

"This deal serves both our interests," Tag said. "You must realize what is at stake."

As the tongue let go of Tag and the beak drew away, Tag took in a deep breath, finally able to inhale normally again. Raktor seemed to be rummaging for something within the cavernous chamber. A vine extended toward them, carrying something in its coils. It unraveled and withdrew to leave behind something that looked vaguely like an acorn. Sofia stepped forward, crouching down to pick it up.

"This is your seedling?" Sofia asked.

"It is," Raktor said. "We trust you will take good care of it."

Two vines extended from the top of the acorn and wrapped around Sofia's arms. She held it close to her chest, and a small beak appeared at the top, letting out a coo.

"We'll be leaving now," Tag said to Raktor, "to ensure we can take your seedling to a new ship."

Sofia's eyes widened as she looked at the dense wall of vines before them. "We'll take good care of it, I promise."

Tag pressed a hand against the vines, trying to force them apart. But more whipped in front of his face, beating him back from the wall, not allowing him to escape.

"Jaroon, Bracken," Tag said. "Stand by with weapons hot."

The pilot lights on the marines' flamethrowers flickered on, and they roved the weapons over the vines twisting and winding all around the group, narrowing in on them like a swarm of angry boa constrictors.

"Captain," Alpha said, her head swiveling as she took in the impending assault, "the current situation appears to support my earlier predictions that Raktor would display an act of aggressive violence."

"We made a deal," Sofia said softly.

The vines careened from every direction, too fast for the marines to even pull their triggers. Flamethrowers fell apart as they were crumpled by huge vines. Tag leapt to the side, avoiding a tree-trunk-sized vine charging past him. In the blur of green and brown, he saw Sofia and Alpha still standing with Coren beside them. Sumo was trying to draw her pulse pistol, but her weapon was batted away. Gorenado and Bull stood back-to-back using knives to slice through the oncoming vines.

Then all at once, the vines retreated, leaving behind only the stalks that the marines had cut off. Tag surveyed his crew for injuries. Everyone was still standing, seemingly unhurt. Everyone except for—

"Lonestar!" he yelled, his heart thrashing against his rib cage.

Lonestar dangled above him, several meters out of reach. Her hands were secured tight against her sides, cocooned by vines that stretched in every direction, and her eyes were closed.

# TWENTY-EIGHT

Tag wanted to rip every goddamned vine from the wall and set them on fire. But making a Raktor bonfire wouldn't bring Lonestar back.

"Why did you kill her?" Tag asked, his voice shaking with anger.

The beak slid down from its perch again, and the remaining crew members circled up, holding whatever weapons they had left. Raktor let out its jarring laugh.

"She is not dead," Raktor said. Her biosigns shone across Tag's HUD. Raktor wasn't lying; she still had a pulse. One of the vines snaked into her wrist terminal, and a jolt of adrenaline spiked through the readings. Lonestar's eyes shot open.

"She is still very much alive. But this is no kind thing yet. And it is no unkind thing, either. This is, I believe, what you humans would call insurance. You bring us back our seedling with its very own ship, and we will return your human. *That* is a deal."

Bull looked between Tag and Raktor. His face burned a bright crimson.

"No," Tag said. "We're not leaving without her."

"Give her back!" Bull roared, shaking his fist in the air.

"We have been betrayed by humans too many times to pretend our seedling is safe with you."

Sofia, still holding the seedling in her hands, turned to Tag. "Should we give it back? It's not worth—"

"No, you will not give it back!" Raktor bellowed. "You will do as promised or this human dies!"

Bull slipped his pulse pistol out of his holster and aimed it toward Raktor's beak. "We've got two warships bearing down on this place. If you hurt her, you and your seedlings will never make it out of this station alive."

Raktor's vines tremored. "Then neither will you."

"Bull, let me handle this," Tag said.

The sergeant seemed about to protest, but Tag stared him down. He didn't want this situation to escalate any more than it already had.

"Raktor," Tag began, "this wasn't what we agreed to."

"We are amending the agreement."

Tag watched the vines coursing around Lonestar. She grimaced and her face turned pale. Tag took a step backward, and the vines relented. The marine's face lost some of its tension.

"You're wasting your time talking to this overgrown tumbleweed," Lonestar said. "Leave without me. Go find those Collectors."

"I judge Lonestar's statement to be accurate," Alpha said. "Proceeding with the amended deal would be the most prudent course of action."

The vines parted, showing Tag and the others the exit as if inviting them to leave the marine behind. Another captain might have. Another captain might have considered how Lonestar had betrayed them, how she had been duped not long ago into thinking Tag and his crew had been the enemy. After all, she had planted a stealth transponder that broadcasted their location to the Drone-Mechs and almost gotten them all killed.

She'd almost gotten this mission nixed before it had ever begun.

Tag didn't consider those things. What he saw when he looked at Lonestar's face was a crewmember who believed in doing whatever it took to accomplish her mission. A marine who embodied the living stereotype that the people of his home, Old Houston, Texas, had long ago outgrown. There were anachronisms in her manners and accent, but they masked a true and noble heart. He had never met someone quite like her. His crew would never be whole if they left her here.

"Lonestar is going with us," Tag said.

The vines whirled around him and the others like a tornado, twisting and whipping faster than gale-force winds. Some sliced against his suit with enough force to shove him backward until he was pressed against the rest of the crew.

"She stays or you all stay!" Raktor roared.

Everything went still. The vines crisscrossed around them like an organic prison cell.

"Go!" Lonestar cried. "Y'all get out of here, now!"

Never had Tag seen her so determined, so fierce, even when in battle with the Drone-Mechs.

"I'll be fine," she lied.

Tag stared at his crewmate. At a life he had been entrusted with.

"Listen to the human," Raktor asked. "Go on your little adventure, and bring our seedling back on its own ship. Bring us back a new Raktor, and this human will be yours once again."

Above Lonestar a thin, waxy vine formed a noose around her neck.

"No!" Tag yelled.

"Human Tag," Raktor spoke calmly, "you leave now or she dies. Then we will pick another human to keep with us. We will keep repeating this until only you are left."

Lonestar locked eyes at him as the vine twisted around her neck and curled under her chin.

"Go," she said.

Tag couldn't let her down now, but if he didn't leave, Raktor would make good on its word, ending the *Argo*'s crew's lives one by one. Lonestar shook her head, and Tag understood what she meant; she would feel just as guilty, just as responsible for their deaths if he stayed on her account.

"Fine," Tag said. "Fine, Raktor. You win. Let us leave."

All the vines retracted, dragging Lonestar with them. She disappeared in the nest of mottled greens and browns, along with the beak. When Tag didn't move immediately, the vines started spilling behind him like an avalanche, ushering them toward the exit.

"Screw you!" Bull roared.

Tag couldn't tell whether the marine was yelling at him or Raktor, but he figured he deserved it just as much as the plant-creature in that moment. Had he really thought that if he lived in Weber's old quarters, sat in the captain's station on the bridge, that he could lead these people? As he glimpsed Lonestar one last time, her hand reaching out before disappearing entirely behind the tornado of vines, he realized that he had a long way to go before he deserved the respect and loyalty of his crew. If he didn't get Lonestar back, they'd never forgive him—and he wouldn't forgive himself.

They ran down the passages with Raktor's vines cascading behind them. And as their boots pounded against the deck, kicking up the slime, Tag vowed that this would *not* be the last time they saw Lonestar.

He would track down the Collectors, discover the answers to what had happened on the *Hope*, and find out where the nanites had come from and how this goddamned station was involved.

And when he was done riddling the last Collector full of pulsefire rounds, he would return here for her.

"Lonestar," he whispered, "we'll be back."

# TWENTY-NINE

Three marines. Somehow, they were supposed to take on a hostile and mysterious alien race with just three marines. The *Argo* had lost its entire contingency of marines once at the hands of the Drone-Mechs. Tag hadn't been responsible then; it hadn't been his fault the Drone-Mechs had caught Captain Weber and the crew unaware in the attack that started him down this perilous race into the unknown.

But this time he was the captain.

As many times as he vowed he would return for Lonestar, it didn't assuage the poison of doubt shifting through his mind, spreading its malevolent influence and threatening to send him in a downward spiral that would lead him to the bottom of an empty gutfire bottle.

He stalked out of the laboratory. As he drew near the mess, the sound of clinking glass and muffled conversation made him pause at the entrance. *Bull, Sumo, Gorenado*, he thought. The idea of facing them was almost physically painful, but he felt exhausted and desperate for something to ward off the fatigue in his brain after working with Sofia all day. With a long sigh, he pushed open the hatch.

The conversation shared by the marines silenced.

Tag gave them a perfunctory nod. Before he could see the inevitable judgment in their eyes, he turned to the food and drink autoserv bay. A quick knuckle tap against one of the terminals spit out a cup with hot, black coffee. He moved toward the exit.

"Captain!" a gruff voice called. "Join us."

Tag glanced at Gorenado and hesitated. Three experiments were running on the sims characterizing the biochemical and genetic samples Sofia and he had obtained from the seedling. None of them would be done for another twenty minutes.

Tag sat with the marines.

"We want you to know," Sumo said without preamble, "we don't blame you."

Gorenado nodded. Maybe those two didn't blame him, but Tag could feel the heat radiating off of Bull. He doubted the sergeant felt the same.

"We had to go back to Raktor," Sumo continued. "We had to get the IDs from its computer room, or we would've wasted too much time. Time that might've meant the difference between the destruction or survival of the *Montenegro*—or some other SRE ship."

"We will stop the Collectors, and we'll get Lonestar back," Gorenado said. He took a swig of whatever he was drinking. Judging by his grimace, it was gutfire.

Bull simply stared into his cup, and Tag didn't prod him to say anything. He wondered if the other two marines were trying to reassure him or themselves.

"We'll absolutely get Lonestar back," Tag said. Now he wasn't sure whom he was trying to reassure either, but he continued, "We're so close, so damn close, to finding those Collectors."

Sumo and Gorenado nodded. Bull's fingers tightened into a fist that turned his knuckles white. For a second Tag imagined the marine slamming his fist on the table and yelling in anger. Maybe it would be cathartic. Maybe Tag wanted to see someone express some anger around here, and Bull was the gods-damned man to do it.

That moment never came.

Tag took a sip of the coffee. The heat slid down his throat, waking him up as it did. Despite their loss to Raktor, the ID codes were still theirs. They would find the Collectors and sneak in through their defenses. "We'll have those bastards begging for forgiveness."

"Damn right, Captain," Sumo said, raising her glass, brown eyes gleaming with an inebriated sheen. "Damn right."

"How much of that gutfire did you all sneak aboard?" Tag asked.

"Why?" Sumo shot back. "You want some?"

He did. He desperately did. "No, not now. But I'm going to owe Lonestar a drink or two when we get her back."

Sumo and Gorenado gave an obligatory laugh.

"Sure you don't want some?" Sumo asked as she refilled her own glass.

Tag checked his wrist terminal. Still had several minutes before he needed to head back to the laboratory. "Fine. Just a little." He offered her his cup of coffee, and she poured what seemed to Tag like a liberal shot. "Why is she called Lonestar, anyway? I'm guessing that as a native Texan, Lonestar got her call sign from acting like one of our old cowboys."

"Not fair to talk about the marine like that," Gorenado said. "She isn't even here to defend herself."

"I'm just curious, that's all. I've never known how marines chose their call signs." Tag held up his hands defensively when the trio stared at him skeptically. "I figured hers had to be a simple explanation."

"It's *not* that simple," Sumo said. "And the whole Texas thing is just a small part of it."

Gorenado raised an eyebrow.

"Ok," Sumo corrected herself. "It's a big part. But it's not the whole story. Let's just say it has something to do with a military space station bar, a few drinks, and a lasso."

"Now I'm intrigued," Tag said, leaning forward and taking another chug of his coffee.

Sumo shook her head and wagged a finger. "Not my story to tell. We'll wait until she gets back."

"Fine," Tag said. He took another sip of the coffee. The combined warmth of the alcohol and the coffee cleared some of the fog of anxiety from his mind. Too much more of the drink would cast an entirely different fog over his mind. He would be of no use to Sofia, much less their mission, if he let the drink inhibit his scientific work. "I won't have to wait long then."

Sumo smiled, understanding the promise behind his words, and Tag left the marines with half his gutfire-spiked coffee undrunk. Beyond the hatch to the mess, Lucky waited for him with her tails sweeping the floor in long arcs. She pranced behind him as he returned to the med bay, and he was forced to shoo her away from the hatch when he entered.

"Sorry, Lucky," Tag said. "Can't have you messing with the experiments."

She scratched at the door when it closed.

From her spot behind a terminal, Sofia said, "That creature will not leave you alone."

"For better or worse," Tag said. "Not sure why. I've never been a huge animal person."

"Apparently, you are now."

Tag walked over to Sofia's workstation. On it, the seedling sat within a polyglass beaker. Its beak opened and closed as it emitted a series of high-pitched sounds that were nothing like the Raktor's baritone voice. Curling green vines sprouted from the top of the acorn-sized creature and draped over the rim of the beaker.

"How's it coming?" Tag asked. Sofia had been charged with rigging up a translation apparatus for the seedling so they could better communicate with it.

"Let's find out." She placed a ring-shaped transponder half as big as the seedling's main body into the beaker, and the seedling wrapped one of its vines around it. Sofia had added a small hole in the transponder which the vine promptly found and went inside. In theory, this would allow the creature to interface with the electronic device just as Raktor had done with the terminals aboard the station.

A rush of static burst over the terminal near the beaker, and Tag recoiled from the sound. Sofia gestured over the terminal to lower the volume. The static faded slowly, replaced by a low murmuring in Sol Standard.

Sofia turned up the volume cautiously, keeping her hand near the terminal.

"—Raktor! We will not be contained!" the words drifted, tinny and light, from the Terminal.

The seedling rolled slightly in its beaker with its vines dancing about like blades of grass in a gentle breeze.

"Raktor?" Sofia spoke as if talking to a child. "We're not here to contain you. We're here to help you."

"Raktor has told us all," it said. Tag assumed it was referring to the *Hope*'s Raktor now. "We know what you want from us."

"Short of letting you take over our ship," Sofia said, "is there anything we can do to make your stay a bit more comfortable?"

"More water!" the voice cried. "More food! I must grow!"

Sofia looked to Tag for approval.

The bio-simulation experiments on the tiny sample of vine they had trimmed from the seedling had finished shortly before Sofia turned on the translation software and device. Blue and green letters scrolled across the screen, representing the nucleotides comprising the Raktor's genetic makeup. Tag's interest was more than purely academic; he wanted to know how a little thing like this became the monstrosity they saw on the *Hope*.

And how they might use that data for their own benefit. "Let's hold off on feeding and watering it for now," he said quietly, pulling Sofia aside. "As much as I dislike the idea of treating the seedling as a prisoner, I don't want our ship to end up like the *Hope*."

# THIRTY

Tag paced in front of the lab's main holoscreen. The scent of sterile air wafted around him. Machines chirped in concert with ongoing experiments, and the bulkheads groaned in that way that let Tag know the fusion reactors were still thrumming along in the *Argo*'s belly, keeping everything alive and healthy.

Every system aboard his ship was functioning as normal, but that might all change with his next order.

They would be jumping into hyperspace soon in pursuit of the Collectors. For now, he had science to distract him and his crew. Alpha stood straight and still in one corner. She looked just like the M3 droid used to when it was powered down and waiting to carry out some medical procedure. The only indication she now possessed synth-bio sentience was through the way her beady black eyes scanned the room.

Near her sat Sofia, picking at one of her nails. The anthropologist had dark bags under her eyes, and her normally ruddy complexion seemed paler than usual. Tag attributed it to her tireless work on the translator and trying to reason with the little Raktor now living in a cubic polyglass container. The constant clink of metal against polyglass sounded as Raktor swung its transponder around, exploring its environment. Sofia had assured Tag that the species was quite all right with living in a confined space. They were damn adaptable creatures, able to live in spaces barely larger than a drinking straw, but there was one thing that drove their choice of living arrangements: ready access to electronics and other digital equipment.

Coren glanced at the Raktor suspiciously but never let his golden eye stray from Tag for too long. The six fingers of his right hand tapped in rhythm along the armrest of his crash couch. Bull stood off to the Mechanic's side with his arms crossed and his forehead wrinkled as though he was angry about something. For all Tag knew, he probably was. The marine seemed to harness anger like it was a damn horse he rode everywhere.

"Thanks to the data you all have uncovered, I think we can make our jump tonight," Tag began. "But I want to make sure we're all on the same page. If anybody thinks we're missing something, now is the time to figure out what that is."

"Before we talk to Bracken and Jaroon?" Coren asked.

"Yes," Tag said. "I want any objections or concerns brought up here and now. Let's get to the easy stuff." Tag snapped his fingers, and an image of the Raktor seedling appeared. "Sofia?"

Sofia gestured at the holoscreen. The image of the seedling morphed, showing a series of currents traveling up and down the length of its vines like marching ants. "We went ahead and added some simulations Tag and I ran to the data we pulled from the Collectors on the *Hope*. I feel ninety-nine percent confident that the Raktor's vines can interact with any computer system in the galaxy. In fact, Raktor are capable of drawing energy from these systems."

Her voice pitched higher in excitement as she continued, "These creatures have adapted to deep space travel and diverse environments so well, it's frightening. The plants we're used to seeing on Earth use photosynthesis to harness solar energy and create complex organic molecules from water and carbon dioxide. This process occurs in a specially designed organelle within a plant's cells called the chloroplast. Raktor possess very similar organelles within their cells."

"Photosynthesis would be inefficient or even impossible to achieve when a Raktor is living aboard a space station like the *Hope* without proper access to full spectrum lights," Alpha said.

"Correct!" Sofia said like a proud teacher. "I've decided to call the organelles I discovered in Raktor's cells *voltaplasts*. Remember that name because I'm copyrighting it now. When they write xenobiology books on the Raktor, you can proudly say you know—"

Tag gestured for her to move on with a slight wave.

"Anyway, these voltaplasts contain organic, magnetic particles that react to the current flowing through a power source, whether it's a wired or even wireless power transfer."

"So Raktor needs to keep the fusion reactors alive aboard the *Hope* to keep eating, more or less," Coren said.

"Yeah," Sofia said. "But again, I'm getting off the point here. Besides allowing the Raktor to leech power, these organelles also allow it to send signals through data connections. That's how Raktor maintained some control over the station and how our little Raktor can control its transponder."

"Okay, great," Bull said, his face screwed up in a scowl. "Thanks for the biology lesson. What's the point of this?"

The corners of Coren's mouth quivered as if he was tempted

ANTHONY MELCHIORRI

to smile. "The point, I believe, is that this thing could be an even better hacker than Alpha. Or me."

"I am surprised you would so quickly admit to this creature's superiority over your technical prowess," Alpha said, cocking her head as she looked at Coren.

"You're getting sharp, Alpha." Sofia grinned. "Most importantly, there's one more feature about these things that Tag and I found. It's a direct biochemical process—I won't bore you with the details."

"Thank you," Bull said.

Sofia rolled her eyes. "This process links the data and computational control skills Raktor learn each time they encounter a new cyber environment. Each encounter rewrites segments of their genetic code so they can expedite the adaptation of their voltaplasts when faced with a similar computer architecture."

"In Sol Standard?" Bull asked.

"Big Raktor has been sitting aboard a space station run by the Collectors and cobbled together from the technology of a huge number of other species," Tag said. "It already knows how to control all those race's computers—even the ones *we* don't know how to access. The only reason we could get all those ID codes before was because the Collectors had created an umbrella computer architecture that hooked all those other ships up to the *Hope*."

"But big Raktor," Sofia said, "knows how to access each of those individual race's computer architectures *and*, thanks to the Collectors' work aboard the *Hope*, it can connect to a Collector computer system."

"Okay?" Bull said. "Big Raktor is still aboard the *Hope*. How does this help us?"

Alpha waved a silver hand like an over-eager student. "Because these genetic changes are imparted to Raktor progeny. Is that correct?"

"Bingo," Sofia said. "Our little seedling should be able to access the Collector computers and, as a result, control their ship."

"Glad to hear you eggheads came up with something helpful," Bull said. "So can you use its knowledge so that *we* can control the ship, too?"

"Uh, not exactly," Sofia said, turning to Tag.

"I'm afraid we can't reverse engineer the changes made to their voltaplasts and adapt it to our equipment," Tag said. "We've still got Alpha and Coren to do things the old-fashioned way, but the seedling is by far the quickest and most efficient way to control a ship."

"Which means we're relying on the seedling's cooperation," Coren said. "How likely is it that it will grant our requests?"

"Definitely likely," Sofia said.

"Definitely?" Bull asked. "Or likely?"

"It's definitely a possibility that it will," Sofia said with a mischievous smirk. "Look, this thing shares its genes with Raktor, but in many ways it's just a baby. We've got the chance to interact with it, to make it our friend."

Bull let out a derisive laugh. "I saw what that ugly thing grows up to be. I'm not about to make friends with it."

"It's our best option," Sofia said.

"I am up for the challenge of befriending this specimen," Alpha said.

Tag admired her enthusiasm and felt proud at seeing her readily volunteer for such a cause. Maybe this is what a father felt watching his daughter grow and take on new responsibilities, building her own identity and life path. He rubbed his eyes. Or maybe he was just getting a little too sentimental thanks to his exhaustion.

"Thanks, Alpha," Sofia said.

Coren scratched at the fur along his arm, studying it intently.

"I do have one concern." He looked up at Tag and Sofia. "Gaining control of the Collector computers through this Raktor seedling is a fine plan. But that involves just one monumental task we haven't yet discussed: getting onto a Collector ship."

# THIRTY-ONE

N ow I'm beginning to see why you wanted us to meet first," Bull said. "Boarding a Collector ship is going to be a real gods-damned pain in the ass."

"I concur," Alpha said. "It will be a tremendous, as Bull says, pain in the ass."

"We will succeed," Tag said. "We'll have the aid of the Mechanics and Melarrey."

"Captain, ships from both their races were added to the *Hope* station," Alpha said. "They seemed to have fared no better than Weber in their attempt to confront and destroy the Collectors."

"Not helping, Alpha," Tag said.

"I am not intending to be helpful," Alpha said. "I am simply reporting the facts."

That sense of pride Tag felt for Alpha was starting to turn to frustration. She still had a way to go in the human psychological development arena. "Look, we've got an interspecies force with all the strengths each can offer, from technical expertise to weapons. Plus, now we've got the ability to spoof the Collector ID codes."

"Those facts are accurate," Alpha said.

"Thank you, Coren and Alpha, for doing that," Tag said. "Now all we need to do is gain access to a Collector ship and get the Raktor seedling on with us. Sofia rigged it with a transponder to translate its communications to us. We can easily outfit that transponder to transmit data to the *Argo* as well. It'll be like vacuuming up everything the Collector ship has on it: locations of other Collector outposts and planets, ships, what they're doing to other species, why they're doing it. Any nanite connections. What happened to the *Hope* and why the Collectors were there. All the answers we're looking for."

"That's assuming whatever Collector ship we manage to hijack has all that information," Coren said.

"And if it doesn't, we leapfrog from there," Tag said. "We find another Collector ship. We learn and adapt like we've always done. It's the only way we can stop whatever the Collectors are doing. It might be the only way to prevent them from destroying the Mechanics, Melarrey, and the humans."

He paused, taking a deep breath. "We have to find out who these Collectors are. This trail, from the first time we discovered nanites and Drone-Mechs, leads to them. If Weber was supposed to destroy them, I want to make sure we do that. But I also think it's imperative we find out what else these things might be planning. Because the gods know if they somehow got Lonestar to work for them, if they have their fingers in the SRE and are pulling strings there, we have to stop them. For all we know, the Collectors and the Drone-masters are one and the same.

"Brute force isn't what got us here today. That won't be what stops the Collectors, either. And that's a good thing, because force isn't our strength." He narrowed his eyes, looking at Bull, then

Sofia, then Coren, and finally then Alpha. "Intelligence. Guts. Pure stubbornness. That's what we've got."

Sofia hooted and slapped the table, and Coren managed a full-blown smile. Bull still seemed skeptical, however, and Alpha merely listened. Tag decided it would have to do.

"Right now the Mechanics, Melarrey, and SRE are in the dark," Tag said. "We don't know who we're fighting. We don't know why. The Collectors have hidden themselves from us for long enough. Let's get ourselves a Collector ship and figure out who it is we're fighting against. If we can get that knowledge back to our people, we'll shine a light into the shadows."

Alpha clapped her hands with a violent sound like the hulls of two ships colliding. It wasn't quite the dramatic applause Tag had wanted at the end of his speech, but at least he had won her over.

"Was that not an appropriate response?" Alpha said.

Sofia clapped Alpha's metal shoulder. "You did fine."

"Anything else before we call a meeting with the other ships?" Tag asked.

"Besides, of course, noting once again that this will be an extremely risky mission with an improbable level of success?" Coren said.

"Yes, besides that," Tag said.

"Wouldn't be any fun if it weren't," Sofia added.

Tag looked around at the others, giving them a chance to speak up. But the only one in the room that spoke up was the seedling, declaring through the terminal, "Raktor is hungry!"

———

A pinprick of light showing the location of the UNS *Hope* and the strange station built around it glimmered in the distance as Tag sipped a cup of coffee alone, his elbows on a table and his eyes glued to the viewscreen. Stars peppered the screen, reminding Tag of the days he had gone camping in a budget OutDome with his family. Their favorite destination was the "Black Hills Retreat," which mimicked the open skies and snow-capped mountains of long-ago South Dakota. As a child, he had been unimpressed with the six-meter diameter dome until the holoscreens had turned on. The images transported him to a camping site surrounded by pine trees. A bonfire burned in the middle, and he could smell the charred wood and smoke mixing with the aroma of the ponderosas. Of course, the images and scents had all been pumped-in forgeries, but he still couldn't forget the simulated night, when, for the first time, he had seen what the skies were supposed to look like without the light pollution clotting his view of space from Earth. He'd felt an almost magnetic pull toward the heavens.

"I want to be there," he had told his parents.

And now he was. The space between stars wasn't so romantic when he faced monstrous plants that took over space stations, slug-like Dreg who were little more than parasites, and the mysterious Collectors who apparently had no ethical qualms about killing and enslaving all citizens of the universe. Still, in moments like this, he couldn't help but marvel at the vast, sparkling beauty of space.

The hatch opened, and Coren strode in. The Mechanic headed straight to an autoserv bay.

"Well that didn't go *terribly*," Coren said without turning to look at Tag.

"Could've been better," Tag said.

Their meeting with Bracken and Jaroon had, unsurprisingly, been filled with a fair amount of doubt in regard to relying on the Raktor seedling. Bracken thought the entire thing was suicidal, but her Mechanic's honor overruled her logical objections, and she pledged to follow Tag and see this mission through. However, she had insisted that they not rely solely on Little Raktor. Tag had agreed that deploying a second, non-Raktor transponder granting their three ships access to a Collector ship's computer systems would be prudent.

At least now they had a backup plan of sorts, and while Bracken had been reluctant to agree to the mission, Jaroon seemed positively ecstatic to go after the Collectors. Tag figured the jellyfish-like alien would follow him into the three hells and back if that's what he asked, and he still wasn't sure why. It didn't hurt to have a constant cheerleader on the team, and the Melarrey did have formidable, if odd, weapons which would come in handy if they were forced to engage the Collectors in battle.

Tag found it oddly comforting that the *Argo* was well-equipped with enough weapons to turn their enemies into a cloud of space dust.

Coren punched a selection on the autoserv bay's terminal and the hot, salty smell of fresh ramen wafted from the machine. Tag's stomach grumbled, and he crumpled his empty coffee cup, following Coren's lead to stuff himself with something more filling.

"You know there is something I find absolutely crucial that I must do, no matter what happens next," Coren said.

Tag's eyes roved over the selections of artificial foods. "And what's that?"

"If I'm going to be a permanent fixture on this ship"—Coren paused and slurped up a mouthful of noodles, wincing as he did—"we're going to need to get a proper food facility here. This human food is as atrocious as human weapons and shield systems."

"I mean, it *is* based on human technology," Tag said, selecting a bowl of fried rice for himself. "What did you expect?"

"You have me there." Coren drained the rest of his noodles with an unceremonious slurp. "After we're done with the Collectors, I will install a Mechanic-friendly food processor."

"Feel free to do so," Tag said. "I'm curious what your food tastes like."

From the open hatch, another voice called, "Don't be." Sofia strode in and made her own food selections. "Imagine pasta that's been overcooked until it's slimy. Then add a liter of hatch grease and that stinky brown stuff Raktor left all over the *Hope*."

"It's that bad?" Tag asked.

"Worse," Sofia said, tapping on an autoserv bay's terminal.

Alpha joined the group next, carrying something under her arm.

"Food?" Tag asked her.

"Absolutely not." Alpha set what she'd been carrying on the table. It was the tank with the seedling. The vines no longer whipped about wildly, and its beak was gently closed, reminding Tag of eyelids closed in sleep.

"Little Raktor's looking especially calm," Sofia said. "What did you do, drug it?"

Alpha clicked disapprovingly. "That is against all human ethics! I would not drug a creature without its consent."

"I know," Sofia said. "Just joking."

"Oh, humor," Alpha said. "I am pleased to report that I have established a data connection with Raktor."

Tag's eyes followed Alpha's arms to a fingernail-sized port where one of Raktor's vines trailed out. "Is that safe?"

"I am controlling all data flow to and from Raktor," Alpha said. "It is unable to control me due to the biological portions of my synthetic intelligence. It can only access computational data *in silico*."

"If you're sure," Tag said. "Why did you establish a direct connection? Is there an issue with the translation device?"

"I decided the translation device is much too slow for efficient communications. Conversations that would take weeks can happen over the course of minutes using this direct link. It is a much more efficient mode of communication than vocalizations."

"And are you two friends now?" Sofia said, leaning across the table. Coren chuffed.

"I suppose that would be one way to characterize our relationship," Alpha said. "We have bonded over the similarities of being computationally oriented beings. Both the seedling Raktor and I would not exist if it weren't for the power and data flow provided by technology other races have made."

"Glad to hear it. But the most important question is," Tag said, "do you think, when push comes to shove, Raktor will help us?"

"That is something I cannot accurately predict at this time."

Alpha loved numbers. Her refusal to provide any kind of numerical assessment signified even her uncertainty.

"So our future may rely on the willingness of an unpredictable immature seedling that can connect with computers to help us and you can't provide any prediction on whether it will," Tag said. "That sounds pretty grim."

"I can assess that statement, Captain," Alpha said, "and it appears that you are one-hundred percent correct. It does sound, as you say, pretty grim."

# THIRTY-TWO

Tag curled his fingers around the armrest of his crash couch. Plasma washed over the ship as they traveled the last leg of their hyperspace journey. Maybe it was just his nerves, but Tag thought the violet and emerald streaks coursing over the viewscreen were more violent and frantic than usual.

Every bit of tension flowing through his fingertips would undoubtedly be felt by his crew. He needed to be the face of confidence, completely assured that they could pull off a heist that would someday be made into a score of shoddily made holo-films and novels distributed throughout even the most distant of SRE colonies.

"Prepare for descent into normal space," Tag said.

Sofia's controls moved forward to meet her waiting hands, and her fingers curled around them, ready to engage manual piloting at the first sign of incoming pulsefire.

"Alpha, have the T-Drive spooling and calculate an escape

trajectory as soon as we descend," Tag continued. "Coren, countermeasures and weapons hot. We're going to try to do this the stealthy way first, but if all else fails, you know what to do."

Coren nodded and punched in commands to his terminal. The whine of the charging cannons reverberated throughout the bridge, along with the metallic clicks and clangs of chaff being loaded. Those weren't the only weapons the *Argo* had to offer this time.

As much as he wanted to destroy the Collectors, especially if they turned out to be the Drone-masters, the thought of launching thermonuclear warheads made his skin creep. Images of a world being turned into chunks of rock swam through his mind. He saw forests turning instantly to cinders, and oceans boiling and evaporating. People crying and screaming, running from a wall of fire and destruction they could never escape.

He was the one with the power to bring those images to life. If he was to carry out Captain Weber's original mission, he wanted to be absolutely sure he was launching those weapons at the right target.

If not…

There was no room for *if*. He had to be certain. "Bracken, Jaroon, are you ready to do this?" Tag asked over the comms.

"We are ready," Bracken said.

"Absolutely!" Jaroon replied.

"Alpha is going to transmit the retreat trajectories and muster point if we get separated. There's no shame in turning back now."

"We are in it as long as you are," Jaroon said.

"As are we," Bracken said.

"Initiate transition into normal space now!" Tag ordered, approving the command via his terminal.

Alpha pulled back on her controls and began the transition procedures. The purple and green waves on the viewscreen crackled and slowed, and Tag fought against the familiar feeling of being thrown forward as the inertial dampeners caught up to the rapid change in acceleration. He braced himself as the images on the viewscreen gave way to a field of stars, half-expecting asteroids to loom into existence before them.

But this time, no asteroids careened toward them, threatening to grind the *Argo* into bits of slagged metal. The holomap at the center of the bridge pinged. It marked a flurry of activity as red dots zoomed in and out of existence several hundred thousand klicks off their bow.

"Countermeasures ready?" Tag asked.

"At your word, Captain," Coren said.

He waited a moment, his gaze intent on the holomap. Bulkheads groaned around him as the alloys expanded and shrank, adjusting to the tremendous output of energy and absorption of heat from their recent transition, but otherwise, no one dared say a word. The crew was poised at their stations, their gazes darting to and from the holomap.

They were all looking for the same thing. Like every encounter with the Drone-Mechs, they expected to see a maelstrom of incoming ordnance sparking across the holomap headed in their direction. The klaxons could go off at any moment to sound the alarm that they were being targeted.

But as they waited, despite the apparent hive of activity on their holomap, nothing happened.

"Jaroon, Bracken, any incoming contacts?" Tag asked tentatively, almost afraid of their answer.

"Negative," Bracken said.

Jaroon next. "We haven't detected anything."

"Maybe the spoofed IDs actually worked," Tag said.

"Of course they did," Coren said with an air of confidence that sounded forced to Tag. "Alpha and I did all the work."

"Even so," Alpha said, "there is a chance for error."

Tag eyed the marker on the holomap that all the activity seemed centered on. "Is that a planet?"

"All sensors indicate it is," Alpha said. "There also seems to be a large station orbiting it."

"Then this is what we came for." Tag took a deep breath. "Take us in closer so we can get a visual."

Sofia pushed the controls forward, and the *Argo*'s impellers roared to life, accelerating them toward the planet. As the marker grew closer on the holomap, Tag watched the viewscreen. He didn't like going in without their energy shields, but ordering Alpha to raise them might make the Collectors suspicious. They needed to pretend like they belonged here for however long they could.

Soon the telltale flare of impellers and thrusters tracing across the viewscreen cut white streaks through the otherwise black void. Ships flew in all directions like shrapnel from an explosion. Several of the drive signatures blossomed into a brilliant splash of white when the ships transitioned into hyperspace. At first, Tag wondered if there was an intense battle already underway. But there were no telltale explosions of torpedoes or pearly ropes of PDC fire jutting between ships.

"Is this a trade colony?" Tag asked.

"Certainly seems like it," Sofia said. "I don't know how else to explain this much activity."

"Unless they're amassing forces for war," Coren said drily.

Tag tried to swallow but felt a lump in his throat. He coughed. "If that's the case, it makes what we're about to do all the more important."

Amid the frenetic movement of ships, now barely visible as specks of dust in the viewscreen, something colossal grew before them. It was a planet with a red tinge, illuminated by the distant star it orbited. The planet had the dusty appearance of Mars but was at least five times bigger according to the holomap's estimates. A planet like that could host billions upon billions of humans—if it had been properly terraformed.

Then the constant flux of ships made sense to Tag. This planet *was* being terraformed.

As they approached, the viewscreen showed all manners of unfamiliar ships headed toward the planet's surface–along with the massive space station floating in geosynchronous orbit.

"Can we magnify the image any more?" Tag asked.

"Yes, Captain," Alpha said. She gestured over her terminal.

The station consisted of an enormous honeycomb structure with long tendrils jutting off all sides like reaching tentacles. Several hundred of those tendrils snaked from the station and seemed to be rooted on the planet's surface. Cylindrical ships— more appropriately, space elevator cars—zoomed up and down the structure.

"Do we go in closer?" Sofia asked.

"Not yet," Tag said.

Scores of ships rocketed into hyperspace, and Tag wondered if they were all leaving because of their arrival. A few more ships transitioned into normal space around the station, but most seemed to enter the station only briefly before taking off again.

"Seems awfully busy," Sofia said. "Maybe there's a party we're missing out on."

"If the Collectors are hosting a party, I'm okay with losing the invitation," Coren said.

"Do not worry. We never received an invitation," Alpha said with a seriousness that made Tag question whether she was joking.

"Now you can bring us in a bit closer," Tag said.

A rash of ships floated above the station like a cloud. They buzzed around the station like flies on carrion, swooping in and out of the open bays of the massive station. The *Argo* moved toward them, flanked by the *Stalwart* and the *Crucible*.

"We're detecting Mechanic ships," Bracken said over the comms. "I'm assuming they are Drone-Mech."

"Likewise, we are seeing Melarrey," Jaroon reported. "But a quick inquiry into our databases shows these ships were reportedly destroyed during the sacking of our planet."

Tag's heart thumped, wild as pulsefire, as Alpha panned the magnified view of the assembled fleet. There were oblong, glassy ships and some that looked more like living creatures than manufactured technology. Many of the ships were similar to the ones that had formed the makeshift station around the *Hope*. Then his eyes fell on one of the ships that was all sharp corners and silver alloy. Seeing the ship felt like a punch in the gut, and he fought to catch his breath.

It was human.

# THIRTY-THREE

Tag squinted at the letters along the side of the ship. *New Blood.* It had no SRE designation, but it had a blue-and-green symbol beside its name that indicated it had been constructed within an Earthen shipyard. The ship was the length of a corvette, similar in size to the *Argo*, but the cannons bristling off its sides made it clear that this was more warship than exploratory science vessel. It was like nothing he had seen in the *Montenegro*'s fleet.

"What is that doing out here?" Tag asked. "Sofia, you know what kind of ship this is?"

"You're asking the woman who spent the past half a decade in underground caves documenting the life and culture of tribal cephalopod-like aliens?" she replied.

"'No' would've worked," Tag said then pressed a button on his terminal that transferred the images on their viewscreen to the holoscreens where the marines were situated in their crash couches below deck. "Bull, any of you recognize this kind of ship?"

"I don't," Bull responded through the comms. There was a brief pause. "Sumo says she does. It's—are you serious? You're positive?" Another stretch of silence. "Sumo said it's an experimental vessel from Starinski Labs. Her uncle works there. The prototype wasn't classified or anything, apparently, but she hasn't actually seen a functioning vessel."

"Why would it be out here?" Tag said. Then the dread filling his stomach with a leaden feeling answered the question for him. "Maybe the Collectors already made it to Earth."

"Or—this is only slightly better—maybe it belongs to whoever infiltrated the SRE," Sofia said. "Maybe this is further proof of the connections between the Drone-masters, the Collectors, and whoever got Lonestar to plant that transponder in the *Argo*."

"I can't believe I'm saying that I hope you're right," Tag said. "But either way, this is not good."

"No, Captain," Alpha said, "this is most definitely not good. Even Raktor agrees."

"You're talking to Raktor right now?" Tag asked, searching the bridge. Raktor was supposed to be stowed safely within the lab during their transition.

"Yes," Alpha said. "I installed a wireless communicator within my chassis so that I can access Raktor's transponder remotely. Raktor needed reassurance as this recent journey into hyperspace was the first time it had experienced a faster-than-light jump."

"You're telling me our little Raktor got scared?" Sofia asked. "Because things are about to get way more frightening."

The motley fleet of ships around the huge space station began drifting in all directions, putting distance between them at an accelerating rate. Several appeared to be blasting in the direction of the *Argo*. Tag held his breath. Still no warning alarms, no weapons locks. One by one, the ships disappeared into the void, transitioning into hyperspace and disappearing from the holomap.

"Shit," Sofia said. "We're going to lose our chance to grab a ship. Want me to follow one?"

"Don't pursue them," Tag said. "Whatever's going on, we've still got that station. I have a feeling that will be far more interesting, and I don't want to attract their attention just yet."

The ships blinked away until the only things moving were the space elevators dumping their cargo onto the planet's surface. Over the next half hour, even the elevators slowed before crawling to a stop. The long tendrils connecting the station to the planet retracted. The remnants of the fleet zipped into darkness, disappearing into hyperspace like the others until the only thing that moved was the space station as it continued its slow rotation with the planet.

"Captain," Alpha said, "I am not detecting any more active spacefaring vessels. The only ships I see are those within the space station's bays."

"What about the planet?" Tag asked.

Alpha manipulated the outboard cam views to survey the planet's surface near the space elevators. Ravines and mountains cut through the landscape surrounding a central plateau. There, the magnified images provided a glimpse at a host of vehicles and lumbering droid-like forms. Squares of gray alloy and skeletal support beams marked construction sites across the dry land. While there were plenty of vehicles and mechanical suits moving on the dusty surface, Tag struggled to find anything that looked remotely like a living being below. He assumed the atmosphere was hostile to whoever was trying to terraform this place. Still, he expected to see *someone* in EVA suits guiding traffic and construction. The scene looked more like something out of an automated factory rather than a colonization effort.

"Don't see any weapons down there," Coren said. "Maybe it's safer than we thought."

"Maybe they don't have any weapons," Sofia said.

"That's hopeful thinking," Tag said.

Movement on the planet caught his eyes. The huge space elevator tendrils burrowed into the surface began to vibrate. Cracks formed in the dirt and rock at their base, fracturing outward. The vehicles and colonization droids didn't seem to care about the earthquake. All continued their assigned tasks with no particular sense of urgency. Soon holes formed at the space elevators' bases, and the tendrils rose from beneath the soil. They shed clouds of dust as they retracted from the planet and ascended back toward the station.

"What's going on?" Sofia asked, leaning over her controls.

All across the space station, ports appeared, glowing an intense cobalt.

"Are they about to fire on the planet?" Coren asked. "Why would they destroy it after just depositing all those machines there?"

Tag began to wonder the same thing. What had they just wandered into? But then he saw the cannon batteries and guns poking off the strange station every which direction. None of these weapons seemed pointed at the planet. Maybe the ports weren't weapons at all, but rather—

His stomach flipped.

"That's not a space station," Tag said. "That's a goddamn spaceship."

"Good gods," Sofia muttered.

"It's larger than any I've ever seen," Coren said. "Larger than anything the Mechanics could even build."

Tag knew that Coren admitting inferiority like that was a sign that whatever they were looking at was beyond extraordinary. It made Mechanic dreadnoughts look like a child's playthings, and a ship like the *Argo* might as well be a gnat compared to the monstrosity before them.

Lurching away from the planet, its space elevators still retracting, the titanic ship's impellers glowed a brighter blue. It was no wonder the rest of the fleet had already taken off. When this thing hit hyperspace, it was going to cause such an intense gravitational distortion that it would practically leave a black hole in its wake.

Tag couldn't believe what they were witnessing. He silently thanked Bracken for encouraging them to go back to Raktor, to find those codes rather than spend weeks sifting through the space station. They might've missed this opportunity to witness such an immense display of technical prowess if not for Lonestar's insistence they leave her as Raktor's hostage.

But the chance to find the answers they'd been looking for was now shifting away from him like water between fingers.

"We have to get on that ship!" Tag said. "Sofia, gun it!"

The *Argo* jerked forward, and intense forces pressed Tag back into his crash couch, igniting pangs of nausea until the inertial dampeners kicked in. All the bays that Alpha had noted before were beginning to close as huge hatches spiraled together.

"Jaroon, Bracken," Tag said, "we're going in!"

The other two ships accelerated next to them in concert. Each aimed for one of the hatches near the base of the presumed Collector ship. Images of when the *Argo* had barely made it aboard the Drone-Mech dreadnought attacking the *Montenegro* resurfaced in Tag's mind. Their ship had taken a beating; it had hardly been spaceworthy afterward. It wouldn't have traveled between the stars again had the *Montenegro* not been nearby to repair them.

Now they had no lifeline. Just three ships—one human, one Melarrey, and one Mechanic—against a monstrous, mobile space station. Tag prayed to all the gods that would listen for help.

He still feared it wouldn't be enough.

# THIRTY-FOUR

A sickly yellow light shone a path into the bay. Tag ground his teeth tight enough together to feel the beginnings of a pressure headache, but he didn't care. It was up to Sofia now, and if she failed, he would have a lot worse than a headache to contend with. The hatch continued closing, faster now as it cinched shut, and Tag resisted the urge to close his eyes and tried not to imagine the *Argo* erupting into tongues of wild plasma when it hit the closed hatch.

They cleared the entrance.

"Gods be damned!" Sofia hooted, immediately pushing forward on the controls to apply reverse thrust. They slowed in a cavernous bay that rivaled the magnitude of the Forest of Light.

"Bracken, Jaroon?" Tag called over the comms. "Please tell me you made it."

"If your ship could," Bracken said, "then of course ours did."

There was a beat of silence. Tag's muscles tensed as he waited for the Melarrey captain's response.

"We're through," Jaroon said, "although we had to perform the matter transmutation process again."

Tag took a moment to survey the immense chamber as Sofia kept the *Argo* at a thrumming hover. While most of the deck space was clear, though marred by black splotches where thrusters had scorched it taking off, there were still dozens of ships inside. Huge bulkheads delineated this bay from the next two where Bracken and Jaroon were now.

"This definitely looks like the Collectors' kind of place," Sofia said, her eyes tracing the images on the viewscreen.

"So many ships, so many races," Coren said. "It is truly frightening to think they may have subjugated so many species."

"I have relayed these images to the lab," Alpha reported, "and Raktor reports feeling truly frightened now."

"What did I tell you, Alpha?" Sofia asked.

"You told me, 'Things are about to get way more frightening,'" Alpha responded.

"Yeah, I did. But that's just an expression."

Alpha continued to look expectantly at her, and after a moment, Sofia muttered, "Never mind."

The bridge returned to silence once more as they studied the ships within the bay. Tag was looking for any sign of life, certain that at any moment hostile forces would appear, weapons blazing. But nothing changed, and no one appeared. Just shadows and ships.

"I guess spoofing those ID codes worked even better than we thought," Sofia said.

Tag undid his restraints and stood. Although they were in what appeared to be the heart of the enemy's forces, there was a certain comfort in knowing they had at last made it partway to their objective. He had thought that boarding a Collector vessel would be the hard part; now he realized that had been easy.

A shiver crept through his spine as he stared into the vacant bay.

"Alpha, go grab Raktor," Tag said. "Everyone else, get geared up."

Alpha split off from the group, heading to the lab, and the others filed down to the armory. Tag grabbed a mini-Gauss rifle. As usual the marines strapped enough firepower to their armor to outfit a small army. All they had to do was find a single computer connected to the ship's intranet and plug in Raktor. If that failed, Alpha and Coren would try their hand at it. Three hells, half of Bracken's forces were also engineers and scientists. They would gladly assist. Maybe loading themselves with this many weapons was overkill.

But Tag preferred overkill to overdead. He shook his head as he jammed a fresh magazine into his rifle.

"Something wrong, Captain?" Sumo asked, clicking her visor down.

"Ever make a pun so bad you cringe just thinking about it?" Tag asked.

"Not a problem I often have," Sumo said.

Tag strapped the rifle over his shoulder and waited at the cargo bay's exit hatch until Coren and Sofia joined him. Alpha came last with a rifle in her hands.

"Raktor?" Tag asked.

Alpha tapped her chest plate. "I stowed it in here for protection."

"If you say so," Tag said. Gorenado and Sumo stood at the front of the group with Bull taking rearguard. "First sign of a computer, we secure the area and go to work. We clear?"

His crew nodded, and Tag once again felt the weight of leading them into the unknown. A quick punch of the terminal, and the cargo bay airlock opened. His sensors reported that the atmosphere possessed similar oxygen, nitrogen, and carbon dioxide concentrations as the *Argo*, along with pressures that were only off by a couple of kilopascals. It didn't take long for the airlock to let them spill out into the cavernous bay.

With the *Argo*'s outboard lights shut off, the light banks overhead illuminated the space with a murky glow that caused every ship within the bay to cast long, twisted shadows. Tag signaled the crew forward. No matter how carefully he tried to walk, his footsteps and those of his crew seemed to crash against the deck, echoing madly in the wide, open space. Long groans reverberated through the towering bulkheads, but otherwise, nothing else made a sound. Tag couldn't even hear the usual whistle of air through ventilation shafts or the roar of the impellers pushing the massive ship through space.

"Hate to state the obvious," Sumo said, "but can we try one of these ships? Maybe they have a connection to the Collector ship."

"Not a bad idea," Coren said. "They may be synced with this mothership."

"Alpha, what do you think?" Tag asked.

"I estimate that it is at least worth the effort to try," she replied.

Tag gazed around the room, looking for a ship they might have some familiarity with. But there were no human, Mechanic, or Melarrey ships here.

"Maybe this one?" Tag indicated with his thumb a ship that looked like an old-fashioned aluminum can. At least with this ship, unlike some of the others, there was a clear hatch with a scoop-shaped handle that Tag presumed would let them in.

Sumo and Gorenado crept toward the vessel, their rifles scanning the zoo of spaceships, before announcing it was clear.

The rest of the group joined them, forming a perimeter

around the vessel. Tag nodded at Sumo, and she reached to open the handle. As she did, there was a flash of light. Sumo pulled back, holding her hand like it had been burned. A spiderweb of blue lightning scattered from the point of impact, revealing an invisible cube around the ship. Sumo held her gloved hand in front of her, examining the damage. Black singe marks cut gouges into her armor.

"You all right?" Tag asked, immediately scanning her biometric signals via his HUD. Everything appeared normal.

"Yeah, yeah," Sumo said. "Scared me more than anything." She flexed her fingers. The joints crunched when she curled them, but at least the armor still worked. "Damn. What is that ship?"

Coren's working eye narrowed, and he leaned into where the blue shield had momentarily revealed itself. "Look." He kneeled and pointed to a centimeter-wide groove in the deck. It traced the perimeter of the ship, perfectly matching up to where the shield had appeared. Coren stood and then indicated the next closest craft. "It's here, too."

Gorenado took a full magazine from a pouch attached to his armor. He ejected a single Gauss slug and flicked the round at the second ship. The round cartwheeled through the air until it hit another blue shield, causing a violent burst of lightning, then shot off in another direction. Tag instinctively ducked as the slug bounced between shields, setting them off as it ricocheted until embedding itself into a bulkhead. The buzz of electricity in the air made the hairs on the back of Tag's neck stand up.

"Looks like we won't be accessing any of the ships," Sofia said.

The shields unsettled Tag. He stood slowly, looking around at the bulkheads and decks.

"There's something else wrong here," Tag said.

"You mean the fact they haven't sent a greeting party to meet us?" Sofia asked.

"Besides that."

He squinted. Something about the alloy making up the interior of the bay was...off. He couldn't quite describe it, but it felt like he was looking at a patient he *knew* was sick but couldn't see why yet. It was the subconscious part of his brain noticing the subtle clues his conscious mind hadn't quite picked up yet.

It didn't take him long.

While the bulkhead and decks in the chamber were massive, dwarfing the ships, there wasn't a single rivet anywhere. Not so much as a line or crease to show where two plates had been joined together. His eyes shot toward where Gorenado's errant round had impaled the bulkhead. There was no hole, no defect, not even the slightest hint that a kinetic slug had torn through it moments ago.

"This alloy—or whatever it is," Tag said. "It's self-healing. I only know one technology that can do that."

"Autonomous nanoparticle-based assembly materials," Coren muttered. "By the machine, I never thought I'd see this type of nanomaterial technology in the flesh."

Then, without any explanation, Coren sprinted back to the *Argo*.

"Hey!" Bull said, bounding after him to provide security.

Tag turned to follow them, but he stopped in his tracks. There was no need to go any closer. He could see what had alarmed the Mechanic from here.

Like every other vessel in the bay, a shallow groove now traced a square around the *Argo*. A weight pulled on Tag's shoulders. He felt ready to drop through the deck as dread filled him. The rest of the crew saw it too, not saying a word.

Bull did the honors of throwing a loose kinetic slug toward the *Argo*. Tag watched it spin through the air, hoping against hope that his suspicions were wrong. But the round pinged when it hit an invisible shield. The same blue lightning crackled in a cubic shield around the *Argo*.

There was no way to get back on their ship.

# THIRTY-FIVE

I t didn't take long for Tag to confirm with Jaroon and Bracken that their ships, too, had been imprisoned by the same strange energy shields. Jaroon's entire squad had left their ship, just like Tag's. Bracken, with the largest crew and ship, left a considerable number of engineers, scientists, and other personnel aboard the *Stalwart*. The shields had still enveloped their ship, and they were too nervous to try moving the vessel to see if the force field automatically deactivated lest the effort end with the *Stalwart* turning into a pile of melted slag.

"I suppose that leaves us no option but to move forward," Bracken said over the comms.

"That's our plan," Tag said, "unless we happen to come across another terminal first."

"If the bay you're in is anything like ours," Jaroon said, "I don't believe you will. The walls here are completely bare."

Tag's group tentatively spread out, combing the bay while

maintaining sight lines with each other, to explore the bay. Tag looked for terminals or maintenance equipment, but he didn't spot a single repair bot. Not so much as a plasma welder.

"Don't they need anything to maintain the upkeep on these ships?" Tag whispered to Coren.

"If they possess self-assembling technology, that is doubtful," Coren said. "Theoretically, such technology could mean that any repair equipment or tools might come from the bulkheads or decks themselves."

"You're kidding," Tag said.

"The one thousand and fourth issue of the Academic Proceedings of Nanotechnology, provided by the Mechanics to my databases, asserts that this theoretical technology is exactly as Coren describes," Alpha said.

"Gods be damned," Tag muttered. "No wonder there isn't a terminal or computer access port in here. It's probably somehow embedded in these self-assembling walls."

"That's my guess," Coren said. "We'd need some kind of code or gesture or something to call the computers up."

"Computers, appear!" Sofia's voice echoed in the otherwise quiet bay. She shrugged when nothing happened. "Worth a shot."

They continued their search for several more minutes, but they found nothing. Nothing other than the strangest and most diverse set of ships Tag had ever laid eyes on. The admirals and intelligence officers in the SRE navy would die for access to technology like this. They'd never come close to setting their fingers on warships from so many of the races from throughout the cosmos.

But as much as he would love to spend his time documenting these ships to send intel back, there were more pressing concerns at hand.

"Let's catch up to the others," Tag said to his group. "I'm beginning to think the sooner we get off this ship, the better."

Careful to avoid the invisible shields, they made their way toward the back of the bay and the center of the massive mothership. At first, Tag feared they would run into yet another smooth wall with an entrance only accessible if they used some gods-damned magical password. He spotted a cone of white light flooding from a semicircle in the bulkhead.

"There," Tag said, pointing.

Sumo and Gorenado led the group toward the opening. When they reached it, they paused. Sumo held out a kinetic slug, wincing slightly, clearly expecting it to go shooting out of her hand. No electric blue shield appeared. She waved her hand through, then passed into the corridor. Tag followed with the rest of the group, and they found themselves in a wide passageway. The glaring light in here was a stark contrast to the ship bay. The light banks were as bright as if they were standing in a field under the midday sun with not a cloud in sight.

Tag looked up and down the white passage. The sterility of the place gave him the creeping sensation that he was in a massively oversized floating hospital drifting silently through space, with only the ghosts of its former patients roaming the halls. Once again, he found no computers. A multitude of hatches cut away from the main corridor. There weren't even any signs to point them toward the bridge or a laboratory or a communications room. Right now, he would settle for a private crew quarters or a facilities maintenance closet. Did the Collectors even have computers?

The tapping of footsteps caused the group to drop low, leaning into the door wells along the passages, their only passable cover. Several humanoid forms raced toward them, sending Tag's heart galloping in concert with their footfalls. He brought his rifle to his shoulder and braced for a battle. But he quickly recognized the black uniforms and orange visors of the Mechanics.

"Bracken," Tag called. "Glad to see some sort of life aboard this thing."

"Likewise," she said, striding ahead of her pack to meet him. The rest of their troops took up positions around the corridor, securing a score of entrances.

"Jaroon?" Tag called. "Are you near?"

"Shouldn't be far from your position," Jaroon reported.

True to his word, he arrived a few minutes later with the rest of his soldiers. Their bulbous forms were encased in sapphire armor to match the alloy of their ship. Shadowy black visors shielded their eyes, and ornate tracings and patterns were carved into the plates covering their limbs and torsos. Each carried a short weapon that looked like something halfway between an axe and sword with a barrel poking out at the end. Normally, Tag thought their translucent, gelatinous bodies were a bit comical, but in their power armor, they appeared strangely elegant. Like knights of old charging into battle—albeit somewhat fat knights.

"Anyone see any signs in here?" Tag said.

"Nothing," Bracken reported. "This place is like a labyrinth."

"*Like* a labyrinth?" Jaroon said. "I'd say it absolutely is one."

"It's certainly huge," Tag said. "Big enough that it's going to take a while for this thing to jump into hyperspace, if it's jumping at all. If exploring *Hope* station would take weeks, this place might take months."

"Agreed," Bracken said. "But if I understand where you're going with this, I don't like the idea of splitting up. We have no idea what we might face."

"We will cover much more ground if we do split up," Jaroon said. "It would be a far more efficient use of our time. Besides, I'd rather figure out how to release our ships sooner rather than later."

"You both have good points," Tag said. "And I think the best option is somewhere in the middle. I want to stick close enough we can lend fire support." He held up a finger before Jaroon or Bracken could interrupt. "But I also don't want to all end up in a single room and all of a sudden those blue shields trap us with no one left on the outside. I say we take parallel corridors directed toward the center. If this thing really is a ship, there's got to be a bridge of some sort. If we don't find a computer anywhere else, maybe we can force someone there to show us a terminal."

Bracken sighed. "I hope you're right. I don't like the feeling of this place. It reminds me too much of being in the Forest of Light when we first encountered the Forinth."

Coren nodded. "You could *feel* that they were watching you, but you couldn't see them."

"Gods, wouldn't that be something if the Collectors were invisible?" Tag said.

"I do not detect any lifeforms in the vicinity across infrared spectrums," Alpha said, scanning their surroundings. "Unless they have thermal shielding technologies, there is nothing to be concerned about in our current environment."

"If they can do everything we've seen so far, I wouldn't put complete thermal shielding past them," Sofia said with a shrug. "But I like to believe you're right. Maybe this whole ship is just one huge robotic hunk of junk."

"You might be right," Tag said. "I didn't see anything living on the planet. Just droids and drones setting up a colony."

"True," Bracken said. "We made a similar assessment. But the logs we pulled from the Mechanic ship at the *Hope* station documented those peculiar blue aliens. Whether this thing is automated or crewed, I still suspect the Collectors are an organic species."

"Only one way to know for sure," Tag said. He pointed to three separate hatches leading toward the middle of the giant ship. "Pick one, and let's find out."

# THIRTY-SIX

Bracken and Jaroon plunged into the right and left corridors with their forces, and Tag took the center. The footsteps of the other groups quickly faded away as the *Argo*'s crew rushed into yet another sterile hallway. Given the enormous ground they had to cover, Tag didn't want to waste time investigating spaces that seemed to promise nothing of interest. Most of the open hatches they passed led to chambers filled with stacks of crates, drones, and vehicles similar to those they had seen on the planet they had just left.

"You think that's all this thing does?" Sofia asked, jogging beside Tag down another long stretch of passage. "Just drops off autonomous colonization equipment?"

"Seeding Collector colonies all over the galaxy," Coren said. "That is not reassuring."

Onward they continued, the scenes repeating themselves until Tag wondered if they weren't somehow running in circles.

Constant checks to Bracken and Jaroon showed they were encountering the same sights. No terminals. No signs of life. Just colonization and terraforming equipment. Tag's group began to run, caution and stealth giving way to urgency and speed. There had to be a terminal somewhere. Maybe even a staffer or tech worker they could hold hostage, someone they could coerce into telling them what they needed to know.

His mind whirred back to what all this had to do with Captain Weber and the nanites and the *Hope*. He felt like Alice after jumping down the rabbit hole, plunged into a world that didn't make sense. A world of strange beings and technology so advanced it felt like magic.

Maybe he was going mad. He would wake up in a regen chamber, having recovered after some accident on the *Argo*.

Sumo slid to a stop, with Gorenado throwing himself to the ground beside her, his rifle whipping up to face some threat Tag couldn't yet see in the next corridor.

No, this was no drug-induced dream. This kaleidoscopic nightmare was all too real.

"What is it?" Tag asked.

"Contacts," Sumo muttered.

The others found cover behind crates or colonization vehicles. A low whine filled the corridor, growing louder as the source of the noise closed in. A layer of sweat formed between Tag's palms and his gloves as he sighted up his rifle, ready for the enemy to appear at the hatch, ready to see the face of whoever was operating this enigmatic vessel.

A vehicle passed in front of the hatch, hovering centimeters above the ground. It had what looked like an operator's cab, but there was no driver. About the size of an air car, the back of it had a mechanical arm, and a few crates were stacked in a cargo bed. Tag held his breath as the slow-moving autonomous vehicle trucked across the massive doorway. He waited for it to stop, to sound the alarm.

It simply trundled past as if it didn't notice anything unusual, and Tag let out a sigh of relief. He signaled to the others to move forward into the next chamber. They emerged into a sudden wave of heat. It washed over them, and it took a good ten seconds for Tag's suit to reduce the temperature slightly. Huge vats of molten metal were being poured into troughs leading to a series of furnaces. The splash of the liquid metal and whoosh of hot air bellowing through the chamber was accompanied by the drumbeat of mechanical arms and hammers.

"Must be some kind of foundry," Coren said, eyeing the machinery as they passed it.

"Plenty of machines, but no computers," Sofia said.

"Then we keep going," Tag said.

They continued for what seemed an extraordinarily long time through the foundry. The walls were no longer the sterile white of shipboard med bays but instead a dirty gray with speckles of black, like soot had been embedded within the alloy bulkhead. The lights were different, too, having lost the glow of the white light banks, instead illuminated by lights that gave off a bluish glow.

Sumo held up her hand again, pointing her gun barrel toward another corridor. The whir of another hovering autonomous truck echoed their direction. Tag waited for it to pass as before. This time, the vehicle paused at the chamber's entrance. He could almost feel the tension weaving between the crew, connecting each of them with electricity as they readied their weapons. The truck's mechanical arm sprang to life, moving in starts and jerks. It grabbed a black crate from its cargo bed. It placed the crate on the deck. Then it lifted another and stacked the crates until there was a line of six at the end of the passage.

Its task apparently done, the truck hovered away. Even as the sound of its humming motor dissipated, Tag heard the sound of another truck approaching from the end of the passage they had just come from. It also placed six black crates at that end of the corridor.

"What is going on?" Sofia asked, her voice whispering over their comms.

"Bracken, Jaroon," Tag said. "We just came in contact with some autonomous vehicles. They left cargo behind. Did you see anything similar?"

"That's an affirmative," Bracken said.

"Likewise," Jaroon said.

For almost thirty seconds the group waited. There were no more whirring hover trucks, and the distant sounds of the thrumming foundry carried on unchanged.

Sumo looked back at Tag and Bull, waiting for some indication of what to do next. Bull flicked his hand forward, and she slowly got up from her position. Her rifle stock never strayed from its spot pressed against her shoulder as she inched toward the exit. The strange black boxes were a meter taller than Sumo and even wider than Gorenado.

Sumo's shoulder brushed against one as she passed, and a reverberating, low roar shook the corridor. The box quivered, then burst into millions of tiny black particles.

Instead of exploding outward, the cloud of particles was drawn back together. Instead of reforming themselves into their original shape, however, they coalesced into a humanoid figure. Long, spindly legs connected to a beastly torso. Thick arms sprouted off its side, and a tiny, faceless head sat atop it.

"What in the—" Sumo never finished her question. One of the massive arms swung at her. A hammer-like fist connected with her chest plate, throwing her backward. Her arms cartwheeled until she slammed into a supply crate, crushing it beneath the weight of her armor.

Gorenado swung his rifle up and fired at the creature. A burst of slugs tore gaping holes in its torso, exposing only more fluid-like black particles. There appeared to be no organs or blood vessels—no wires or servos, either.

"Machines be damned!" Coren yelled. "This thing's made of the same nanomaterials as the decks in the ship bay!"

"They're like some kind of…golems!" Sofia yelled.

In response to Coren's booming voice, the other eleven crates transfigured themselves into humanoid monstrosities. Their feet slammed against the ground in unison, sending tremors through the deck. Tag almost lost his footing as he aimed at one of them. He let loose a flurry of kinetic rounds that sliced through its shoulders and head, sending its arm crashing against the floor. The limb burst into thousands of tiny black globules like so many marbles scattering over the deck.

The others unleashed a fusillade of kinetic rounds into the monstrous nano-golems, and the first few fell apart, forming black puddles.

"Take that you pieces of robotic shit!" Sumo yelled, pushing herself up from where she had fallen. She unloaded a magazine into one of the golems. It stepped forward against the incoming rounds even as its limbs disintegrated. The monstrosity fell, face-planting against the deck, and exploded in a spray of particles.

All around Tag the sound of gunfire and splattering golems swirled. His rifle shuddered against his shoulder as he unloaded round after round, desperate to stop the constructs before they hurt another crew member. Amid the sounds of the skirmish, he heard the faraway echoes of Jaroon's and Bracken's forces engaged in their own fights. Sweat poured down Tag's forehead, and adrenaline surged through him as he dodged one of the monstrosities.

It pummeled at the deck, chasing after him, and he felt an almost wild thrill as he fired on it, taking grim satisfaction each time one of his shots sent pieces of the golem splashing against the floor. With only one arm and half a leg left, the golem dragged itself at Tag. A small mouth formed in its cylindrical head, opening and closing like it was gasping. A shrill sound spilled out from its mouth until Tag tore it to shreds of fluid-like metallic slivers that spilled across the deck.

Tag roved his rifle across the room, looking for his next target, the next golem dying for a taste of his mini-Gauss. His ears thundered with his pulse, churned on by the electricity exploding through his nerves. His finger itched next to the trigger guard, but all he saw were the other crew members standing over the remains of their vanquished enemies. He almost wanted to laugh. These Collectors were supposed to be extraordinarily advanced, and he had expected a more impressive defense.

"Oh, gods, no," Sofia said.

Tag whipped his head around, following her gaze. His heart seemed to go still. A sound not unlike human shrieking came from a black puddle of particles. Something was growing from it. First came a head, then a torso. Then the arms and legs.

The same shrieking exploded from the other puddles as the nanotech repaired the rest of the constructs.

The one nearest him brought its arm back, an eerie whine sounding from its head, and then it punched a block-like fist straight at Tag's chest.

# THIRTY-SEVEN

Tag dove to the side, barely dodging the nano-golem's fist. He rolled, already feeling the bruises forming in his elbows, and he sent the rest of his mini-Gauss's magazine careening through the golem. The rounds tore a hole in the golem's torso big enough for Tag to jump through, and still the monster came at him as though he had called the damn thing's name. All around him he heard the yells of his crew entangled with their own regenerating adversaries. No matter how many rounds he pummeled the thing with, it kept coming back.

"Bracken," Tag managed to grind out. "How are you fighting these things?"

Bracken sounded just as exhausted. "They keep…regenerating. Damn self-assembling particles."

Tag's mind sprinted even as he ran from another self-assembling golem. He fired at it, but as soon as the round cleared its torso, the particles reformed.

An idea hit him with an almost palpable force as he slid across the deck, escaping another slicing blow. No physical round would tear these monsters apart…because they were barely put together to begin with. Bullets and slugs would do no more damage to them than they would do to a cloud of water vapor.

But if these little nanomachines were reassembling when they were torn apart, there was a way to defeat them. Tag was certain he could figure it out, if only he had a few minutes to think. He crawled under a huge truck loaded down with colonization supplies. One of the golems pummeled the side of the vehicle, tearing the metal panels as it tried to reach Tag.

Traditional firearms weren't going to do anything to the golems. He needed to think on the nanoscale, to destroy the nanomachines that were actually responsible for the large forms. Another golem charged toward him. Tag fired on it, watching the particles spread then reassemble like a school of fish avoiding a barracuda. Not only were the kinetic rounds ineffective, but the nanomachines were quickly adapting to the physical blows, re-forming faster than before.

The mini-Gauss rifle was useless. Tag slung it over his back and pulled out his weaker pulse pistol. Orange bolts of pulsefire burned into the golem. This time, instead of the particles simply falling away, they glowed bright red, like molten metal, and then splattered on the deck and cooled in large globs of silver. To Tag's happy surprise, they never reformed.

"That's it!" Tag said. "Overload them with energy. Short the nanomachines' circuits. Melt 'em!"

Another golem careened toward him. He fought back with a renewed vigor, knowing that these things *did* die. They might not bleed, but they weren't invincible—and that was all that mattered. Pulsefire rang out from around the room as the crew switched from kinetic slugs to energy rounds. Each time a bolt from an energy weapon hit one of the golems, more slag burned off in sparks of red and orange, signifying millions of tiny nanomachines melting into an unfixable mess.

A golem bore down on Coren. Its legs were practically sponge-like, full of so many holes that Tag couldn't understand how it was still running. Before it reached Coren, a tongue of white-hot flames spat from the Mechanic's wrist-mounted weapons. Fire consumed the beast, and the thing glowed in a chromatic symphony of white, then red, then orange as it finally cooled into an oozing pile of silver.

"That's the right idea!" Sumo said, switching her pulse pistol out for a flamethrower.

Between the glow of pulsefire and flames spurting from the marines' weapons, the room resembled the foundry. Golems wilted away, and Tag hooted in victory even as sweat matted the shirt under his suit to his skin.

Any feeling of victory was short-lived.

The telltale whir of more incoming trucks whispered down the hallway. Tag knew that whisper would soon turn to a shriek when more of the golems transformed and renewed the assault of their fallen comrades. Yes, they had proved the golems could be defeated. But this time, they faced only a dozen golems. Next time, only the gods knew.

Their flamethrowers wouldn't last forever, and neither would their stamina. Now, more than ever, they needed to move. They needed to find a goddamned computer to figure out what twisted plans the Collectors had for the galaxy.

"We're moving," Tag called to Bracken and Jaroon. "More golems are incoming."

"Copy," Bracken said. "On our way."

"As are we," Jaroon said.

Tag called to his crew to move out. They sprinted down the

passages, barely slowing to look into more chambers as they passed, all filled with the same smooth bulkheads and decks, no terminals in sight. There had to be some way to access the computers here, some way to turn off the shields surrounding all the ships back in the bay. There *had* to be.

If not...

Tag hated to think about the alternatives. If they never came across a living soul they could force to help them. If they never found a terminal. Never found a way to shut down those auto-generating shields or stop the flow of vehicles delivering more of the golems to pursue them.

If they couldn't do any of those things, then this place would turn into their prison. A lifeless, automated tomb. If the golems didn't kill them, they would eventually succumb to starvation or dehydration.

*No,* Tag said, *that won't happen.*

He would find a way off this ship, if only to save his crew.

And there was still Lonestar to rescue. He couldn't leave her on the *Hope* for an eternity with Raktor. The alien would be *terrible* company for spending an eternity.

The constant buzz of other trucks delivering the regenerating golems chased them on, accompanied by the clamor of the heavy machines that sent tremors through the deck. It felt as if the entire ship was falling part. The forces amassed like a tidal wave, building and gaining on them.

Bull slid to a stop and removed the rocket launcher from his back. He flicked a switch on the launcher, and a rocket flew from the tube, spiraling to meet the oncoming horde. It collided with the first golem and exploded in a spray of white sparks that danced over the rest of the advance guard. Fire consumed the nanomachines before they had a chance to reassemble. Sofia whistled appreciatively as half a dozen of the golems melted.

"Thermite rounds," Bull said with a grin.

Tag tried to grin back, but it turned into a grimace. Pain stitched through the muscles in his side. His recent workouts had certainly helped, but he couldn't sustain their current pace. Golems swarmed over the melted forms of their fallen comrades, unwavering in their dogged pursuit, and Tag pushed his reluctant body into a jog.

Suddenly, Alpha sprinted ahead of the group and darted into a side chamber. She emerged a moment later, grunting as she pushed a stack of metal crates, each the size of an air car. The others ran to join her. The crates leaned precariously before tumbling across the deck and blocking the entrance of the hatch.

"This should afford us approximately four extra minutes in which to escape," Alpha said.

The cacophony of the oncoming stampede roared beyond the barricade of crates. Tag stole a glance behind them as they continued to run. Echoing clangs burst through the chamber when the golems slammed into the crates. The jarring high-pitched squeal of metal scraping against metal battered Tag's eardrums. He watched, one hand around his pulse pistol, the other still pumping madly as he ran. At any moment, he expected the crates to explode outward, broken to jagged shards by the golems' relentless assault.

Instead, something more disturbing happened. Black liquid seemed to ooze between the cracks of the makeshift barricade. It pooled on the floor, and Tag watched in horror as golems began to form from the puddle of nanomachines. Rockets and rounds flew from the marines as the group pushed forward, churning deeper into the ship.

Their surroundings seemed to be a constant repetition of sterile passages, storage rooms, then strange foundries and factories. As they littered the ship with globs of melted nanomachines, he wondered if there would ever be an end to the flow of attackers. A shiver snuck through him as the effects of adrenaline wore off and exhaustion took its place. What if all the factories and foundries they'd seen were endlessly pumping these golems out?

"What do we do now?" Sumo yelled over the comms.

She had stopped, pointing at something ahead. The others slowed, raising their weapons. Beyond the next chamber, with its rows of conveyer belts and robotic assembly machines, a line of golems was advancing toward them, their raised arms transformed into a variety of anachronistic weapons ranging from scythes to lances and axes.

"What in the three hells?" Sofia said under her breath.

Tag could only stare at the constructs. Some of the ensigns back in Tag's training days used to play a game, hypothetically pitting an SRE soldier against a medieval army or a legion of ancient Roman soldiers to predict who would win. They had always laughed at the scenario, mocking the crudeness of ancient warfare tactics. The SRE soldier, armed with the best military science and technology had to offer, would invariably come out victorious.

Faced against the brutal weapons now, Tag felt none of the certainty he had back then. The hypothetical had become frighteningly real.

"Captain, what do we do?" Sumo repeated.

# THIRTY-EIGHT

There was only one order Tag could give under the circumstances. "Fire!"

Thermite rounds exploded against the newcomers' ranks, accompanied by the whistle and blaze of pulsefire. Between blasts of their weapons, Tag heard the labored breaths of his crew echoing over the comms, each of them scrabbling to take down another golem, desperate to ensure their survival. There were fewer golems ahead than behind, so Tag signaled their advance against the enemy, occasionally taking cover behind one of the robotic assembly machines still dutifully doing its job while it absorbed damage from the *Argo*'s crew and the golems alike.

"We can't hold out much longer!" Sofia said. She dove away from a half-melted golem. Globs of molten metal dripped from where her pulsefire had hit, but it lumbered after her like a zombie driven by a single-minded hunger.

"We need to regroup!" Tag yelled over the comms to Jaroon and Bracken.

"On it!" Jaroon said.

"We're facing heavy opposition," Bracken said, "but we'll be at your position in a few minutes."

"*We* won't be at this position in a few minutes," Tag said. "But the golems will be."

"Understood," Bracken said. "We'll try to regroup in the next set of chambers."

One of the golems in front of Tag's group charged, swinging a punch at his head. Just before the blow landed, the fist transformed into a spike. Tag barely dodged the lancing strike and peppered the golem with pulsefire as it swung its fist around again, this time as a blade. Ducking and weaving, Tag engaged in a deadly dance with his opponent where any mistake would leave him short an arm or, worse, his head. He turned to the side as the golem hoisted an arm into the air, preparing to slam it down on Tag like a hammer. But when he tried to dive, his left foot didn't move.

His boot was caught in a puddle of cooled slag, essentially welded to the floor.

Then a swathe of orange flames curled around the golem, and Tag had to put an arm up to shield his visor from the bits of molten metal flecking off his attacker. The construct crumpled in the inferno, sinking to the deck.

As it fell, Tag saw who had saved him. Sumo stood with her flamethrower still growling and spurting fire.

"I got your back, Captain," Sumo said. "Always."

Tag's gaze slid past her. "Look out!"

A huge form raised a single arm—the only arm it had left. Half of its body was burning bright orange as thermite ate through it, but it was still determined to attack. Tag leveled his pistol at the thing's shoulder, firing. Sumo's eyes went wide for an instant and then she twisted out of his line of fire. She wasn't quick enough to avoid the golem's wreckage. It fell over her already damaged power armor, and her head slammed against the deck with a wrenching thud.

Tag fired at the slag cementing his foot until it sprayed and melted away. He sprinted to Sumo. Behind her visor, her eyes were closed. The helmet had protected her from external injury, but it could do nothing to prevent her brain from rattling around inside her skull.

"Sumo!" Tag said over the sound of the battle raging on all around him. "Sumo, can you hear me?"

Blood trickled from one of her ears, a dark rivulet dripping over her hair. That was not a good sign. At the very least she had suffered a concussion.

Another golem lumbered toward him, and Tag cut it down with pulsefire. Gorenado covered him with his flamethrower while Coren and Sofia held off others with salvo after salvo of pulse rounds scorching the air around them.

Tag tried to shove the remains of the golem off of Sumo, but it wouldn't move. "Alpha! Help me out here!"

Alpha leapt over the head of a golem while simultaneously riddling it with pulsefire. The golem fell away in melting globs before Alpha landed. If Tag weren't so worried about Sumo, he might've admired the synth-bio droid's acrobatics. She had come a long way from the struggling, nonverbal creation she had been when he'd first brought her to life—which was lucky, since he needed her help now more than ever.

"We need to move this thing," Tag said. He supposed he could burn the golem away, but he didn't want to risk injuring Sumo any worse than she already was. Melting globs of nanomachines over her armor could be just as devastating.

Alpha positioned herself on the other side of the golem, and together they lifted it enough to move it off Sumo.

"She's hurt," Tag said. "I can't carry her."

"Do not worry, Captain," Alpha said. She scooped her arms under Sumo and lifted her form with ease.

*Thank the gods I chose a medical droid chassis for her,* Tag thought. M3 droids were especially suited for moving injured patients.

Another golem hurled itself toward him, and he fired on its shoulders, rendering its arms useless before taking potshots at the torso. Bull launched another thermite round into the golems catching up from behind, but Tag could see they would be overwhelmed soon. It didn't help that one marine was incapacitated, and Alpha was encumbered by carrying Sumo.

"We've got to go," Tag said. "Jaroon, where are you?"

"Here," Jaroon said simply.

Tag looked around and spied the cobalt glimmer of the Melarreys' power armor. Huge swathes of green light exploded from their weapons, disintegrating the golems they touched. When the golems came too close, the Melarrey swung their weapons like axes. The blades on them glowed red, slicing easily through nanomachine particles. Each strike sent orange lightning coursing through the golems' bodies.

*Some kind of thermal weapon,* Tag realized. Everywhere the orange lightning arced, drops of molten metal sprayed from the golems.

The *Argo's* crew worked side-by-side with the Melarrey to defeat the last of the golems that had charged from the center of the ship. A final golem disintegrated, leaving the crew gasping for breath. The constant hum of the conveyor belts and the hammering of machines punching into metal was punctuated by the click of fresh batteries into pulse pistols.

Tag wanted to catch his breath. The healer in him wanted to examine Sumo, while his role as a captain meant he should probably be checking on the rest of his crew and making a plan to get them off this ship. But the stomping of the golems behind them gave him no time to do anything. There would be no reprieve from the advance of their regenerating opponents.

As they jogged away from the factory chamber, Tag spotted movement on their left. He feared the golems were coming in for a pincer maneuver, attempting to surround them again. His heart settled when he realized the incomers were Bracken's Mechanic forces. Two of them were limping, moving only with the aid of their comrades. They paused long enough for Bracken's forces to converge with the others.

"We would not have lasted much longer," Bracken said. "We can't keep running indefinitely. This is getting to be an exercise in futility."

"There are no other choices," Jaroon said.

"We could stand and fight," Bracken said. "Hold our ground until we take down the last one."

"The way those things keep turning up, I doubt there *is* a last one," Tag said.

He led the way into another chamber. This one was different from the warehouses and factories they'd encountered. All manners of crops were growing from what looked like carefully manicured rows. Plenty of fruits and vegetables Tag recognized grew alongside others that appeared to be from planets even more exotic than Eta-Five and the Forest of Light. There were bushes and trees and stalks jutting up all around the space, and the cloying fragrance of the various plants intermingling in the air sifted its way through Tag's air filters.

"This is a welcome change of scenery," Sofia said. "Not so depressing as the rest of this damn ship."

Throughout the fields, huge pieces of equipment moved, dispensing water, pruning leaves, or tilling soil. Additional hovering golems seemed to be surveying the fields, occasionally dipping down to take a soil sample or clip off a leaf before drifting away through another hatch toward the end of the massive enclosure. While all kinds of machines operated through the fields, each specialized for a particular task as they maintained the agricultural space, Tag noticed one striking similarity between them.

There were no operators.

And try as he might, he couldn't find any terminals either.

But *something* had to be controlling all these automated pieces of machinery. Something had to oversee the factories and foundries. And that something was probably also in command of the golems hounding them at every corner.

Tag looked at Jaroon, then Bracken. "We have to find the central command center. It's our only hope of getting off this ship alive."

# THIRTY-NINE

Nano-golems spilled into the fields, entering from corridors all around the giant agricultural chamber. They trampled the crops and tore through the bushes and trees as they charged straight toward the intruders. Other automated equipment continued working, either unaware or not caring their work was being ruined by the deadly machines.

"There!" Tag pointed to where he had seen a small hovering drone disappear into a hatch. It had taken with it a sample of some kind of purple, apple-like fruit. If they were going to find a computer system nearby, a laboratory seemed to be a good place to look.

He rushed ahead of the others as they began firing on the attackers. Energy rounds split the air, and flames danced over the waving grain and drooping trees caught in the flurry of crossfire. Smoke wafted up from the burning plants, the acrid scent seeping into Tag's suit and overwhelming the formerly pleasant atmosphere of the agricultural chamber.

One of the Mechanics reached the hatch where the drone had disappeared before Tag did. The others followed, first the ragtag crew of the *Argo* and then the slower Melarrey.

It took a second for Tag's eyes to adjust to the light, but he quickly realized this was not a laboratory for soil and harvest samples. The hovering golems followed a route that took them through the ceiling to some other destination. But though they hadn't found the lab where the samples from the agricultural sector were being processed, they had certainly found a lab of some kind.

Huge tubes carried liquid to columns arranged throughout the lab. In each column Tag saw something suspended in the dark liquid. His heart began to climb into his throat as he approached one. He had the curious sensation of blundering into a place of worship. The liquid within each translucent column was murky, but Tag feared he already knew what would be hidden inside.

This place was eerily similar to the specimen storage room aboard the *Hope*.

"I don't like the looks of this," Sofia said.

Tag turned on his helmet-mounted lights to pierce the gloom within the chamber. A figure was suspended within, wrapped in cords and tubes.

Sofia gasped. Coren took a step back.

"It's a human," Coren said.

Mechanics and Melarrey spread throughout the room. They reported finding the same thing in other tubes.

The strange feeling he had back on the *Hope*, back when he had been prowling between the decaying bodies and fetid chambers of the alien zoo, gripped Tag once more.

"There were no humans on the *Hope*," he said to Sofia.

"You're right," she said, her eyes wide behind her visor. "Alpha?"

Still holding Sumo's limp form, Alpha was silent for a moment. "The data we recovered did not indicate anything regarding humans within the specimen storage files."

"But Raktor confirmed that humans left the *Hope* only fifty years ago," Coren said. "That doesn't make any sense. If there were humans aboard the *Hope* long after the time the Collectors had taken it over and turned it into a space station, surely the Collectors would have studied and characterized them, too."

Bull, standing nearby, stared back through the hatch they had come through. "No time for your mystery science discussion. Golems are almost here."

A few Melarrey were perched in the doorway, sending waves of fire out into the attackers.

"Is there another exit here?" Sofia asked, looking around the lab.

The other Mechanics and Melarrey were scrambling around the bulkhead, searching for a way out. As each reported they could find no exit, Tag felt a leaden weight drag itself through his torso. He didn't want to believe it. They hadn't come this far without anything to show for it.

Maybe they still had a shot.

"Jaroon, keep your group at the hatch," Tag said. "Hold it as long as possible. Bull, Gorenado, help them out. Bracken, I've got a job for your people." He looked at the smooth bulkheads, then the columns, each home to a slumbering human form suspended by tubes and wires.

It was those wires that had drawn his attention.

"What do you have planned?" Bracken asked.

"Try forcing an exit through the wall," Tag said. "You've got plasma cutters in your suits' weapon systems, right?"

Bracken nodded. "We do, but these bulkheads look like the same material we saw in the ship bays."

"Still, we've got to try." Tag was desperate, and he knew the idea sounded crazy. But what else could they do?

Bracken appeared skeptical, but she still sent a squad of Mechanics to the opposite wall. Plasma jetted from their wrist-mounted weapons, carving into the bulkhead. If they could cut a hole just large enough and kept the nanomaterials back with their plasma cutters, they just might be able to escape.

And if that failed, Tag had another, even crazier idea. "I want another squad dismantling one of these tubes. All those wires and apparatus have to go somewhere, right?"

Now Bracken nodded vigorously. "And if they do, we can follow a hard connection to this ship's network."

"Exactly," Tag said. "And..."

He let the words trail off. The whine of Mechanic plasma cutters clashed with the stomping feet of the approaching golems.

It seemed Tag's darkest suspicions about this facility were right. The surge of golems sweeping into the fields was endless. No longer could he see the green foliage speckled with a rainbow's worth of colorful fruits and vegetables. Instead all he saw were the dark forms of the golems swarming over the landscape like a flood of shadows.

Bull launched another thermite round, and sparks flew from the golems it hit. Several fell, lost under the trampling feet of the others around them.

"I'm out," Bull said, dropping the launcher. He pulled out his pulse pistol and fired in concert with the Melarrey. Gorenado followed his lead, peppering the golems. But as frantically as the group's defensive forces tried to fend off their enemy, there was no denying the inevitable collapse of their meager barricade. Even a wall of pure pulsefire wouldn't stop their enemy now. The only thing that would change the tide of this battle was Bracken's squad, toiling away without taking their eyes off their work.

"We can't break through this," one of the Mechanics at the bulkhead shouted. "It's not working. No matter what we try, this thing is faster."

"It heals as soon as we cut it!" another yelled.

Sofia locked eyes with Tag for a second. It was long enough for him to see what she was thinking. Worry and despair shot out at him from that glance. He felt it, too—a rising heat of anger coursed through him, battling with the icy grasp of dread.

No wonder the *Hope* had been taken by the Collectors. No wonder the Mechanics had fallen, so easily turned into Drone-Mechs, and the Melarrey had perished before they could put up too much of a resistance. This technology was more powerful than any of their races could have imagined. More relentless and frightening than Tag's darkest nightmares.

A hulking golem made it to the lab's entrance. It went down in a flurry of fire but was quickly replaced by another. The next golem managed to send one of the Melarrey flying backward into a bulkhead before the defenders tore it to slag.

"The polyglass isn't self-healing!" a Mechanic shouted victoriously from the specimen chamber. Liquid began seeping out of the widening hole. A drizzle became a flood as the human within, along with the wires and tubes, was sucked out of the hole and poured across the floor.

The Mechanics bent to the wires, pulling them out of the human, showing no reverence for the man's body as it lay pale and naked beside them. Tag didn't blame them, not now. One of the Mechanics pressed a cut end of wire into the data port built into his wrist terminal.

"I'm picking up a—" The body of a Melarrey crashed into the Mechanic, sending them both tumbling backward. They fell in a jumble of armored limbs, liquid oozing out from broken joints in both their armor, and neither moved.

Another Mechanic struggled past them, reaching for the wire but was forced to duck when a second Melarrey was thrown toward them.

"Hold the line," Jaroon bellowed, his cobalt armor reflecting the green light from his weapon.

Bull and Gorenado stood stalwart next to the Melarrey, with Sofia offering fire support.

"Alpha, help the Mechanics!" Tag yelled.

She scrambled over the wreckage near the broken suspension chamber, set down Sumo gingerly, and bent over the wire. Tag couldn't watch for long. A whine like a sawblade chewing through wood screamed from the lab's entrance. Tag only had a second to duck under another body being thrown backward.

"Bull!" he yelled as the marine sailed over his head.

The ranks of the golems pressed against the entrance, swinging and slicing as the defenders fired desperately, cursing in several different languages. Like an ocean swell, the golems crashed into them, threatening to overwhelm them. Once the golems made it in the lab, if Alpha or the Mechanics didn't find a way to shut them down, it would be over.

Tag feared there wasn't even a way to surrender to these automatons. He had led these people—Mechanics, Melarrey, and humans, all—straight to their death. And for all their sacrifices, they had achieved nothing. They had discovered no intelligence to send back to the SRE or Meck'ara. Nothing to warn the other races what they had seen here, what terrifying technologies the Collectors possessed. What they might yet unleash—if they weren't already—on Earth.

"Don't let them through!" Jaroon bellowed, radiating courage in the face of almost certain death.

Tag sprayed pulsefire into the torso of the nearest golem, and its body split into two overheated halves as more energy rounds riddled its flank, turning it into gobs of melted metal. Alpha worked frantically at the data connection to the broken stasis chamber with another Mechanic.

They just needed to hold out a moment longer. If they could keep the golems at bay for a few more minutes, Alpha would find a way to shut them down.

Then the line broke.

# FORTY

The golems had no concept of mercy or restraint. Melarrey bodies flew past Tag. Gorenado slammed into a suspension chamber. Shattered glass pinged across the deck as the murky liquid spilled out, carrying with it the intubated body of a naked human.

All those still standing retreated, firing in waves at the golems. The voices of the Melarrey and Mechanics filled the comms in a disjointed din of curses and cries of pain. Bodies slammed together or smacked against bulkheads. More chambers spilled open like broken eggs, revealing the nascent embryos within.

Golems filled the chamber like darkness after a sunset. Tag watched in horror as the bodies of the Melarrey vanished under their masses. Then came Gorenado, still swinging his arms and firing. Tag saw the last few orange pulsefire rounds lance up from where the marine disappeared, then silence.

Tag backed away from the horde of shadowy machines. The

meager pulsefire streaming from his pistol felt horribly inadequate as the monstrous forms descended on him.

"Alpha!" Tag said. "What's going on?"

"I am trying!" Alpha replied.

Something touched Tag's shoulder, and he spun to face Sofia. She stood next to him, sharing only a momentary glance, as they guarded Alpha and the Mechanics' work. He thought he saw a wet sheen in her eyes, but he didn't look long enough to confirm it. Couldn't look long enough. The golems demanded his undivided attention. One by one, they overwhelmed the remaining defensive forces throughout the room.

"It was an honor to serve with you all," Bracken said before disappearing in a wave of golems. Her anguished cry tore over his comm, and then she went abruptly silent.

"Come on, Alpha," Sofia said. "It's now or never."

"Success!" Alpha said, standing up suddenly. "We have—"

A huge golem's fist scooped her up.

"Looks like it's never," Sofia said before another golem grabbed her.

Tag was the last one standing. He dodged a grasping claw, then leapt over fingers scooping toward him. He wasn't sure why he was continuing to fight, why he was trying to survive when everyone around him had been vanquished. But a tiny voice called at the back of his head, telling him he had to keep fighting. He had to make their efforts worth something. He somersaulted under another attacker, glancing at the wires Alpha had left behind, her wrist terminal still clamped to the data cable.

He could do this. He *would* do this.

His fingers stretched toward it, missed, and then he snatched the wrist terminal. The small holoscreen reported a stable connection with the ship's network. Alpha had been working on a command that seemed like it would disable the ship's defenses.

Tag ducked under another incoming blow and selected the command. His finger traced over the holoscreen, ready to initiate the shutdown.

He never got the chance.

A golem wrapped its claws around him and tore him away from the wrist terminal. The device fell from his grasp. The claws cinched tighter, crushing the plates in his suit. A rib popped, and he yelled in agony. Nanomachines from the golem's fingers crawled across him like ants and pierced the joints and filters in his suit. They trickled over his skin like water up his chest, then his neck, and then his face until he could no longer stop himself from screaming.

No sound came out. Just the creeping sensation as the nanomachines filtered into his helmet, soaking into the comms system poking into his ear canal and filling his HUD until he saw nothing but black.

He waited in the deafening silence for the golem to finish him off.

The agony in his chest turned to a dull throbbing as the painkillers administered by his suit kicked in. Still the drugs couldn't quell the burgeoning pain in his head. He tried to speak, to call out over the comms for someone, anyone.

His voice seemed to die on his tongue, muffled by a ringing in his ears. His muscles tremored as he fought to push his arms out and break the grip of the golem. But he was locked into place, imprisoned in his own body.

Soon he felt the golem moving at a steady rhythm, carrying him out of the chamber. He could neither see nor hear, so he tried focusing on the one sense that seemed to be working normally: smell. His nose was filled with the scent of metal. He could taste it, too. Almost like he had been licking an alloy bulkhead or something. It had to be the nanomachines.

In his mind's eye, he pictured them swarming through his flesh and into his bloodstream, poking at his cells and taking over his body. Maybe that was how the Collectors had accumulated so much information on other species.

Maybe this was how they had created the Drone-Mechs.

There was no telling what the Collectors had planned for him. Would he end up in a suspension chamber, just another anonymous soul preserved like a specimen in a jar? Or worse, would he be turned into a mindless soldier for the enemy?

*You won't take me,* Tag thought. He tried to think of a way to prevent the nanomachines from overtaking him like a swarm of parasites. There must be a way. He would rather die than become a tool for the Collectors.

He wondered if this is what the Mechanics had felt when the nanites crept into their brains. How many of them had tried to fight it, tried to fend off the psychological changes commanding them to betray their own race? Had they felt the horror of losing control?

Maybe they were prisoners, just as he was now. Maybe there was still a conscience trapped beneath the nanites controlling the Drone-Mechs. The thought of being forced to kill his friends, his family, his people—it was too much to bear.

*No,* Tag thought, *I won't let that happen to me. I won't.*

If he had a chance to fight back against the nanites, he would take it no matter what.

And if he could not win that fight, he'd die before becoming one with them.

# FORTY-ONE

Tag was falling. He tried to put an arm out to brace himself, but his body wouldn't move. His muscles were as useless as his non-existent voice. He slammed into the hard deck, and the impact sent a bright pain through his side, radiating from the rib he feared was broken. He couldn't do anything but wait for his suit to kick in with fresh painkillers.

Then something else was thrown to the floor beside him. *Sofia.*

She lay on her side, unmoving, her brown eyes wide. Dried blood crusted around her nostrils. She didn't blink. Just stared straight back at him with a look that wasn't accusatory or damning or even angry.

It was just sad.

A single tear rolled from the corner of her eye as more bodies hit the floor next to them. Black shadows skirted around Tag's periphery. He couldn't turn his head to confirm it, but he had no doubt those were the golems. He hoped the thumps of other things smacking the deck signaled that the others had been spared death like him.

*Still alive,* Tag marveled.

His mind whirled back to when they had first encountered the golems. Their intentions had been clear—to kill, not to capture.

What had changed?

The mere fact that *something* had changed its mind, had decided to keep them alive, gave Tag reason to hope. There must be someone he could bargain with. If he could just talk to one of the Collectors, there was a chance, however slim, he could convince them to let him and his people go.

The last of the bodies was tossed to the floor, and the sound of heavy footsteps faded as the golems left them. For far too long, the only other sounds Tag heard were the rasping of his own breath and the pounding of his pulse within his eardrums. He wondered if the nanites had control over those involuntary physiological functions. Could they stop his heart or cease his lungs without warning?

He continued to stare at Sofia, unable to avert his gaze even if he had wanted to, and she stared back. In a strange way, it was as if they were sharing in their mutual feeling of utter isolation.

Then he heard a new sound. Like heavy boots plodding against the deck. A thicker, richer sound than the mechanical smack of the golems' footsteps. Without warning, his body was lifted from the ground.

No, not lifted.

Rather his body stood on its own, without any input from him. Then he began marching to a massive viewscreen. All the stars of space shone across the void. Some were painfully bright, glaring at him. Others were wrapped in curtains of color, dust illuminated in the distant swirl of another galaxy. And at the center of the screen floated the planet they had just left.

Tag hadn't expected to see it again. Large and round, a ball of dirt and rock undergoing an autonomous terraforming procedure that would forever change the face of the lifeless sphere.

"Beautiful, isn't it?" a voice said from behind them.

Whoever it was had spoken *his* language. It had a strange accent, nothing like any SRE world he had ever heard, but it was nonetheless Sol Standard. There was also something else odd about the voice. It contained a rich array of sounds, like a whole chorus ranging from sopranos to basses, delivering the words in perfect unison.

"Everything is ready to be molded," the voice said. "Like a block of clay waiting for a sculptor. Brand-new opportunities. Nothing to stand in the way of achievement but the desire for perfection itself. I relish these moments."

Tag tried to ask, *Who are you?* Other questions—*what do you want, what are you doing to us, why are you doing this*—clamored in his mind.

The words died in his throat.

He wanted to turn and see who it was that had taken him and the others prisoner. But he was still just as paralyzed as before, functioning as nothing more than a puppet with invisible strings. His eyes remained fixed on the planet.

"This world is one of many," the voice said. "It is the future. *Our* future."

More footsteps, like someone was pacing behind Tag.

"Everything we have is built on the backs of planets like these. Each one is a chance to reclaim what is rightfully ours. We deserve to live."

*So did everyone you've killed, you bastard,* Tag thought.

"We deserve a chance at life." There was a sigh. "But others would prevent us that. Even our own people would try to regulate our progress under the guise of false prophets like morals and ethics. Now we stand victorious. The gods have granted us an opportunity unlike any other."

The voice paused, his words still resonating in Tag's mind.

"We have a chance to *become* gods." Another pause. "Is that something you would pass up?"

Tag wanted to yell at this *thing* to quit its proselytizing and face him, to explain itself without being obstinately vague. Then a hand slammed on Tag's shoulder. Long gloved fingers wrapped around it, squeezing slightly.

"I was surprised to see a Sape here. It must have been a long, messy trail to reach this point, and I'm sure now you are wondering why you and your little band of unevolved misfits are still alive." The fingers tightened around Tag's shoulder. He wanted to wince, but the nanomachines wouldn't even allow him that much movement. "*You* impressed me. I hate to admit it, but a Sape like you deserves an opportunity."

The fingers released Tag's shoulders, and the multi-octave, harmonious voice continued, "I have met other Sapes. Surely you noticed the ships when you arrived here. Those Sapes were easily manipulated, won over by promises of money and greatness." The voice laughed. It was a disharmonious sound, full of piercing high-pitched notes that clashed sharply with lower, grating pitches. "You are something else. You are driven by another desire, and I haven't quite figured out what exactly that is."

Tag felt the thing lean over his shoulder, its body bent low so its cheek was practically touching his. From the fringes of his vision, he saw only a glimpse of the cerulean flesh of the creature's face. This must be a Collector, just like the ones reported in the Mechanics' ship's log at the *Hope* station.

"You're a failure," the thing said. "A failed officer of the bridge. You were offered another chance to succeed as a scientist and medical officer. But you failed to save your crew when the things you call Drone-Mechs attacked your ship. You failed to save the *Montenegro* fleet from almost complete destruction." That grating laughter, again. "The ship was limping when you got there. How many died because you couldn't be there sooner? You failed to save the Forinth on Eta-Five, you failed to prevent the deaths of so many Mechanics who sacrificed their lives when you promised to get their planet back.

"And how long will they hold that planet? Was the sacrifice worth it? They'll die now anyway, and we will take back what was ours."

The Collector took a step backward and yanked off Tag's helmet. Hot air rushed in around him, smelling at once sweet and putrid, like flowers stabbing up through a garbage dump.

"Now you have failed to stop *us*. Failed to warn the rest of the Sapes still shoving their way around the stars like toddlers. Everything that happens next is, in a way, your fault. How does that make you feel?"

The Collector's words fell harshly on Tag's ears like a rain of pelting rocks, battering his mind.

*No,* Tag thought. *I haven't failed. We still saved the* Montenegro. *We still saved Meck'ara. We still found the* Hope. *And we found you.*

He vowed not to let the Collector control his emotions as it did his body. Slowly his body began to turn, his muscles involuntarily swiveling him away from the viewscreen. His eyes remained fixed ahead, unable to look away as the Collector at last moved into his field of vision.

And then, despite his promise, Tag lost control of himself. Although he could not make a sound, inside he was screaming with mind-shattering horror.

# FORTY-TWO

The Collector towered over him, skinny as a Mechanic, but corded with muscles that pressed against the thin suit covering its body. It stared down at Tag with three eyes. Two mirrored Tag's own, with another in the center of the Collector's wide forehead. Its jawline was striking and square, like a champion Turbo player, but covered in blue flesh.

And yet, even though the Collector was most decidedly not a human like him, it *was* human.

"I can only imagine the expression that would be on your face," the Collector said, "if you weren't pumped full of nanites controlling your body."

The Collector put a five-fingered hand over where Tag presumed its heart was. "Welcome to the *Dawn of Glory*. I am Ezekiel." It jabbed Tag's chest with a long finger. "My grandfather was a Sape like you. And in three generations, look at what we have accomplished!"

Ezekiel paused as if he expected a response from Tag. Then he snapped his fingers.

"There," Ezekiel said. "That should be better."

Tag's eyes went wild, searching for what had changed until he realized it was *him*. "Wha...wha...how are the others?"

He tried to walk, but his body locked up. His eyes were free to rove the vast room. There was a chair in the center, large enough to be a throne. Before it stood a single terminal with a holoscreen—the only gods-damned computer Tag had seen in the vast *Dawn of Glory*. Behind it lay the bodies of his crew alongside the Melarrey and the Mechanics. He couldn't tell if they were still breathing.

"They're crawling with nanites, of course," Ezekiel said, "but they're alive. Even that abomination of yours—the one you call Alpha—is functional."

Tag spotted her silver form. Her chest plate lay open as though Ezekiel had been toying around with her insides.

"Did you do something to her?" he asked.

"She'll be fine. They'll all be just fine."

Tag opened his mouth to speak again, but Ezekiel cut him off with a snap.

"So very impatient," Ezekiel said, "just like all the other Sapes." Ezekiel motioned to the planet, then to the interior of the *Dawn*. "But before you go rattling off a dozen questions, let me explain a few things."

"Fine," Tag said. "I'm listening."

Ezekiel laughed, and Tag found himself wanting to cover his ears again.

"Very good," Ezekiel said. "Let me bring you up to speed. You are a basic human: Homo sapiens. I am what you might call a post-human. I still share much of the same genetic information as you, but you will never be like me. For all intents and purposes, we have taken a leap in the evolutionary scale, bounding past the false hurdles of natural selection, making our own biological destiny. That was the dream of my grandfather's generation."

"You altered yourselves, tampered with your DNA to force drastic changes in the human species."

"Exactly," Ezekiel said. "My ancestors traveled the UNS *Hope*. But human bodies weren't meant to travel beyond Earth. It was meant to be a mission of exploration, but instead generations lived and died in a metal hellhole." Ezekiel prodded Tag again. "Your bodies are weak. Humans thrived on Earth, but post-humans will thrive beyond it."

Tag's darkest suspicions about the *Hope* and the Collectors seemed to prove true. There had been no humans within the specimen chamber back on *Hope* because they were the ones doing the collecting. "That's why you studied all those poor captives on the *Hope*. You were selecting traits from other species, weren't you?"

"Good deduction," Ezekiel said. "I knew there was a reason I wanted you alive. You are correct. My ancestors collected that data and experimented on themselves. All of that, of course, was strictly against UN regulations."

"Because it's inexcusable. Imprisoning other sentient beings so you can experiment on them and then genetically altering humans with total disregard for the long-term effects of those changes…it's horribly irresponsible."

"Maybe it seems that way to you," Ezekiel said. He slouched into his crash couch, looking like a lonely king in an empty kingdom. "But we saw it differently. Or at least, my predecessors did. Technology was a gateway for us, a preemptive defense. Because without it, without this forced evolution, we would be extinct."

"Extinct?" Tag asked. "The human race is thriving."

Ezekiel raised a wide, hairless brow. "Thriving? More like fumbling. Your own colonies have erupted in ill-fated rebellions, and you've faltered against unfriendly races. In the face of these dangers, we have done what is necessary for the survival of our species. There is no room—nor time—for moral quandaries when our very survival is at stake."

"What are you talking about?" Tag asked. "The most dangerous thing I've run across in our travels is *you*."

"Because you haven't traveled long enough," Ezekiel said solemnly. There was no wry smile or expression of smug superiority across its face, just a deep sympathy that surprised Tag. "There are things out here that you wouldn't understand. That you couldn't *hope* to understand." Ezekiel looked away, his lips curling into a frown. "Things that even we don't understand."

Tag's body twisted, jerking around to face the center of the bridge. A holo bloomed to life there showing a familiar sight: the corridors of the *Hope*. Only now they weren't covered by Raktor's draping vines. Normal humans walked the passageways wearing the old-fashioned uniforms of the UN navy.

Then something appeared within the corridors. A flash of light. It ran between five of the crew members, and all five disappeared. The other crew members screamed and fell against the walls. One of them began clawing at a bulkhead like he was trying to tear through it.

The holo flickered off.

"I don't understand," Tag said. "What was that?"

Instead of offering an explanation, Ezekiel waved his hand over his terminal and the same holo appeared again, this time zoomed all the way in on one of the flashes of light. It vaguely resembled an explosion, but between the spikes of spreading light, Tag thought he saw something like a hand, and another area that appeared almost like a face without eyes.

"Is that...is that some kind of alien?" Tag asked.

"Your guess is as good as mine," Ezekiel said. "Whatever it

was, those crew members who were taken never reappeared. The other witnesses never recovered either. They all died screaming and crying, hooked up to machines to keep them alive until someone finally let them die."

"Did you ask the other races you encountered about these things?"

Now a smile spread across Ezekiel's face. It wasn't a nice smile. "We tried. Some listened to us, some said we were crazy. A few reported similar occurrences. But we had already made our decision at that point. It didn't matter much what these other races said or did. We had already determined that we would control our own destinies, harnessing whatever technology and science could grant us to advance our species. To ensure that we would progress, that we would survive."

"All of this was inspired by those creatures your ancestors saw?" Tag asked skeptically.

"Yes, that was the catalyst," Ezekiel said, pointing at the vague holo forms still floating in the middle of the bridge. "We must find out who they are, and what they are."

"This doesn't make sense," Tag said. "The crew of the *Hope* was so scared after a few crew members got killed by some unseen alien or weapon that you went around massacring other races, conducting experiments that would make Dr. Frankenstein cringe, and doing this to yourselves." He jerked his head toward Ezekiel, still unable to gesture with his hands.

"It wasn't just a few crew members," Ezekiel said. "I showed you only one image. Half of the *Hope* was killed that day. Half of them dead, gone within seconds. Much of the surviving population went insane. There were only a few humans left, deep in space, isolated from the rest of civilization. They did what they had to do."

Ezekiel stood, clenching his fists, his voice rising to a pitch and volume painful to Tag's ears. "The UNS *Hope* was a vanguard for the new era in human expansion. It was to be the harbinger of everything that was good about exploration and discovery. But instead the *Hope* was shattered. This new dawn, the idyllic future of humans in space, was destroyed before it began."

An intense fire burned behind Ezekiel's three eyes as he stared at the planet far below. "But in that day"—the Collector put his hand on his chest—"*we* were born from those ashes."

# FORTY-THREE

Tag wished he could shake his head in disbelief. Everything Ezekiel had said was insane, and yet the post-human continued talking as though his ancestors had taken the only logical course of action.

"You thought the best way to react to a new threat was to massacre all your possible allies," Tag said. "That's ridiculously short-sighted."

"We tried diplomacy," Ezekiel said, "but it is a tedious affair. It soon became clear that we were wasting our time. There were far easier methods of convincing others to do what we want."

"The nanites," Tag said, confirming his darkest suspicions that the Collectors and Drone-masters were one and the same.

"Precisely. It's efficient. I had hoped you would appreciate that as a scientist."

"I can't condone slavery in the name of efficiency."

Ezekiel leaned forward on the crash couch, all three eyes

narrowing as if he was annoyed. "It's a matter of survival—both for our race and for these other lesser races. They refuse to protect themselves from the threat that our ancestors witnessed. We created better humans, a better race than the likes the natural universe has ever achieved. And as an unintended, but I believe benevolent consequence of that, we now have parts of all these species within us. We also have the ability to recreate any species at our leisure. We are the failsafe the universe needs against the monsters that once wreaked havoc aboard the *Hope*."

"This is insane," Tag managed, still trying to process everything Ezekiel had said. He marveled at both the technological prowess of these post-humans and at their disregard for other lifeforms as nothing more than tools and pets. Had it really taken just three generations to turn humans into the creature before him?

"Insanity? Maybe," Ezekiel said. "I'm reminded of that ancient parable about Noah's Ark. The old story says Noah was considered insane when he rounded up specimens from all over Earth in preparation for an existential threat unlike that which the human race had ever seen. We post-humans are no different. We are simply preparing for that which everyone else seems to be too blind to see."

"If you were really champions of science, you would gather data on those light creatures instead. You would investigate them, and use evidence to show others that you're right."

Ezekiel laughed. "Don't think we haven't tried, Sape! The beings in question are testing the bounds of our own understanding of physics and biology."

Tag was silent for a moment. Everything the post-human said seemed to answer—or at least started to answer—the questions he and his crew had amassed up to this point. Ezekiel's tale also posed frightening new ones. Tag began with the one that had been troubling him the longest. "Why did you infiltrate the SRE? And how?"

Ezekiel smiled. "Despite our superiority, we do have a soft spot for our ancestral past. It's difficult not to look at you Sapes with nostalgia. We also knew the UN—and, more recently, the SRE—did not see things our way when it came to advancing biological technology, so we offered to support certain individuals and organizations interested in real progress. My hope is that they, like you, will come to appreciate what we can offer the human race."

"Who in the SRE is on your side?"

"I'm not going to list names," Ezekiel said. "Instead I want to focus on what you can do for me."

"I'll never help you," Tag spat.

"Just hear me out. There's a way for you and your crew to come out of this situation alive."

Tag's eyes went wide. "What do you want?"

"See? I am more benevolent than you give me credit for. Running the *Dawn* by myself has gotten a bit lonely, or maybe I'm just getting sentimental. Colonization is one of the more mind- numbing duties required of us on these awfully boring ships."

"There are more ships like the *Dawn*?"

"Of course! You see, one problem with our new post-human race is that we haven't had enough time to populate. We've been forced to divide and conquer—to sow our seeds, if you will. Eventually, we'll be able to come back and live on these planets, but the initial process requires an intense amount of automation. There are dozens of ships like this depositing what we call 'colony seeds' onto barren planets."

Tag looked at the dusty planet. "All the robots, vehicles, drones–none of them are manned?"

"No," Ezekiel said. "I run it all on my own, controlling everything from up here. I'm literally the brains of this operation."

At least Tag now understood why he hadn't seen a single terminal anywhere about the ship. "If you can automate so much of this, I don't understand why you don't just use your army of golems and drones instead of enslaving other races?"

"Let me put this in terms you will understand," Ezekiel said. "Nature and evolution have given most races a tremendous advantage in the form of an adaptive immune response. Our bodies learn to fight new diseases. Sure, sometimes a disease culls the weakest from our ranks—and there are many diseases, even for us post-humans. But the glory of our genetic diversity is that even when a disease runs rampant through our population, we still have some who are resistant to fight on."

"What does this have to do with your golems?"

"Simple enough, really. For all the glories of advanced computational technology, golems and drones and AI are remarkably weak. It is a shame to admit, but if someone were to impart an effective computer virus into the *Dawn*, the entire thing could come to a grinding halt. Our networks do not possess adaptive immune systems, and there is certainly no such thing as genetic diversity in a million drones and golems who are all constructed the same."

Tag considered this, the scientific side of his nature drawn into the discussion despite himself. "So it's the same reason a pure clone army wouldn't work. One exploited weakness, and they all go down."

"Aren't you a clever Sape," Ezekiel said. "Mindless golems work for now as tools, but they are vulnerable to exploitation and not adaptable enough to survive all that the universe has to throw at them. Therefore, we have successfully recruited a variety of other races like your so-called Mechanics."

"You mean you've enslaved them."

"Semantics." Ezekiel lifted his huge shoulders in a shrug. "Truth be told, I don't want the fate of post-humanity to rest on the shoulders of aliens or mindless golems. I want more control over it." Ezekiel gestured to Alpha. "She's an interesting creation. You did something we had written off long ago. You created an AI that is both sentient and biological. If we could introduce synth-bio intelligence into our golems, we would have a smarter workforce with more adaptive immunity to cyber threats."

"That's why you kept us alive? You want me to build you an army of Alphas?"

"No, that's not the only reason," Ezekiel said. "The droid merely drew my interest to you when I pulled that data from your ship—thank you for landing so nicely in my bay, by the way. Mainly, I brought you here for my own amusement."

Tag's muscles began to shake as he tried to clench his hands into fists. "Your amusement?"

"Even I get bored when things like colonization no longer pose a challenge." Ezekiel paused. "You do care about your crew, don't you? Even the xeno and the synth-bio droid?"

Tag hesitated, unsure of where this was going. "I do."

"I watched you give orders to these other xenos." Ezekiel motioned to the paralyzed forms of Jaroon's and Bracken's troops. "You have gotten these other aliens to follow you all the way here onto my ship."

Tag didn't respond this time, unwilling to give anything else away to Ezekiel.

"We had a difficult time with the Mechanics and Melarrey, hence the deployment of the nanites," Ezekiel said. He paused, a calculating look on his strange, unsettling face. "Look, I'm feeling generous, so I might let you live."

Tag sensed there was a catch.

And he was right.

# FORTY-FOUR

Ezekiel stood, towering above Tag, and strode toward the bodies of the others frozen by the nanites coursing through their flesh. Each step he took sent shivers through the deck that Tag could feel even in his own paralyzed limbs.

"These Mechanics and Melarrey follow you like you are their master," Ezekiel said. "The data from your ship shows these creatures have sacrificed for your missions. I wonder, how do you like the power?"

Tag couldn't help himself. "The power?"

Ezekiel balled a fist in front of his chest. "The power you have over these pets of yours. Does it drive you? Do you like calling yourself captain now? Do you like how they look up to you, how they revere you?"

Tag remained silent.

"I think you do like it," Ezekiel said, striding toward Tag. He leaned in over him, uncomfortably close. "I think you revel in it.

It's a rush; I can tell you that from experience. But I want to see how you use it."

"This is ridiculous," Tag said, his skin crawling as he tried to flinch away from the Collector. "Why not let us go? We could share your message, warn the SRE. It doesn't have to be like this."

"Diplomacy is useless," Ezekiel said. "We've been down that road before, and it takes far too much time."

"Let me try," Tag insisted.

"See? You *do* think you have power. You think after recruiting a handful of xenos to your side, you can make a difference." Ezekiel grinned. "You cannot."

He motioned over his terminal, and a pool of black nanites flowed in from a vented panel behind his crash couch. With a raise of his hand, the nanites swarmed upward and formed into a golem. "You see? I have all the control here. I'll remind you that these things are in your body, in your crew's bodies. You will do what I want or"—he clenched his fist, and the golem exploded into a spray of particles that drifted back into the pool—"I will crush all of you."

Tag's teeth gritted. "What do you want?"

"I had hoped, since you were a scientist, you would appreciate what we're trying to accomplish. I hoped you would want to contribute to it, in fact. Your efforts, as primitive as they are, could be helpful. I would allow you and your crew to live on that planet"—he pointed out the viewscreen to where the *Dawn of Glory* had deposited its automated colonization equipment—"and continue your synth-bio research unperturbed by silly things like your Sape government."

"I won't be your pet scientist."

"That's the only way your crew gets off this ship alive."

Tag considered the offer. Once he and his crew were stranded on the planet, they might fashion a courier drone to send word to the SRE of what happened. Certainly Alpha had the schematics for a drone in her data storage. There had to be enough equipment and raw materials that they could cobble one together and send it off when Ezekiel left this system for wherever he was meant to colonize next.

At least getting off this ship would mean no one was killed. They would be alive, whether they were indentured servants or not.

"I'll need the *Argo*. My vessel has the most advanced lab—"

"How stupid do you think I am?" Ezekiel said. "I'm not letting you back on that ship for a second. I've already got all the data you need off it, and our fabricators will produce a lab for you planetside."

Tag was glad the nanites wouldn't let him move, because they kept his expression neutral. He'd never had much of a poker face, and right now he felt like grinning. He had known Ezekiel wouldn't let him have access to the *Argo* again, but he had gotten valuable information. Access to fabricators would be even better. Surely, he could use them to build a drone, if not a goddamned spaceship once Ezekiel was gone. Ezekiel would undoubtedly put other safeguards in place, but Tag would work around them. The Collector seemed to underestimate the intelligence of Tag's crew, and it would be easy to use against him.

"Fine," Tag said. "Send us down there."

"Not so quick," Ezekiel said. "You don't need *all* of these beings down there."

Tag's stomach twisted. There was always another catch. The Collector made a few swift gestures, and the nanites reacted accordingly. The crew stood robotically and split into two groups, each facing Tag. On one side stood Sofia, Alpha, Sumo, and the Melarrey. On the other stood Coren, Bull, Gorenado, and the Mechanics.

"I want to know how well you have trained your pets," Ezekiel said. "You have two options. First, you choose one side. They have to kill themselves. Every single one of them. I don't care how they do it, but they have to commit suicide. Order them to do it."

"No!" Tag cried.

"That's why I'm giving you two options. Your second is to organize a little fight. One side against the other. Fight to the death until half of them die. Whoever is left will be your crew."

"They won't fight each other."

"I can make them," Ezekiel said. "The nanites, of course, have that ability."

Tag's eyes flicked from one familiar, eerily calm face to the other. "You can't do this."

"No, I won't. I'm asking *you* to do it." Ezekiel cocked his head to the side, laying his cheek in his open palm like a bored teenager. "I suppose you do, in fact, have a third choice. Do nothing, and I kill them all and you."

The third choice was no choice at all. Tag couldn't let them all die here. Not when they still had a mission to finish. Not when they still needed to get word to the SRE and Meck'ara about what they had learned. He had promised that, given a chance to complete what they had started, he would pursue it to the end.

The crew—his friends—shared wide-eyed looks of fear or steadfast anger or immeasurable worry. Tag looked between them, measuring each side.

If it came to a hand-to-hand fight, there was no telling who would win. Each possessed their own advantages. The Melarreys' brute size and armor versus the Mechanics' agility and wit or Alpha's unparalleled strength and knowledge.

Tag could not let his crew tear each other apart. Doing so might relieve him of the burden of choosing who lived and died.

But it would also mean every survivor would be haunted with the memories of those they had killed.

No, he couldn't shoulder this decision onto his crew. Even if they forgave him, he would never forgive himself. This decision had to be his and his alone.

He caught Sofia's eyes. At first, she appeared stricken, afraid. But when she saw he was looking at her, her face turned stoic. Next to her, Sumo's chin jutted out as if she was standing at attention, and she stared straight ahead, fixed on some point only she could see. Tag was surprised to see her standing at all after the concussion she'd undoubtedly suffered, but he wrote it off as the nanites. Across from her, Bull appeared as red and angry as ever, full of lava and hungry fire. Coren's working eye looked as dead as his disfigured one. No emotion.

"I have planets to colonize, Sape," Ezekiel said. "Your decision?"

Tag surveyed both lines. No one looked to him, begging for their life. No one would condemn the others to die. He thought he saw Sofia's fingers twitch, but when he looked at her, she was as still as ever. No one would make this choice easier.

"You make a decision now," Ezekiel said, his three eyes narrowing. "Or I make it for you. And I promise you won't like it."

"Fine," Tag said. His arms shook with the anger rushing through him. He took one final look at the people—alien and human—who had entrusted their lives to him. They had known this mission would be risky. They had known they might not return to their homeworlds. But none of them could ever have predicted it would end like this.

Then he noticed Alpha. She was the only one willing to meet his gaze. And when their eyes locked, she did something that surprised him.

She winked.

Tag knew exactly what his choice would be.

# FORTY-FIVE

L et them fight," Tag said.

"I'm surprised," Ezekiel said, blinking. "That is more ruthless than I expected."

"I'm sure it is," Tag growled.

"This will be far more entertaining than I thought," Ezekiel said, no longer looking at Tag. He faced the two lines of combatants and lifted his large hand into the air. His fingers came together with a snap to switch the nanites into fight-mode and force the sides together in combat.

Bull turned first, yelling in unbridled ferocity. Sumo collapsed when the nanites no longer held her up and lapsed back into unconsciousness. Alpha twisted next, leaping over the heads of the Mechanics, and Jaroon cocked a fist back as he ran. Coren ducked low and charged, and Sofia took a plasma blade from its sheath, switching it on with an electric hiss. The forces came together in a blur of bodies.

But they didn't attack each other. Tag tore a blade from one of his sheaths and pounced. The blade dug deep into Ezekiel's broad shoulder, spilling dark blood. The Collector threw Tag against a bulkhead. Before his head slammed against the hard surface, he saw the confused look in Ezekiel's eyes, the question burning clear in his three pupils: *How?*

Pain swarmed through Tag's skull, and he blinked away the snowflakes in his vision as he renewed his assault on the post-human.

Ezekiel tried to snap his fingers again, this time undoubtedly to make the nanites tear apart their hosts from the inside. The gesture did nothing.

Mechanics, Melarrey, humans, and a synth-bio droid descended on Ezekiel. Blades flashed, fists flew. The post-human towered above the others and swung wildly, defending himself with unparalleled strength and a deftness that spoke to his forbearers' skill at splicing genes. Punches from Ezekiel cracked power armor and sent aliens and humans flying.

Tag wasn't sure how Alpha had done it, but when she had winked at him, he'd understood that she had somehow taken control of the nanites. He had curled his fingers together and made a fist, something that he shouldn't have been able to do if the nanites had still been controlling his body. The others had remained still as if they were still being held prisoner by the nanites, with Alpha somehow the one actually governing the nanites. Whatever Alpha had done, however she had done it, Tag wanted to know.

Later. First, they had a would-be god to deal with.

Ezekiel threw another Melarrey into a pile of Mechanics, knocking them all backward. He tried to wave an arm over his terminal even as Sofia clung to his back and jabbed her knife into his spine. Every time a wound opened, it seemed to heal almost immediately. It appeared as though nothing they were doing actually caused him real harm.

Tag didn't let that dissuade him. He saw the desperation bleeding through Ezekiel's face. The post-human fought like a cornered dog—one that already knew the battle was over but was going to fight it out anyway. He managed to gesture over his terminal, and the nanites that had pooled on the deck from earlier reformed into a squad of golems. They joined the fray in a flurry of slicing limbs and grasping claws.

Everything became a haze of red and blue and black. Tag tried to keep up with the battle, tried to help. It was too much, and he lost track of the action as pain and exhaustion threatened to overwhelm him. But just when he thought the golems had pushed the battle into Ezekiel's favor, when he thought Ezekiel was actually going to fulfill his promise of killing them all, the golems fell apart, spreading across the deck like a puddle of oil once again.

Ezekiel stared in horror at what was left of his guards. Coren grabbed one of the post-human's arms and dug deep into the muscle with his knife. Bull charged, attempting to tackle him, while Jaroon levied another powerful blow into Ezekiel's stomach.

Through it all the post-human still stood tall, seemingly invincible.

Tag roared and leapt at Ezekiel, brandishing his blade at the post-human's face. The others followed, desperate and disorganized. Even so outnumbered, Ezekiel should have won. He'd been engineered to be faster, stronger, smarter. He had every advantage, but one.

They were angrier.

Ezekiel didn't even stand a chance.

The constant bombardment and unrelenting attacks brought the post-human to his back. Lacerations wept with crimson blood, and even his fast-healing body couldn't keep up with the others' assault. Ezekiel went down, his head cracking against the deck. Tag mustered his remaining strength and leapt. He delivered a blow that sent shivers of pain through his fist. But none of that bothered him. The pleasure of seeing Ezekiel wince more than made up for it.

Finally, Ezekiel's limbs went still. His chest rose and fell in racking gasps.

"How…how did you overcome the nanites?" he asked, a trickle of blood dribbling from his lips. "You were never supposed to be free. The nanites would've made you fight to the death. You could never turn on me like that. It makes…it makes no sense."

"Guess you aren't as smart as you thought," Tag said, willing a triumphant smile across his face despite the pain and exhaustion seeping through him. It was worth the pain to see the post-human look thoroughly bewildered at the turn of events. He would never give the post-human the satisfaction of knowing the truth, even in these last few desperate moments. "And humans, Mechanics, Melarrey, we *are* better than you."

Then with a look of humiliated disappointment, the post-human took his last breath.

Tag's chest heaved. He planted a boot on Ezekiel's bleeding ribs and waited a moment to ensure the post-human had stopped moving. Everyone had seen what Ezekiel could do and had done; they weren't going to give him a chance to regenerate himself, even if his pulse had stopped. One of the Mechanics took it upon himself to guarantee he stayed down by the expedient measure of removing his head. Tag forced himself to watch as the blade sawed through the post-human's neck.

The battle was over, but they were far from safe.

"Alpha," Tag gasped, "monitor Sumo's suit. Make sure she's stable."

"Yes, Captain," Alpha said, bending over Sumo's once-again limp form.

"What did Ezekiel say about this ship, Skipper?" Sofia asked. "That he was the brains of it?" She wiped her bloodied blade across Ezekiel's pant leg. "Looks like we've dumbed down the ship. Everything's going haywire."

"I think someone else did that," Tag said, looking to Alpha as she gently situated Sumo against a bulkhead.

Sofia raised a brow. "So when you made your choice to start the whole gladiatorial combat thing, you did know the nanites weren't working anymore, right?"

"Thanks to Alpha's wink," Tag said. "I had never seen her do that before, so I knew something was up."

"Good," Sofia said. She paused, standing next to Ezekiel's headless body with her hand on her hip. "If you had to choose one half of us to live, which one were you going to pick?"

Tag shook his head. "Thank the gods I didn't have to make that decision."

"I mean, you would've wanted to keep me on your side. That's basically a guarantee," Sofia said.

Tag smiled enigmatically. The truth was that he hadn't had a chance to decide, and he would be eternally grateful for it. If he'd chosen, even in his mind, he wouldn't have been able to live with the guilt. He clapped a hand on Alpha's shoulder. "I cannot thank you enough for hacking into the *Dawn*'s system. How did you do it?"

"I did not do it," Alpha said. "It was Raktor. The seedling fought for control of the nanites and won, using them to hold us in place until Ezekiel gave the signal. Instead of allowing the nanites to make us fight, Raktor simply disabled them completely. When Ezekiel tried to regain his control, Raktor superseded his command."

"Was Raktor not affected by the nanites?" Coren asked.

"It was not," Alpha confirmed.

Bracken sauntered toward them. "And how is that? Are Raktors not susceptible?"

"I believe they are," Alpha said. She opened her chest cavity. Tag remembered how it had been lying open when he had first seen Alpha on the bridge. Apparently, she had done it to herself. "But Raktor isn't here."

"What do you mean?" Bracken asked. "Where is it?"

"Raktor is currently breaking through various firewalls within the *Dawn*'s intranet," Alpha said. "Just as Ezekiel said, machines can be manipulated and defeated rather easily if you can find a weakness to exploit. Raktor are especially suited for exploiting such machines. When I couldn't access the data line from the suspension chamber myself, I left Raktor behind just before the golems took us."

"Good thinking," Tag said.

"It was I believe what you would call a gamble, Captain. I estimated the success rate at less than ten percent. Because Raktor still has the transponder, we were able to maintain internal communications, and it realized it had to access the nanite controls in order to help us."

"I feel like I owe our Raktor much more than just the ship I promised it," Tag said. "That thing saved all our lives."

"I believe it would say that it has done a kind thing," Alpha said with a ghost of a smile on her lips.

"A very, very kind thing indeed," Sofia said.

Bull looked less impressed. "Come on. Even Raktor isn't that dumb. The little plant knows that without our help, it'd be stuck here. Ezekiel would've fried that viny bastard the moment he found it."

"Whatever its motivation, we're alive," Sofia said.

A rumbling shook the *Dawn* from deep within the vessel's belly.

"It will count for a whole lot more if we can *stay* alive," Bracken said.

A single red light flashed from the terminal, and an alarm barked. Soon it was joined by the distant chorus of alarms echoing through the passages. The trembling of the ship continued, and the viewscreen showed the massive planet beginning to loom larger.

"Looks like we're drifting toward the damn thing," Bull said.

"Alpha, what's going on?" Tag asked.

"It appears that with Ezekiel's death, the *Dawn* is undergoing an automatic shutdown process. All systems are being deactivated and the data aboard the ship is being summarily deleted as a safety precaution. At least that is what Raktor has been able to tell me."

Another rolling wave of tremors quaked through the bridge.

"Can't Raktor stop this?" Tag asked.

"It's trying," Alpha said. "But the data port there isn't giving it access to all the *Dawn*'s systems. Getting through the new firewalls and security measures from that limited port is proving to be a slow process due to the automated shutdowns. Raktor needs direct access to the ship's controls."

Tag looked at the sole terminal at Ezekiel's crash couch. "We need to bring it up here."

"I can do that, Captain," Alpha said. "I have a map of the ship now, thanks to Raktor."

Tag was ready to agree but then thought better of it. "Transfer the map to my wrist terminal. I need you here, along with Coren and Sofia. I want you guys working with Bracken's crew to break into the terminal if you can. That's Plan A. We'll retrieve Raktor for Plan B." Bracken nodded as she ordered two of her engineers to Coren's side at the terminal. "Alpha, what's the situation like with the *Dawn's* defensive forces?"

"They are presumably all shut down," Alpha said. "But there are several errant golems that may yet be functional. Warnings indicate that the *Dawn* is attempting to reboot its security measures."

"Marines, on me," Tag said. "Jaroon, want to go for a run?"

Jaroon nodded, clicking his visor back down on his power armor. "Ready when you are."

A half-dozen Melarrey fell into ranks behind him. With Bull and Gorenado at his side, Tag took off into the depths of the post-human ship.

# FORTY-SIX

They sprinted down a wide passage. Unlike the bare, sterile halls they had passed to get here, this one was filled with holopaintings and sculptures like an art museum floating through space. There were humanesque shapes Tag faintly recognized with multiple arms. One had an elephant's head. He saw others that were amalgams of humans and hawks, cats, alligators, or other animals. Then there were paintings depicting humans looking down from lightning-filled clouds.

"What's with the awful artwork?" Bull asked the question on Tag's mind. "I didn't think post-humans would be so obsessed with us 'Sapes.'"

Tag could hear the air quotes in the way he pronounced Sapes.

Gorenado, still keeping pace with the group, stared at the holopaintings as they passed. "These aren't normal humans. They're gods."

Tag looked at the huge marine. The question must've been clear in his expression.

"I like studying ancient mythology and religion," Gorenado said. "See, there's Horus? And that one? Ganesh. Zeus. Odin." He continued to name the gods they passed as they ran down the corridor. The scent of burning plastic hung heavy in the air as they passed a sculpture of a half-woman, half-cat.

"Through there!" Tag said as an indicator on his HUD lit up. He twisted into another passage. At the end of it, he saw the bright greens of the agricultural sector.

"We were so damn close before," Bull said.

The heavy footsteps of the Melarrey pounded after them, crashing through the narrow passages until they burst into the rows of crops. Many of the stalks were trampled, evidence of the golems' assault here. A few trees still burned, their leaves blackening and curling, as smoke drifted toward the high ceilings. Embers blew on an artificial wind. Maintenance bots were attempting to put out the flames, while still other farming bots roved the fields, tending to their responsibilities as though nothing had changed.

Another quake trembled through the *Dawn of Glory*, and Tag fell forward into the wet soil. He picked himself up, mud clinging to his suit, and saw that most of the farming bots had started to shut down. The overhead lights fizzled off, and the room went dark. Tag listened to the others fumble around in the darkness until they had turned on their helmet-mounted lights. A swathe of white light shone before Tag when he switched his on, and they continued forward, albeit a bit slower now.

"Alpha, what just happened?" Tag asked over the comms.

"The terminal is reporting that approximately eighty percent of the ship's power systems are going into dormancy."

"What about engine systems? Are we still headed toward the planet?"

"We are," Alpha replied. "Raktor has been unsuccessful at accessing drive and impeller controls from its current position."

Tag's legs pumped harder, his boots digging into the mangled crops and dirt at his feet. Beams of light bounced off a patch of trees ahead, and they entered what appeared to be a small forest. They wound between the tree trunks. A rotten smell akin to carrion slithered into Tag's suit. He almost gagged as he tried to clear the copse of trees and their malodorous fruit.

A dark shadow loomed to his right. At first, he thought it was just a bulky Melarrey, but the fist crashing through a tree next to him proved it wasn't a friend. Tag dodged another leaden blow as the shadow morphed, falling away and reforming within seconds. It looked like someone trapped within a plastic bag. Spikes jutted from its nanoid flesh, then disappeared to be replaced by more conventional humanoid limbs. All around Tag and the squad he'd dragged down here, more shapes appeared.

"Nano-golems," Bull grunted.

"They're going insane!" one of the Melarrey shouted.

"Alpha, can you find out what's going on with the golems?" Tag asked. "I thought Raktor took care of them."

"Raktor is now attempting to manage multiple systems at once, including the defensive systems," Alpha replied. "It is reporting minimal success."

"We can see that!" Bull said, firing at an encroaching figure as it morphed between a humanoid golem and a ball of spikes.

A torrent of energy rounds spit from the human and Melarrey weapons. Orange and green bolts of pulsefire crashed through shadowy figures, and the attackers fell away in waves of molten metal.

"Keep moving!" Tag said.

At least, the automated golems were in disarray and attacked only in fits of aggression. The group soon cleared the trees. More golems appeared across the field, limping toward Tag and the others. The only thing keeping these things hindered right now was Raktor. As soon as they loosed the alien from its mount within the lab, all control over the golems would be lost.

The alternative was leaving Raktor there and losing complete control of the *Dawn* as it continued its shutdown procedures. Neither one was particularly appealing.

"Alpha, any chance anyone on the bridge has learned how to control the *Dawn* yet?" Tag asked.

"No, I am afraid not, Captain," Alpha replied. "We are capable of reading current ship activities but unable to influence them."

"Damn," Tag said. He swung his pistol around on another swarm of golems surging toward him. The marines opened up on the mutating machines. Another hatch appeared in the bulkhead across from them over a field full of melted golems. It was the lab, the site of their last stand.

"Straight ahead," Jaroon bellowed. The Melarrey formed into a spearhead and charged into the golems. They hammered the creatures with their weapons and lanced out with flashes of green pulse rounds and blades. The dark spray of melted nanomachines flew from the golems like gore, singeing the crushed vegetation.

Tag dashed along the path they cleared and ran through the hatch, straight toward a broken suspension chamber. Next to the human corpse was a tangle of wires. A small plant no bigger than a tumbleweed sat in the nest of wires, its vines leeching into the central data cable.

"Raktor!" Tag said. "We're getting you out of here."

The vines from Raktor's central body whipped around as it began detaching itself from the cables.

"Good, let's go," Raktor squeaked. "It is becoming far too difficult for us to deal with all the security systems from here and take control of the flight systems."

"Can you at least shut down the defensive systems?"

"We can, temporarily," Raktor said. "But the golems are beyond control from here. The automated shutdown procedures are triggering all the defensive systems to go live. Every time we shut them down, another signal is sent from the bridge to turn them back on."

"Understood," Tag said. "I want you to put all your energy into shutting them down for as long as you can. We need to make a run for it."

"We will try," Raktor said.

The Melarrey and marines milled about the entrance to the lab. Their weapons lit up in bursts as they fired on the golems managing to hobble their way forward. Everything played out like a horrible case of déjà vu until the golems all suddenly disappeared, falling into black puddles in the furrows and craters of the field.

"We will not have long," Raktor said. "We should run now!"

Its vines waved in the air above the seedling, like a toddler begging to be picked up. Tag scooped it up, carrying it under his left arm. Vines curled around his biceps, holding on tightly.

Tag sprinted toward the others. "Move! Now!"

They spilled into the fields, rushing back toward the bridge. The lights from their helmets provided dim cones of illumination over the quivering pools of nanomachines struggling to reassemble. Each time Tag jumped over one, he half-expected claws to shoot from the puddle and grab his ankle.

Faraway red emergency lights sparked in his vision.

"There's the passage," Tag said, pointing to the open hatch.

In Tag's periphery, the shadows shifted, just outside the reach of his helmet-mounted light. He turned enough to see the golems beginning to form. Like phoenixes rising from the ashes, they rose from the scattered nanomachine remnants. This time, without

Raktor to interfere with their programming, they became whole again without the jittering they had exhibited before. Masses of the golems poured after the group as they reached the corridor back up toward the bridge.

"Gorenado!" Bull yelled. "On me!"

The two marines took rearguard, blasting fire into the closest golems with the Melarrey providing support. Tag continued on, not even pausing long enough to see how the marines fared against the machines. Raktor squeezed his arm tight enough he could feel it through his suit. The living plant was nervous, and somehow that made Tag even more determined to outrun their pursuers.

Sounds of gunfire and stomping boots, weapons clanging against the bulkhead, and curses from the crew chased him. But he never looked back.

He *had* to get to the bridge. Rounding a corner, he entered the art gallery depicting all the ancient gods, and he found himself praying to his own gods that they would survive this.

Gunshots echoed from the bridge before Tag reached it. His heart pounded, and stinging sweat dripped into his eyes.

"Alpha!" Tag yelled.

"Captain! Over here!" Alpha called back from the center of the bridge.

Pulsefire ricocheted against the bulkheads, coming from a corner where several of the Mechanics and Sofia had been herded by golems. A river of black particles drained from an overhead air vent. As the particles hit the deck, they formed into more golems with slicing claws and sword-like appendages. A wall of them stood between Tag and the terminal where Alpha and Coren were working furiously, defended by a few valiant Mechanics.

Even if the Melarrey and marines caught up to Tag, he wasn't sure they would have enough firepower to swat down all the golems now streaming into the bridge like water from a spigot. There was only one way to stop them now.

"I'm sorry about this, Raktor," Tag said.

# FORTY-SEVEN

Human, what are you planning to do?" the tiny plant-creature squeaked.

"Just brace yourself," Tag said.

He hefted the seedling in his palm. Raktor seemed to catch on, because it wrapped its vines into a protective ball. Alpha locked eyes with him as he cocked back his arm. Summoning all the power in his muscles, he threw Raktor toward the terminal. The seedling's vines whipped centimeters above the grasping claws of one of the golems. Alpha leapt with her arms outstretched and snatched the seedling out of the air, then disappeared behind the wall of golems once again.

Pulsefire still rang out from all corners of the bridge as the golems surrounded the separated groups of Tag's forces. The dusty red-brown planet blotted out the view on the screens now. Tag could already make out the thin veins of silver and gray that were the trains of colonization vehicles and drones working to create the planet's nascent infrastructure. They would drone indefinitely until someone issued them any order to stop.

If the golems didn't kill them, the collision with the planet soon would.

A few golems turned his direction and stomped ahead with weaponized arms raised. He saw the marines fighting to reach him, but in his mad dash to the bridge, he'd left them too far behind. Now he stood against a small army. He lashed out with pulsefire, severing an arm from one golem, then a leg from another, encumbering them with energy-ridden injuries as fast as he could.

But his back was soon pressed against a bulkhead. A claw slashed into his leg. Sharp pain followed a second later as he felt blood soak through his pant leg. He dodged another raking claw and then the heavy blow of a hammer that dented the bulkhead. The dent was soon filled in by the self-repairing nanomaterials, but a strike like that against him would not be so easily fixed.

"Alpha, I need an update," he said over the comms as he dodged another blow.

"We are working on it," Alpha said in her annoyingly calm voice.

Tag tried to avoid another hammering punch by a golem missing a leg, but the fist connected with his shoulder and sent him reeling. His back slammed against the bulkhead, and a shuddering pain resonated up through his spine and into his skull. Stars glimmered in his vision. He could barely see straight, much less dodge another attack. He fired blindly into one of the dark shadows moving toward him.

And then the golems fell away.

His vision began to settle in time to see the golems break apart like cinders blown by the wind. The others regrouped, their chests heaving and their weapons still hot, as a layer of deactivated nanites blanketed the floor.

"Defensive weapons systems are shut down," Alpha said. "Permanently."

A few of the Melarrey hooted in victory, and even the Mechanics seemed relieved underneath their stony appearances. But Tag didn't breathe a sigh of relief.

They were still headed straight for the planet.

"Raktor, can you correct our course?" he asked, running toward the terminal.

The seedling was perched atop it with vines intermingling in a bed of wires that Alpha and Coren had exposed. "Quiet. We are attempting to do so."

The flashing red lights turned steady white, and the alarms went silent. Without anywhere to sit or secure themselves, the crew found handholds along the viewscreen or grabbed hold of the terminal to brace themselves. The ship shuddered under the immense strain as it curved away from the planet, its massive impellers rumbling. Soon the planet disappeared from the viewscreen, and the ship leveled out.

"Thank you," Tag said to Raktor.

The seedling chirped happily. "It is our pleasure. We did not want to see the post-human succeed. He likes very much to do the unkind things."

"We damn well owe you a kind thing or two," Sofia said.

"We did promise it a ship," Coren said.

"Can we have this one?" Raktor asked.

"I think I'm going to need this one," Tag said. "It might prove handy."

"What about the *Argo*? We enjoyed our time there."

"No," Tag said. "That one is off-limits. So are Jaroon's and Bracken's."

"Then we would like this ship."

One of the vessels from the ship bays showed as a holo in the center of the bridge. It rotated slowly before them. The data scrolling underneath the three-dimensional image reported the ship to be at least twice as big as a Mechanic dreadnought. At first, Tag was hesitant to gift the seedling—and, indirectly, the larger Raktor back on the *Hope*—a battleship.

"That's a great choice," Sofia said, pointing to the ship's description with a smirk.

Apparently, the ship, named the *Peace of Spring*, had been used as nothing more than a cargo transport for a species called the Raundins. The Raundins hailed from a tropical environment, and the ship was equipped to sustain a hot, humid environment. Perfect for a creature like Raktor.

"Fine," Tag said. Then a thought struck him. In his mind's eye, he saw the humans that had been imprisoned in the suspension chambers. He had seen only a small fraction of the ship. Maybe the crew of the *Peace of Spring* was aboard this ship, imprisoned somewhere and awaiting release. If so, Tag didn't want to give the ship away under the noses of its owners. "Are there any Raundins aboard the *Dawn*? Or for that matter, anyone else besides the humans we found?"

"No," Alpha said. "There are not."

"And how do you know?"

"While the *Dawn* was running through its automatic data deletion methods, I thought you might want me to save as much as I could for reference. I could not interfere with the ship's procedures at the time, but I could read the data," Alpha said. "I started with the laboratory files and logs. The only test subjects aboard this ship are the humans."

"There aren't any prisoners?" Coren asked.

"That is correct."

"There are hundreds of ships in those bays," Gorenado said.

"Makes you wonder what happened to all the people they belonged to," Sofia said, her smile fading.

"No kidding." Tag's thoughts turned toward another prisoner. One they could still rescue. Lonestar was waiting for them. "Raktor will have the *Peace of Spring*. And the rest of you need to return to your own vessels."

Bracken crossed her thin arms over her chest. "I suppose that thing can release our ships."

The terminal glowed red, then blue.

"All permissions are granted," Raktor said. "You can access any system on the ship from here."

Tag settled into Ezekiel's crash couch. He felt like a child in the driver's seat of an air car.

"Should I prepare the *Argo* for launch?" Alpha asked.

"Yes," Tag said. "But I won't be joining you."

Coren and Sofia shot him skeptical looks.

"Someone's got to command this thing," he said, patting the arm of the crash couch.

# FORTY-EIGHT

With Raktor's help, Tag found piloting the *Dawn of Glory* to be surprisingly easy. Sofia had tried to convince Tag that he should let someone else ride shotgun with him in the ship. Unfortunately, there wasn't a single additional chair anywhere on the hulking vessel. The only other restraints capable of safely securing a human during a hyperspace jump were the suspension chambers in the laboratory. When Tag had mentioned that, Sofia's insistence that someone stay aboard with him beside Raktor quickly faded.

The jump back to *Hope* station proved to be uneventful. Just like when Tag took the *Argo* to hyperspace, waves of purple and green plasma played over the *Dawn*'s viewscreen as Tag settled into the huge crash couch for the ride. His only company was little Raktor, but the plant-creature wasn't the best conversationalist. The seedling complained that Tag spoke too slow and it lamented the fact that the human couldn't establish a direct data link with it like Alpha had. Together they perused the files that Alpha had saved. They found plenty of files on various races and creatures the post-humans had encountered in their campaign to colonize the far reaches of space. There was another subset of files documenting the atmospheric, environmental, and surface composition of planets that Tag presumed this particular colonization ship had visited. According to the logs, Ezekiel had spread the post-human colonies to fourteen planets already.

"We think these post-humans are doing very many unkind things," Raktor said. "We do not support these actions."

"That's good to know," Tag said, tapping at the terminal. "Have you found anything out about the humans we found in the suspension chambers?"

"Yes, we have. The people were brought here from Earth and deposited within the chambers for experimental purposes."

"What kind of experiments was Ezekiel running on the humans?" Tag asked.

"We will show you," Raktor said. It hummed to itself a moment, and then a holo erupted in the center of the bridge.

Tag felt his jaw drop to his chest. He didn't know what he had expected, but what he saw made his blood turn to ice. "My gods."

"Did we do a poor job?" Raktor asked. "This *is* the information you requested, is it not?"

"It's not you," Tag said. "We need to call an emergency meeting. Now."

Moments later holo images of Alpha, Coren, Sofia, Bracken, and Jaroon appeared.

"What's up, Skipper?" Sofia asked.

Tag shared the holo with all of them. He could hear the collective gasps over the comms as the more scientifically oriented ones got it.

The visible nerve bundles behind Jaroon's eyes glowed in electric colors. "What is this?"

"These are modified nanites," Tag said. "They're based off the original technology that started this whole mess, going all the way back to their development on Earth."

"Just like the ones that turned my people into Drone-Mechs," Bracken said.

"Exactly," Tag said. "But these have a bonus feature." He gestured over the image, and a series of helix shapes uncoiled. "They deliver a set of DNA vectors. Within those vectors contain the codes that turn people into Collectors, just like the post-human we met."

"So what do we do?" Jaroon asked. "Does this change our mission?"

"No," Tag said. "We've done what we promised Grand Elector L'ndrant we would do. We found the enemy, and we have a good idea what they're planning."

"What will we do next, Captain?" Alpha asked.

"We get Lonestar, then we take this ship back to Meck'ara," Tag said. "I propose we leave it there. The surviving humans Ezekiel was using as test subjects on the *Dawn* are still in stasis. I'd like to keep them that way until we figure out what Ezekiel did to them and whether we can safely wake them. Your people can take the rest of this thing apart, search every square centimeter of it, and see if we can't take any useful tech from it."

"We would greatly appreciate the opportunity to do that," Bracken said. "But I take it from this project Ezekiel was working on that the Collectors will be headed to the SRE. It would be prudent to prepare your government for the attack by giving them a glimpse of the enemy. You're sure you do not want to bring it to Earth?"

"I am," Tag said. "We still don't know who duped Lonestar

and infiltrated the SRE." He pictured the Starinski's *New Blood* warship leaving the *Dawn* before they had boarded it. "But I think we have a much better idea of at least one organization complicit in the Collectors' plans. I have a sneaking suspicion the drones sent from the *Hope* to Earth and the SRE over the years were attempts to communicate with human collaborators. We haven't identified who is or isn't compromised, so I don't trust anyone but us right now."

"That is a sound decision," Jaroon said. "My crew is still ready to carry out whatever we need to do next. From what we witnessed, it seems these Collectors have far more allies than just a few Drone-Mechs and human collaborators. Our mission is not yet over."

The Melarrey was right. They had a long road ahead of them. "We'll need to identify all those ships we saw departing the *Dawn*. Since all we really have left of Ezekiel's data is his scientific work, I don't know *why* those ships were there or where they were headed when they all left."

Alpha looked dispirited. "I apologize I was unable to save more useful data."

"Don't sell yourself short, you sappy tin can," Sofia said. "You did good."

"Really good," Tag said. "You and Raktor saved us."

He looked at Raktor meaningfully. "You did a very kind thing."

Even Bracken managed a smile.

"Speaking of kind things, how is Sumo?" Tag asked.

"She responded well to treatment. I have restricted her to bedrest, which she is most unhappy about, but she is healing well."

"Good," Tag said. He felt more than a little relief at hearing those words.

"She did ask when you will join her and the marines again for a round of gutfire."

Tag laughed. "Of course she did. You can tell her I will as soon as we get our lost marine back."

"And after your revelry and our visit to Meck'ara," Bracken said coolly, "do you have a plan for where we will be headed next?"

"We? You're coming with us?" Tag asked.

"I am. So long as my crew doesn't mutiny at the prospect."

"Excellent," Tag said, a genuine smile dawning on his face. He wasn't sure what the future held, but he felt better—stronger—knowing that he would have such brave and capable allies at his side.

# FORTY-NINE

The four ships transitioned into normal space. On the viewscreen, the other vessels looked like dust motes compared to the monstrosity he was piloting. Before them, drifted the familiar hobbled-together *Hope* station. Every nerve in Tag's body began to fire as they approached.

"Ready?" Tag asked Raktor.

"We are ready." Raktor secured the transponder it had used to communicate with Tag and the others to the terminal. "You should have complete remote control of the *Dawn* now."

"Thank you. You have done us another kind thing."

"You will do many kind and good things for others if you carry on with this mission," Raktor said. "The equation is balanced. It is only mathematics, not kindness."

Tag smiled. He seemed to be doing a lot of that lately. There was no way the huge ship would dock with the station, so Tag commanded the ship to drift next to the station. He held out a hand, and Raktor climbed up his arm, its vines wrapping around his shoulder to hold it in place. They made the long journey down to the ship bay and boarded the Raundin vessel. The *Peace of Spring*'s interior looked and smelled like a jungle that had decided to take to the stars. Raktor seemed at home in the humid atmosphere even as Tag's suit struggled to keep the resulting condensation of the humid environment from fogging his visor.

"We like this ship," Raktor said, bouncing on Tag's shoulder.

"That makes one of us."

Tag took them to the bridge, which was filled with terminals and seating elements not even close to compatible with human anatomy. He was thankful the trip from the *Dawn* to the *Hope* station would be a short one.

Stretching his arm toward one of the terminals, Tag let Raktor take control of the vessel. "This baby's yours now."

"Thank you, human Tag," Raktor said.

The *Peace of Spring* rumbled into a launch, and it wasn't long before Raktor was slipping into one of the station's docking ports, forcing an uneasy connection between the Raundin and human technology.

They departed the *Peace* with little Raktor once more aboard Tag's shoulder. Through a grimy porthole on the *Hope*, Tag saw the *Argo*, *Stalwart*, and *Crucible* dock with the station. Tag had insisted that he take the seedling to the mature Raktor alone. He didn't want to risk losing anyone else.

Besides, if big Raktor decided to pull some last-minute stunt to put Lonestar and himself in danger, he had the support of three ships waiting outside the *Hope*.

Seedling Raktor bounced on his shoulder as they passed through the familiar passages filled with the odor of decay. Finally, they reached the forest of dense vines, which parted as they made their way to Raktor's central chamber.

Its booming voice greeted them as its massive beak lowered from the ceiling. "We see the seedling. What about the ship?"

"You'll find a Raundin vessel, the *Peace of Spring*, attached as best we could to a docking port," Tag said.

The little Raktor bounced. "It will be our new ship! It is a kind thing to have a new ship we can fly!"

Tag swore the massive Raktor beak smiled. "Very good. We are proud our seedling will have this vessel. But why is our seedling not there now?"

"I wanted to show you it's still very much alive and in good health. I'll return it to the ship as soon as I make my way back to my own."

Big Raktor seemed to consider this for a moment. "We do not understand."

"This human Tag is a doer of kind things," little Raktor said. "It says the truth, as I learned from our new friend Alpha."

"If the seedling says so…" Big Raktor unfurled its vines, lowering something covered in brown gunk to the deck.

Lonestar stood from the mess, wiping off her visor. "Captain, it's damn good to see a human." She smiled from behind the grime smeared over her helmet. "Spending all my time with that overgrown tumbleweed was getting old. Never thought you'd return."

"There was a moment I didn't think I would either," Tag said. "Multiple moments. But we did it."

"Can't wait to hear all about. Really, I want to know everything y'all did without me. But first things first, I really want to get out of these clothes and take a long shower. I mean, really long."

"Sounds like a plan," Tag said. He looked up at the grown Raktor's beak. "Thank you, Raktor."

"You kept up your end of the deal, human Tag," Raktor replied. Tag figured it was the closest he was going to get to *you're welcome.*

Tag left the chamber with Lonestar and the seedling. Their first stop was the bridge of the *Peace*, where Tag deposited little Raktor on the terminal. He felt a twinge of guilt leaving the seedling there alone.

"Will you be all right?" Tag asked.

"Of course," the seedling replied. "We would like to offer our assistance if you ever need it."

"I'll have Alpha patch in a direct relay from your ship to mine."

He wasn't sure when or why they might want to contact the seedling, but it was better to have more allies in this universe than go it alone like the Collectors.

Pausing as he exited the bridge, he turned back to Raktor. "Thank you again. We wouldn't have made it without you."

"Likewise, human Tag."

Lonestar waited until they were within the *Argo*'s airlock before speaking again. "Weird things, aren't they?"

"You and big Raktor didn't bond while we were away?"

"Oh, we bonded as much as a farmer bonds with his corn. And in this situation, I think I was the corn."

"I'm not sure how to interpret that."

"You'd understand if you spent days with a plant-creature patting your head and keeping you rolled up tighter than a hand-made cigar."

When the airlock opened into the *Argo*, Lucky curved her back as if she was preparing to pounce. But instead, she wrinkled her nose and ran away, hissing at Lonestar.

"I'm guessing she doesn't like to be reminded of her old home," Tag said.

The other marines welcomed Lonestar back with far more enthusiasm than Lucky, and after the ship was safely underway on its hyperspace route to Meck'ara with the *Stalwart*, *Crucible*, and *Dawn* in tow, they gathered in the mess. Tag took a seat next to

Sumo, whose head was bandaged, and Coren. The Mechanic had already taken it upon himself to start upgrading an autoserv bay to produce Mechanic cuisine, and he was nursing a foul-smelling beverage. The crew passed around gutfire and shared jokes, often followed by Alpha asking someone to explain the punchlines, and they retold their latest adventure with plenty of dramatic embellishments. Not that it needed any. Lucky wound between them, begging for scraps of food and hissing at those who refused to provide her with ear scratches or pets. It seemed almost as if everything that had happened to them was merely something they had read in a book or seen in a holo.

But as Sumo poured herself a glass of water—Alpha had her under strict orders to avoid alcoholic beverages as her brain recovered from her concussion—Tag knew that it had all been real. They'd endured so much together, but they weren't done yet. There was no telling how many other Collectors would descend on them now that they had taken one of their ships, and there were still lingering questions of who in the SRE had established back channels with the enemy. They also hadn't determined the nature of all those other ships swarming around the *Dawn* when they'd first seen it. The prevailing hypothesis shared by Tag, Jaroon, and Bracken was that most of those ships must've been commandeered by nanite-enslaved races.

At least, that's what they wanted to believe. None of them wanted to suggest that other races might be collaborators. They hoped the subterfuge and incursion into other governments was so far limited to the humans, but of course they couldn't know for certain. Now, every time they encountered a new race among the stars, they would have to wonder whether the aliens were enemies or allies.

All this uncertainty made celebrating today all the more important.

"Skipper, you're looking tense," Sofia said. "Share one with me?" She passed him a shot of gutfire.

"Here's to having Lonestar back." Tag raised his glass to the cheers of the others. With his elbows on the table, he leaned over to her. "Now, I feel you owe us the story of your call sign, *Lonestar*."

Lonestar's cheeks burned a bright crimson. "Aw, come on, you don't really want to hear that."

"Being an actual Texan," Tag said, "I have to say I do."

"All right, here goes," Lonestar drawled. She regaled a tale involving a station bar made up to look like something straight out of a cheesy Western holo with a mechanical bull and Western memorabilia ranging from six-shooters to buffalo hides festooning the walls. After having a few drinks, what she thought was an SRE private from the planetary army branch of the military began showering her with attention. She had thought the young man was interested in her until she noticed he was just distracting her while an accomplice tried to make off with her wrist terminal. She'd pulled down a coil of rope from the wall and successfully lassoed the thief, then hogtied him until the station's police arrived.

"That's pretty damn tame," Sofia said. "I expected something a bit more embarrassing."

"She's not done," Gorenado said.

Lonestar rolled her eyes. "I stood there with one boot on the fella until the police got there."

"And..." Sumo prodded her.

"I was singing a ditty about being a sheriff in the great state of Texas."

"I would very much like to hear this song," Alpha said.

"Not going to happen," Lonestar said. "That was a one-time performance."

"I'm really kind of disappointed," Tag said. "Sofia's right. I thought we were in for a much more scandalous story. Sumo, how about yours?"

"How about I tell you after you save me from living the rest of my days with a giant talking fern?" Sumo said.

"You really want to make that deal?" Bull asked.

"I wouldn't take it," Lonestar said. "Captain's crazy enough to turn this ship around and take you right back to Raktor."

"We also have access to the seedling Raktor," Alpha said, "if that is more convenient."

"Now there's an idea!" Gorenado said.

Sumo shook her head, grinning. "I think that concussion gave me amnesia. Can't remember a damn thing about my call sign."

"Fine. We'll let it slide tonight," Tag said.

The group shared in a moment of companionable silence, sipping their drinks as, for once, they weren't being chased by horrendous creatures determined to kill them. Lucky settled into Tag's lap and purred as he scratched her scaly neck.

The peace wouldn't last. As much as they had already been through together, Tag feared things would get worse.

Much worse.

At least, they'd seen the face of their enemy. The Collectors, the mysterious Drone-masters—by any name, they were the greatest threat humanity had ever faced. Maybe those strange lightning-like aliens on the *Hope* were indeed a very real and dangerous threat, too. The SRE might run into them as the crew of the *Hope* had. But Tag couldn't justify the Collectors' response to that single event. The genocide, enslavement, and experiment… it made Tag nauseous. A twisting knife tore at his gut as he realized the Collectors had sprung from humanity, from *his* people, separated only by a few centuries.

As Tag looked around at the marines, at Sofia and Alpha, even Coren, he was also reminded of the SRE's mission in the universe, dedicated to exploration and progress, to finding new races and civilizations that shared their goals. Sure, there were growing pains. But where those principles persisted, there was hope. *Hope* that when the storm passed, Tag and his allies would prevail. The post-humans had stolen their strengths from the races they enslaved, and in doing so had become monsters. But Tag and his motley band of humans and aliens—from haughty Bracken to brave Jaroon, and even the Raktors—were stronger because of their differences. Working together, they had defeated Ezekiel. They had succeeded against overwhelming odds, and Tag felt confident they could do it again.

When the time came, when the Collectors made their move against the SRE, Tag vowed they would not back down. And, once again, they would win.


## THE END OF BOOK 3

Dear Reader,

Thank you for reading the *Shattered Dawn*. Would you like to know when the next book in The Eternal Frontier series comes out? Sign up here: http://bit.ly/ajmlist

I love to hear from my readers. If you want to get in touch, there are a number of ways to reach me.

Facebook: www.facebook.com/anthonyjmelchiorri
Email: ajm@anthonyjmelchiorri.com
Website: http://www.anthonyjmelchiorri.com

Sincerely,
Anthony J Melchiorri

# ALSO BY ANTHONY MELCHIORRI

### The Tide Series

The Tide (Book 1)
Breakwater (Book 2)
Salvage (Book 3)
Deadrise (Book 4)
Iron Wind (Book 5)

### The Eternal Frontier

Eternal Frontier (Book 1)
Edge of War (Book 2)
Shattered Dawn (Book 3)

### Black Market DNA

Enhancement (Book 1)
Malignant (Book 2)
Variant (Book 3)
Fatal Injection

### Other Books

The God Organ
The Human Forged
Darkness Evolved

# ABOUT THE AUTHOR

Anthony J Melchiorri is a scientist with a PhD in bioengineering. Originally from the Midwest, he now lives in Texas. By day, he develops cellular therapies and 3D-printable artificial organs. By night, he writes apocalyptic, medical, and science-fiction thrillers that blend real-world research with other-worldly possibility. When he isn't in the lab or at the keyboard, he spends his time running, reading, hiking, and traveling in search of new story ideas.

Read more at http://anthonyjmelchiorri.com and sign up for his mailing list at http://bit.ly/ajmlist to hear about his latest releases and news.

Made in the USA
Middletown, DE
30 December 2021

57334031R00179